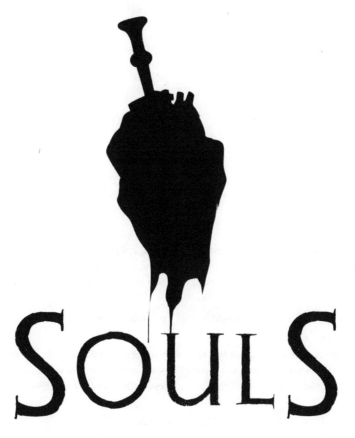

SOULS

The SOULS Series: Book 1

KAHILAH HARRY

FIRST EDITION

Book design by Damonza.com
Editors: Rarebirdediting.com
Jessi Elliott

ISBN 978-1-7368459-0-5 (paperback)
ISBN 978-1-7368459-2-9 (ebook)
ISBN 978-1-7368459-1-2 (hardcover)

www.kahilahharry.com

To myself. Congrats, you're officially a published author.

1

"This is the fifth murder this week, and we still have no witnesses or credible evidence. We can't let boss give the case to someone else," Caspian spoke as we walked away from the body.

I ran my hand through my curly auburn hair. "Which is why I've been working on some leads of my own." I grabbed the coffee he bought me out of his hand.

His pale blue eyes widened as he took a sip of his own coffee. "Excuse me? Are you *trying* to get yourself killed?"

"Cas, don't start. I'll be okay." I sighed and placed a reassuring hand on his arm.

"Yeah, until you end up like this guy." He nodded to the corpse on the ground as one of our guys placed a white sheet over it.

"I won't end up like him, Cas. Trust me, okay?" I smiled at his grim scowl. He wasn't going to continue this conversation. Linking my arm through his, I led us to our precinct SUV. Caspian was upset about me taking the investigation into my own hands, so it was a quiet ride toward headquarters.

"What if something happens and I can't save you this time, Meadow?" Caspian finally said.

1

I frowned at him. Like I actually needed saving. Okay, maybe I needed a tiny bit of help, but I didn't need him bringing it up every time I wanted to take risks.

"Yeah, yeah, let's not talk about that. You're so negative. I'm going to solve this case so it isn't taken away from us. Also, I need closure. *We* need it. I'm going to need your help in achieving this, okay?" I pleaded with him with my eyes.

He glanced at me and sighed heavily. Once I set my mind on something, it rarely changed, especially in a situation where my pride was involved.

We arrived at headquarters and separated to our own offices and piles of evidence. At my desk, I went through everything I'd found. All five bodies had one thing in common: they were unusually pale. As if the bodies had been sitting out in the open for a while, even though they were usually fresh by the time we got to them. Caspian told me it was normal, but I did my research, and it wasn't. The paleness might be a part of the killer's M.O. If I found out why, I might be able to narrow down how all five victims were murdered.

I needed way more evidence for my theory to be convincing. Once the M.E. sent the C.O.D., it'd definitely narrow it down.

Ugh. I hated depending on others for information. I needed my own now, or I was going to burst. I tapped my pen against my face, trying to connect the dots of this case.

All males. Different hair color and height.

All abnormally pale for a freshly deceased person.

All male, all pale.

I didn't mean to rhyme, but it gave me an idea.

I jumped out of my chair and headed toward the one place that guaranteed answers. The cold case section. The place I wasn't supposed to enter without the okay of a higher up. It was a little room with boxes of unsolved, old—super old—cases. I greeted the other employees as I walked quickly to the large room before anyone could stop me.

Shutting the door softly behind me, I turned on the light. Old, dusty boxes, just crying out to be solved, surrounded me. I scanned for one that may have something to do with a pale murder. Or something like that. After about an hour, one caught my eye. I wiped the dust off the label.

Ghost murders.

I almost let out a squeal but remembered to be discreet. Eager to search its contents, I placed the box on the floor, not sure if I was ready for what waited for me in the files. Before I opened it, I checked to make sure no one was coming my way or patrolling the hallways. Once I was sure I was safe, I opened the box and dropped the lid. I thumbed through the massive number of unsolved murders in the box, and my heart squeezed with pain. There were hundreds of files. Hundreds of people with no closure.

I passed my hand over the tops of the files, sad for everyone involved and all the time spent trying to find answers. Filled with new confidence and determination, I searched each file for clues. A super thick file close to the middle had more odd similarities to my current case than the others.

The similarities sent a cold shiver down my spine. In the cold case, the victim had no identification on him, but had a cross carved into his wrist. Male and abnormally pale. I slammed the file shut. But how? How was this possible?

The case was almost identical to mine.

I needed to get to the morgue and inspect my John Doe's wrist. I shook my head, trying to keep my mind from jumping to too many conclusions.

The date on the back of the file read *1995*. Another file that read *2008* was basically like reading the first file. Male, pale skin, engraved cross. I selected two more random files. *1983, 1977*. Same thing. The whole box had 100 plus records dating all the way back to 1866. All of them said the same thing on the medical examiner's report.

"No, no way. *No way,*" I whispered. All of these murders were basically identical, and none of them had any leads. Not one. So many questions, and I needed more information. More answers.

I grabbed the oldest file, *1866,* and the most recent file, *2008,* and placed the rest in the box and the box back on the shelf. Now to get out of here without getting caught by anyone.

I hurried out, closing the door softly behind me, and rushed toward my office.

I turned the corner and ran straight into my boss. Duke's kind brown eyes widened as he steadied me. We both bent to retrieve the files that flew out of my arms.

"Oh my god, I am so sorry! Don't worry about these, I got them."

He picked up both files anyway and studied the labels. Kneading the space between his eyes, he sighed heavily and looked up at me with accusing eyes. "Meadow—"

"I know! I know! You told me to wait until the M.E.'s report came in and for you to come up with a theory before I go snooping in the cold cases, but I couldn't help myself."

He scratched his sandy-blond head and smiled, handing the files back to me.

I looked at him quizzically, waiting for his standard speech. When I tugged on the files, he held them tight.

"Look, Meadow." *Here we go.* "Whatever you get from this, it better be good, got it?" He smiled, so I knew I was off the hook.

I smiled back. "Got it, boss. Thanks."

He let go of the files, and I hurried into my office. I flopped down in my comfortable, bouncy chair, fingers itching to go through the archives I uncovered.

"What are you getting yourself into this time, Meadow?"

My eyes snapped up, scanning my office. I didn't see anyone. I could've sworn I heard someone speak.

"Hello?" I stood, confused. I went to my office door, opening it. No one was there. Peeking out just a bit, I scoped out the hallway, but it was empty. Hm. Closing the door, I went back to my chair.

"Meadow."

I sat up straight, rubbing the goosebumps suddenly peppering my arms.

"Caspian, is that you? I don't have time for games right now!" I listened for a response. I checked my office for hidden bugs, recorders, or anything like that. Nothing. Sitting back down, I shook my head.

"Now I'm imagining things," I muttered. It had been a stressful day. After a few hours of digging into the files, my brain felt fried.

6:43 p.m. Time to go anyway.

During my drive home, I couldn't help thinking about the creepy voice in my head. It was crazy, but I wasn't actually sure if it was all in my head or not. Maybe it was Caspian playing a trick on me again, and I just didn't find the device. Or him. I chuckled. Of course, that was it. I tapped the speaker icon on the smart screen of my car.

"Call Caspian."

"What?" Caspian's voice came through my car with a hint of annoyance.

"Grumpy."

"I need sleep. But boss isn't done going over evidence."

"I totally understand. I'm sorry, Cas. I'm on the way to my house now." I paused, wondering how to bring it up without sounding weird or crazy. "So today, something strange happened to me in my office." I bit my lip.

"Mhm, what happened?" Caspian sounded distracted. Keyboard keys clacked in the background. That might be a good thing, so he didn't realize how crazy I sounded.

"Well, I was about to start going through some clues I found today when suddenly, I heard someone say my name. I think it was like a whole sentence, I'm not actually sure. But I definitely heard my name."

My engine hummed in the silence between us. I glanced at my smart screen to see if the call dropped. Caspian's name was still on display, and the time continued.

"Hello? Caspian?"

More shuffling, and then his voice came through. "I think you cut out. You heard your name in your office?"

I sighed, not really wanting to repeat myself. "Yes, and the voice was deep. Like yours. Were you hiding somewhere in my office? Or had a mic or recorder or something, trying to scare me? Because it definitely spooked me out."

Caspian cursed, followed by a loud thump on his side. Then silence.

"Cas, was it you or not? I heard you curse, so to me, that's you admitting. So just say it." There was no way it was anyone else besides him. Right?

He cleared his throat. "It wasn't me. Maybe you were daydreaming or something."

I rolled my eyes. I'd expected him to say something like that. "Okay, whatever. Thanks for the help." I hung up on him. Even though he said it wasn't him, I didn't really believe it.

I reached my loft and inside, I took off my gun and the holster, placed it in its designated cubby on the wall, and strolled to the kitchen.

I stretched and ran both of my hands through my hair, massaging my scalp. I really needed a spa day. Tension had my muscles bunched everywhere. Opening my fridge, I reached for a carton of orange juice.

A prickling sensation tripped along the back of my neck, and I quickly straightened up. Someone was in my loft.

2

Walking into my living room, I passed my hand over the head of the black couches. Nothing looked out of place. I fluffed one of my black pillows and was about to go back to the kitchen when the prickling sensation returned. I froze. Clenching my hands into fists, I tried to calm my rapidly beating heart as I prepared to defend myself.

"Whoever you are, I want you to know that I have a gun in my waistband, and I will shoot you if you don't leave right now," I lied.

I listened for breathing and didn't hear anything, but I couldn't shake the feeling that someone was there. I counted to three in my head and whipped around with my fists up, ready to attack, but abruptly froze mid-swing.

A stranger loomed in front of me, and no matter how hard I tried, I couldn't move. Not an inch.

"Meadow."

My heart rate spiked at the bass of his voice. He stood quite a few inches taller than my 5'8" height. I had to bend my head back uncomfortably to look at him properly. He wore an all-black suit with black shoes. His inky black hair was slicked back stylishly, and his piercing gray eyes bored into my soul. His eyes nor his face held a hint of any emotion, his face stern and stoic as if he rarely smiled.

The pressure of a force holding me in place dissipated, so I took a cautious step back.

"Who are you, and how do you know my name?" My eyes flitted around the room, looking for the best escape route. He was blocking the quickest path to the front door.

His eyes followed every move I made, and his eyebrows scrunched in confusion at my question. I started inching forward. A plan started to form.

"You really don't remember me?" He didn't react to my moving toward my front door. Now my back was facing the door.

I tilted my head, shaking it side to side.

The stranger turned and faced my new position, his features hard as stone. He had a little black cross dangling from his right earlobe. The left ear had a simple black stud. The cross was an intricate shape, and it looked familiar.

He stalked toward me as slowly as I moved toward my gun.

"Looking for this?" He tilted his head and tossed my gun aside.

I expected it to hit my couch with a muted thump, but it disappeared before it landed. My jaw dropped, and I gasped. My eyes were wide as I stared at the stranger, fear seeping from every pore in my body. I couldn't stop shaking. How in the world did that gun disappear into thin air? How did he get into my loft?

"What are you?" I whispered.

Mr. Stranger locked his gray eyes to my hazel ones and started walking toward me again, taking his sweet time. I didn't even realize he had stopped, I was so caught up in my thoughts. I tried to take a step backward, but for some reason, I couldn't move. I watched in fear as he came closer, with a curiously intent look on his face.

He stopped when he was literally toes away from me. Still immobile, I could only watch as he raised his hand and slowly brought it to my cheek, resting it there. A warmth spread through it, leaving me with a tingling sensation.

"How do you not remember?" He whispered and squinted at me, trailing his fingers down my cheek. The warmth turned into a chill.

The chill moved from my cheek to my chest. I tried to make a sound, but I couldn't. My breathing sped up. He leaned in close to my face and stared deeply into my eyes. Suddenly, he smiled a cruel smile that didn't reach his eyes.

"Well, I'll handle this later." He stood up straight and crossed his arms over his chest. "I can't have you remembering this and alerting that dreadful Caspian, so to sleep you go." He reached out his arm and tapped my forehead.

The last thought that crossed my mind was to warn Caspian.

———

MY ROOM WOULDN'T STOP SPINNING. It was the weirdest feeling. Usually, if a room was spinning, I'd feel nauseous, but I didn't feel anything. I felt hollow. Different. Like part of me was missing. I stared at my black and white spotted ceiling until the odd feeling went away.

The last thing I remembered was going in my fridge for some orange juice. I massaged my temple to try to help myself remember more.

Nothing.

I guess I was so tired I fell asleep...in my work clothes. I hopped out of bed. A wave of dizziness hit me, and I stretched my arms out to steady myself. Once I felt balanced enough, I trudged to my bathroom.

"Oh, mercy," I groaned, passing a hand over my face. The woman in the mirror looked nothing like me with her pale brown complexion and smudged eyeliner. "Pull yourself together, Meadow."

First, I needed a quick shower to wash away this stressful day and help clear my head so I could look at the files with a fresh mind. As I went through my nightly routine, a blurry image hovered on the edge of my mind, but every time I closed my eyes to focus on it, the image disappeared, leaving me with a sense of emptiness. More than that was this nagging feeling that I forgot something important.

It'll come to me eventually. I pushed those thoughts away, grabbed my files from the dresser, and sat on my bed. The business card someone left on my desk a week ago taunted me. It was blank on the back and the front only had a question and a phone number.

"Yes, I do want answers," I said to no one as I gave in and called the number. Less than ten minutes later, after the most cryptic phone call of my life, I had a meeting set up and a plan of action. I flipped through the recent files and saw nothing about a cross on the wrist. Only no identification, abnormally pale skin, and male victims.

I huffed and opened the cold case files, hoping they would give me more insight. As I scanned the pages, I started noticing specifics, like the engraved cross on the victims' right hand. I went back to the recent files—no medical examiner's report for the first four murders. I should've had those reports by now.

I groaned and tossed the files to the side on my bed and leaned back on my pillows, tracing a crack in my headboard as I brainstormed about what I could do.

Wait.

I shot up in bed. Caspian should have the reports. He told me he would get the reports and give me the copies. This could be the missing link I needed. Excited, I grabbed my phone and dialed his number, tapping on my bed, anxious for him to pick up the phone.

It went to voicemail.

3

I arrived at headquarters, glancing at my watch as I made my way to Caspian's office. Perfect, I had enough time to speak to him before I left for my meeting. He was so deep into whatever he was doing on his computer he didn't even realize I was standing there.

"Ahem."

He jumped in his chair, his blonde hair falling in his face. "Geez, May. Ever heard of knocking?" He adjusted his shirt and leaned back, gesturing to the seats in front of his desk.

I sat down and folded my hands together, staring him down.

He pressed his lips together and nodded in my direction, waiting for me to speak.

"First of all, don't call me May. You know I hate that nickname. It sounds like the old aunt that everyone hates," I started.

He chuckled and rolled his eyes.

"Second, I'm here because you never gave me the autopsy reports for the four other ghost murders."

"Ghost murders, May?" He shook his head. "You came up with a name for it already? A silly name at that." He wagged his pen at me and laughed again.

I folded my arms across my chest, not amused with his mockery.

"What's so funny, Cas? That's a perfect name for the case. Plus, I dug through some cold cases with the same name, that's where I got it from, and—"

"Wait, you went through the cold cases?" Caspian raised his hand. "You know that's against the rules until we get concrete evidence to compare." He was judging me. Of course.

"Look, I needed something, *anything*, okay? You were supposed to get the reports for me. Where are they? I need them now," I demanded. I hated wasting time. Plus, I had something else important planned that could help with our case. I waited for him to make a move for the reports, but he just sat there staring at me. He reached out his hand and placed it on top of mine, smiling.

"Do you know how gorgeous you look when you're frustrated?" He asked softly, giving me a cute little puppy-dog stare, trying to trap me with his beautiful irises.

I yanked my hand back from under his. "Caspian! This is serious. Stop trying to sweet talk me out of this!" I growled.

"I'm kidding! Christ, I didn't get the paper copies yet, okay? But I did see them." He studied a document on his desk. "There was nothing we didn't already know on it."

No way. I sank back in my chair. "Are you sure? Not even anything about a cross on the wrist?"

Caspian's head snapped up with narrowed eyes. "Where did you get that detail from?" His fingers drummed quickly against his desk, brows scrunched in suspicion.

"Do you know anything about that? Because if you do, you need to tell me." I stood up and towered over him, trying to intimidate him just a little.

"There wasn't anything like that in the report. You need to calm down and move on." He turned back to his computer dismissively.

"Then what was the cause of death?" He was hiding something, and I didn't like that. Partners should tell each other everything...well, mostly everything.

He groaned softly and looked up at me again. His office door opened. Duke poked his head in and spoke.

"Agent Galanis." Caspian nodded, and Duke turned to me. "Agent Saar, I have to show you both something regarding your case. I think it will be very beneficial."

Caspian grabbed his suit jacket, following Duke. "Let's go, Meadow."

He didn't have to tell me twice.

Duke led us straight to the building's morgue. We were finally going to get some answers—from the medical examiner himself I assumed, which was even better than a report.

Inside the room, the M.E., Harold, stood over a body with his back toward us.

"Harold, my agents are here to see you about the fifth body in their case," Duke said.

I stopped and stood on the opposite side of the body on the table, facing Harold.

He smiled at me, took his gloves off, threw them away, and then put on new ones.

"Hello there, agents. I'm Harold." He reached out his hand, and I shook it. Caspian shook his hand also, and then discreetly wiped his hand over his pants. I nudged him with my foot and gave him a look. Harold had literally just changed his gloves, so his hands weren't even dirty. Yet.

Caspian shrugged.

I turned my attention to Harold. "We know who you are, Harold. We've met plenty of times before on other cases."

He hesitated and chuckled awkwardly. "Oh yes, of course, I remember."

An awkward silence filled the room.

"Harold here made a discovery, a connection of sorts that could help your case. I'll be in my office if you need anything," Duke told us as he headed toward the exit.

Harold shifted his weight from one leg to the other. He ran a gloved hand through his hair and cleared his throat. "There's something peculiar about these five corpses. This one, for example." He pointed to the body on the table.

"I don't see anything out of place or weird. Except for the fact that it's basically the color of a fresh white sheet of paper," I said. *Male and pale.*

Caspian looked bored.

I sighed inwardly. He wasn't going to be any help here, obviously.

"Precisely. Now look over here when I move the arm." He lifted the arm up slightly, then turned it so that the wrist faced our direction.

A small cross was carved in the middle of the wrist.

I gasped. "Oh my god! That's what I found in the cold case files. The bodies all had crosses engraved in their wrists. See, Cas, this is what I was talking about!" I jumped a little with glee. I was right.

Caspian didn't look excited. He looked displeased.

"Caspian, what's wrong? This is the break we've been looking for. We're this much closer to the solving point. You should be excited." I frowned.

He sighed and clasped his hands behind his back. "I am thrilled about the discovery, but I'd like more evidence than a cross on a wrist before getting excited."

I rolled my eyes. "Are you serious right now?"

He nodded.

I scoffed, turning to Harold. "So, what about the other reports about the other bodies? Is there a reason why we haven't gotten the paper copies yet? I always need paper copies." I looked at my watch, impatient because I needed to leave for my meeting. I didn't want to miss it because there was a chance I wouldn't have that opportunity again. Ever. I looked back at Harold, and he looked confused.

"What do you mean? I gave it to Agent Galanis a few days ago. He told me he'd share the information with you."

I slowly turned to Caspian and his eyes widened. If looks could kill, Caspian would've literally disintegrated from the look I was giving him.

"Care to explain this, Agent Galanis?" I growled through my teeth.

He glared at Harold.

I moved to block his view and snapped my fingers in front of his face.

"Helloooo, I'm speaking to you! Explain why you have had the reports for days and didn't share them with me and then lied to me. *Now.*"

He huffed and locked eyes with me, his mouth forming a thin line. "I was trying to protect you," he growled back at me, crossing his arms over his chest.

I chuckled in disbelief and started pacing. "Protect me from what, Caspian? No one is after me. I'm not in any danger!" I threw my hands up in the air.

He grabbed my shoulders, stopping me in my place. "It's my job to protect you, Meadow. I have to, no matter what."

I shrugged his hands off and took a step back. "Stop trying to protect me all the time!" I stormed toward the door. I didn't have time for this when I should be preparing for my meeting.

"Dmitri!"

I stopped in my tracks.

Caspian took in a deep breath and sighed. "I'm protecting you from Dmitri Makris."

4

―――――――――――――

"Dmitri?" I whispered, squinting at Caspian in disbelief.

He nodded, eyes focused on the ceiling instead of me.

I stared at him for a few more seconds and busted out laughing. "So, you really expect me to be afraid of a person you literally just made up? Just so I can forgive you for lying to me?" I scoffed and shook my head.

"Meadow, please listen to me. You have to believe—"

I held up my hand. "Don't even, Caspian. When I get back, those reports better be on my desk, or else." I gave him a pointed look and walked out of the morgue. I couldn't believe he would lie to me. *I'm his partner, for goodness sake*, I grumbled to myself as I grabbed my jacket and purse from my office. I didn't have time for Caspian and his lies. Though he wasn't the only one withholding information. He didn't know anything about my meeting.

He liked to play by the rules, but me, not so much. Especially if it meant I was helping the victims of my cases. I'd break almost every rule for that.

As I made my way over to the location my mystery person gave me, I tried to prepare myself. I didn't know who I was meeting, and that made me anxious.

They controlled everything. The meetup spot, the person I was to meet, the plan they had outlined, *everything*. The only power I had was what I did with the information they gave me. I let out a deep breath and nodded. *I got this.* I reached my destination, according to my GPS. It was a small café on a busy corner of the street.

A cute café like the kind where you would expect to see a grandma behind the counter, baking for everyone. I'd expected to meet up in a sketchy abandoned building or an alleyway. Not this. I parked my car and grabbed my files.

Showtime.

A bell chimed when I opened the door and the fresh smell of coffee and pastries hit my nose. Those two smells combined let my tastebuds know it was breakfast time, but I'd have to miss out at the moment.

I scoped the area. It was a little crowded, and I wasn't a fan of crowds. I headed to a booth in the back that offered a great view of the front door.

I was about ten minutes early, which was on time for me. Being first gave me enough time to get my thoughts in order.

I reviewed my files.

Fifteen minutes later, the mysterious person hadn't shown. I pinched the bridge of my nose, squeezing my eyes tight. Five more minutes and I was out of here. The time ticked past, and still, no one showed up.

As I got up and started grabbing my files, shoes appeared by the table. I looked up at the owner of the shoes and came face-to-face with a woman. An unnaturally blonde woman with dark contrasting eyebrows and striking green eyes. Her outfit, a baby-pink tracksuit with spearmint-green tennis shoes, went well with her hairstyle, a short-cropped bob. She looked like a soccer mom, and she was in the way.

"Excuse me, I just need to get past you." I fake smiled, inching forward into her space.

"I don't think so." A gleaming fake smile crossed her face as she sat and gestured to the empty space in front of her.

I hesitated, and she pulled out a folder from her purse and placed it on the table. The folder read 'Confidential.'

"Sit," she commanded. Her nice soccer mom facade crumbled.

When I was seated, she slid the folder toward me and tapped it twice with her freshly manicured nail. All of her nails were almond-shaped and painted baby blue. Not that any of that mattered at this moment.

"I'm Donatella Stiles. I'll be in charge of making sure you complete the task given to you."

"Why would I need someone to make sure I complete the task? I gave you my word. I plan to keep that."

Donatella smirked and folded her hands together. "Open the folder, sweetie, and you'll see why I'm needed."

My hand hovered over the folder, not sure if I really trusted the information inside. I was told that it was a small task and nothing illegal. But then again, I was already in too deep and I did give them my word, so it wouldn't really matter what was in the folder. I would have to complete any task that was in it. I read over the papers inside and closed it quickly.

"There is no way I'm helping you do this. You guys said no killing and nothing illegal. This is both." I stabbed my finger on the folder. "I'm an agent. I cannot be caught in the middle of this shit storm. I could lose my job. I'm out." I stood.

"Agent Saar, you don't have a choice if you want to solve this case of yours. You *can't* solve this case without us. You will continue to go in circles unless you help us complete this one task." She tapped the folder again. "Look at the picture behind the instructions and then let me know what you really want to do." She smirked as I slowly sat back down.

I opened the folder again, lifted the instructions, and froze when I saw the picture. It was obviously taken at night, but I could clearly see the silhouette of a figure crouching over a body on the ground. The body was an unnatural color, and I couldn't see the wrist, but this was enough for me to sigh in defeat.

Donatella grabbed her purse and stood, smoothing out her

unwrinkled jumpsuit. "I'll be texting you specific instructions and I expect you to follow through. Have a great day, agent." She flashed me an innocent smile and strutted away from the booth.

I groaned, losing my appetite for breakfast. In fact, it was starting to smell a little nauseating. Why did I put myself in this situation? Stealing firearms from the department's closed off facility and putting down anyone that got in the way...I wanted to help the victims of my case, but this price, stealing and possible murder, could cost me everything I'd worked so hard for. Maybe I should've listened to Caspian.

5

The secret facility did not look like a gun storage facility like us agents were told. It looked like a building where secret science experiments happened. It was a tall glass building with a fantastic structure surrounded by a heavily wooded area. A vast building, yet I didn't see any armed guards walking around inside or outside.

Weird.

Donatella stepped out of one of the SUVs, in head-to-toe black like me.

I approached her. "I thought you said we were only taking guns, nothing else."

She smiled with no teeth and placed her hand on my shoulder. "Of course, darling, we are. Then *you'll* leave, so *we* can get what we actually came here for." She patted my shoulder and turned her attention to the two men standing silently behind her.

"Slate, Shar. Help the agent with her comms, please. Then get in position."

They were both over six feet tall and obviously super into working out. They kind of looked alike, but not in a twin way. Maybe siblings. One had short, cropped black hair, and the other had long black hair slicked back in a ponytail. Both of them were masters at frowning. No hint of a smile on either of them. Great.

The one with the ponytail approached me. "Slate. Follow me," he commanded.

I nodded and followed him to one of the SUVs. He opened the trunk, which held a variety of comms and tons of weapons that they definitely should not have. Still, I couldn't tell them anything, no matter how badly the agent in me wanted to.

Slate handed me something small and black. "Here. It goes in your ear," he gruffed, placing the earpiece in my hand.

I inspected it before putting it in my ear. It fit perfectly.

"Can you hear this?" Slate turned the dial on the device in his hand.

There was suddenly a loud ringing in my right ear, making me wince. I covered my ears instinctively and gave him a thumbs up. "Yep, definitely works."

He nodded and put the device back in the trunk.

Donatella came into view from the side of the vehicle and clapped her hands twice.

"All right everyone, listen up. We're here for the guns they keep hidden away in this facility. The agent"—she pointed to me—"will help us retrieve those guns." She grabbed three pistols and tossed one to each of us. "That's all you should need. Your skills should help with the rest." She closed the trunk and moved closer to me, whispering in my ear, "Agent, you're coming with me on the inside while these two will be on the lookout outside." She patted me on the back, and smiled.

I shook my head. "No, that wasn't part of the—"

"Too bad." Donatella cut me off. "It is now."

I groaned quietly as she brushed past me and spoke to Slate and Shar, low enough for me not to hear anything she said. Of course. I walked around the vehicle, wiping my sweaty palms on my pants. This wasn't right. There had to be another way to get this information. I glanced up at them, taking in their stances as they spoke to each other. I could easily make a run for my car and drive out of here.

No! I couldn't do that. All of those unsolved murders, current open cases, they all needed me. This was for them.

Alarms pierced the air, red lights flashing from the building. Around five armed guards came running from the side of the building to our direction.

"Here we go, guys. Showtime." Donatella clapped her hands, holstering her gun. "Everybody, fan out! Slate get to the left, Shar get to the right. Agent, stay in the back and make sure no one gets past you." Donatella turned and looked me in the eyes. "If anyone gets in your vicinity, you know what to do."

I tightened my lips and nodded. I was on the same team as the guards, but in their eyes, I was the enemy. The thought didn't sit well. Surely those of us on the right side of the law could take down these criminals. But if I was wrong, and we lost, Donatella would destroy the evidence I wanted. For now, I'd have to play along.

"Move forward." Donatella's voice came through the earpiece.

We advanced.

One of the brothers stepped on a twig of some sort, alerting the guards to our location.

"Slate, go!" Shar yelled.

Slate took off running, and yelled as he charged after one of the guards in front of him. Time seemed to slow down. Grass flew from Slate's feet as he ran, floating slowly in the air, then back down quickly. The guard lifted his gun to shoot. Slate bulldozed him. A hard grunt came from the guard as their bodies collided.

I was so focused on what Slate was doing, I forgot the other fight happening to the left of me until I heard a scream. Donatella fought with not one, but two guards. Watching her was like watching a madwoman from the wild. She jumped up and kicked her legs into the guards' chests, causing them to stagger backward, clutching their chests. Before I could see what else she was going to do, something whizzed by my right ear.

Ducking quickly, I whipped out my gun and pointed it, frantically searching for the culprit.

Found him.

A guard a few feet away from me, holding his gun in front of his face. When we made eye contact, he lowered his weapon and nodded. That was a warning shot. I nodded back. His eyes lifted as if he were smiling. I scrunched my eyebrows. Out of all the guards, I got the one that wanted to play games.

Getting up from my crouched position, I ran at him. He tossed his weapon to the side and started running at me as well. I tucked my gun in its holster and ran even faster. We reached each other. He ducked and slid on the ground, kicking my legs from under me. I fell hard. A sharp pain shot through my wrists as I caught myself. I groaned inwardly, getting a little pissed.

No more games.

I jumped up, throwing a punch at his face, but he blocked it and hit me in the stomach with a force that took my breath away. The guard laughed as I staggered backward and clutched my middle, coughing. I inhaled sharply. My anger rose like energy inside me, building...like an adrenaline rush. I embraced it.

Screaming, I charged after the cocky guard.

This time, my jab connected to his face. He staggered just enough for me to throw two more punches into his middle. I ducked his next blows and threw more punches into his ribs and back. He wheezed and hunched over. I searched for something to knock him out with. He wanted to do this the old-fashioned way, so I didn't pull out my gun. But I couldn't find anything.

The guard staggered my way. I charged at him and chopped my hand against his exposed throat. His hands flew to his throat, and I swept my leg under his feet, and he hit the ground hard, wheezing. Dropping down with him, I hurried and wrapped my bicep around his throat, squeezing in just the right way until he passed out.

I huffed and sat on my heels, catching my breath. I placed my fingers on his neck to feel his pulse.

"You should do a better job of choking someone out, *Meadow.*" His eyes snapped open, gray irises locking me in place.

My mouth dropped. He grabbed my arm and shot up, twisting it behind my back and slamming me into the ground. I gasped from the force and gritted my teeth, squirming to get out of his grasp.

"My, my, Meadow. This is quite embarrassing, isn't it? I'm sure I trained you better than this, but don't worry, I'll get you to remember and *oof*—"

His grip loosened. I broke free, ready to attack.

Donatella stood over the guard's body with a log in her hand. Her other hand graced her hip. "Really, agent?" She shook her head. "Pathetic," she grumbled as she walked toward the building.

I let out a pent-up breath and glanced at the unconscious guard. Something about his eyes reminded me of...I don't know. It reminded me of something important, but I couldn't quite put a finger on it.

My head started pounding. Nothing made sense. How did he know my name? I followed Donatella to the building, and the question remained on my mind.

It was a light gray, modern, square-shaped building. The windows seemed easy to break into, but there were barriers on the other side that blocked anyone from going in. Plus, an alarm would be triggered when unauthorized personnel entered the building, like the other buildings we owned. Which was also why I didn't understand why Donatella was willing to risk it all for some petty guns she could probably get from the black market.

"Let's go, agent. This should be quick. In and out." She scanned a badge, and the door beeped and turned green.

The inside lights were dim but bright enough to see where we were going. It was a typical storage facility, a stark contrast to the modern-looking outside. There were crates and boxes everywhere. It was going to take a while to search every box and find these guns.

Donatella let out a happy squeal and turned to face me. "We are in, agent! That's your card I used, by the way, so good luck explaining that to your bosses." She laughed as realization dawned on my face.

I gritted my teeth and willed myself to stay calm. Only a little longer until I got my hands on the file to help me solve my case. "Whatever. Let's just get to work. What are we looking for specifically?"

She clasped her hands together and smiled evilly. "Well, these weapons are special. I know I said guns, but that was so no one else would know what I was really after." She paused for dramatic effect, and I moved my hand in a circle, coaxing her to hurry and finish. "As I said, these weapons are extraordinary. I'm talking as in made out of a dangerous element. Only a few weapons were forged from this element, and two of them are right here in this very facility." Donatella twirled in a circle, smiling.

"I'm sure it's not that hard to find, and some chemists can probably make it for you," I scoffed.

She sighed. "Agent, this is no common element. Its origin is unknown, but the power it wields is indescribable," she explained with so much passion.

I didn't care about this so-called powerful element. I just wanted information. But then again, she had me a little curious. "Why do you want it?" I walked around, passing my hand over the dusty crates.

"Because my boss wants it, and it's my job to make sure it ends up in his hands." She clapped her hands twice. It annoyed me a little bit. "Now, let's start looking for the weapons. Both of them will be shaped like daggers. They will look like antiques, really beautiful. Golden handles with blue and white flecks on them. The blade itself will be a beautiful ocean-blue color, the ocean's color when the sun is at its peak."

I watched her face morph into awe as she described the daggers. "Let's get on with it." I turned to the crate closest to me and opened it. I dug around for at least twenty minutes and there were still hundreds of containers to go through. Donatella didn't look like she was going to give up anytime soon.

Of course not, I chuckled to myself.

She would literally go through all these boxes for days if she had to. I took a little break.

It was dimmer on the opposite side of the facility, but there was something off about the wall. I made my way over to it to get a better look. One of the tile squares wasn't symmetrical. It was connected by intricate shapes that seemed familiar, and after some pondering, I realized why.

The shapes were crosses.

The same crosses found on the corpses in the morgue. Interesting. Running my hand over the surface, I felt for a button or anything, but found nothing. I traced the whole shape, drawn in by the intricate crosses.

Everything around me seemed to disappear, and I became one with the shape. I pressed my hand against the middle of the wall. Locks clicked open, and I jumped.

The little crosses each ticked off the seconds as they turned to a vertical position. After the last cross finished turning, the locks stopped clicking and so did the creaking. The silence that followed was deafening, broken only by my shallow breathing and Donatella's annoying gasps.

"How on earth did you do that?" She whispered loudly.

I looked down at my hands and then back at the square. "I...I have no idea," I whispered back.

The feeling inside me was still strong, luring me back to the square like the pull of a magnet. A tingling sensation prickled my arms, up to my chest, and down to my fingertips. I walked back to it slowly. I lightly touched it with my index finger. It rumbled and popped open forcefully, slamming back against the wall, revealing a hole. When it seemed safe enough to move, I started forward.

Donatella put her arm out to stop me. "I'm in charge of retrieving the daggers. They belong...to me." Her voice got deeper as she finished, her face changed into one of greed.

"It doesn't matter who retrieves them in the end." I glanced back at the opening. "Plus, we don't even know if the daggers are in there."

She looked at me as if I had grown another head. "There is a secret wall in the building where they are keeping the most valuable weapons in the world, and you don't think the daggers are in there?" She scoffed and started walking toward the wall. "Idiot," she muttered as she walked away.

I laughed to myself and shook my head.

She made it to the square and stopped. "No way." She gasped. She put her hand in the hole, patting the inside frantically. She looked inside and started growling. "There's nothing here!"

I peered inside, and she was right. I really didn't want to go through all of the crates in the warehouse. Turning back to the empty hole, I gazed into it, wishing the daggers were in there, and brushed my hand over the cold surface. The connection I felt before came back, the same tingling sensation prickling my arms, all the way up to my chest, back down to my fingertips.

The odd sensation built inside me until it bordered on overwhelming. I pulled my hand back, but it didn't move. My face scrunched as I kept trying to move it without alerting Donatella. The sensation in my chest faded, and all I felt was the tingling in my hand. A shock shot through me. I gasped and finally managed to pull free. "Crap!" I clutched my hand. "What in the world…?" I muttered to myself, inspecting my hand. It showed no external sign of damage. Once I was sure that my hand wasn't going to fall off, I looked back at the hole and froze. My skin prickled.

How…?

A blue light shone from the opening. I didn't know how, but in the hole that had been empty sat two blue-bladed daggers.

6

"**D**on't even ask me how I did that because, at this moment, I have no idea how any of this happened," I said before Donatella could say anything.

The daggers were beautiful; Donatella definitely didn't lie about that. The blue from the blades gleamed from the hole.

"Yes! This is it!" Donatella gasped with glee. "This. Is. it." She slowly walked to the hole, still in awe, and gently picked up both daggers. She pulled a brown cloth from her pocket, wrapped the daggers inside of it, and smoothed out the wrinkles in the fabric. "Now, let's get that information you want so badly." She walked out of the facility, and I followed her back to the vehicles. One of them was missing.

"Uh, where are the brutal brothers?" I scanned the area to see if they were close by.

"Don't worry about them, darling. Worry about this." She whipped out an orange envelope and dangled it in front of my face. When I reached out to grab it, she pulled her arm back, tsking. "This information is crucial to your case. But it is also the key to your life." Her voice got more profound, and her eyes widened as if to make me take her seriously.

I scoffed and snatched the envelope out of her hand. "My life is perfectly fine, thanks." I laughed and sloppily saluted her goodbye, walking away and praying that I never had to see her again. Unless I was arresting her. *Now, that's a sight I would love to see.* I chuckled to myself.

I made it home after taking multiple detours to make sure that Donatella didn't follow me. Could never be too careful. As I placed the envelope on the table, my phone rang. I picked it up. "Saar speaking."

"Meadow, what the hell did you do?" Caspian whispered fiercely.

I froze. How did he find out so quickly? "What are you talking about?" I asked, deciding not to give myself away in case he was talking about something else.

"Don't play dumb with me. Duke came straight to me after being alerted that your card was swiped at a facility you should have no knowledge about. What is going on with you lately?" He sounded more concerned rather than upset.

Crap.

I blew out a breath and paced, trying to think quickly on my feet. "I—"

"Hold that thought. Duke and some other suits are coming my way. You better get here now and come up with the best damn excuse because it's not looking good for you right now." He hung up.

"Thanks," I said to no one. I tossed my phone on my couch and ran upstairs to change into one of my best suits. As I got ready, I tried to think of any valid excuse for being at the facility. Maybe I could say that I had insider knowledge that the criminals would try and steal essential items.

No, not good. Why would I, out of all the important people above me, be informed about something like that? I huffed as I tried to get my pants on. Oh—I could say I was kidnapped and forced against my will. Held at gunpoint and everything.

Ugh, no. No good. If there were cameras, I would totally be caught in a lie. I wasn't good at lying; that would be more Caspian's avenue. I was done getting ready and didn't have any more time to waste, so I ran downstairs, grabbed my phone, and bolted out of my place.

The drive there, I was so anxious, I ran over some lane dividers, pissing off other drivers. When I made it to headquarters, I went straight to my office. I turned on the light and yelped, my hand flying to my chest.

Caspian was sitting in my chair at my desk, hands folded together. He frowned, something he rarely did. He was disappointed.

"Caspian, I can explain—"

He held up a hand.

I sighed and sat down in the chair in front of my desk.

"Why didn't you tell me about your plans?" He asked, keeping his voice low.

I ran my hand through my hair and scoffed. "Look, you already know how you get when it comes to trying anything that doesn't necessarily align with the code, so you shouldn't even have to ask that question," I stated, crossing my arms over my chest.

"Okay, fine. Why did you go alone?"

Like that question was any better.

"Because if my own partner doesn't care to be a little reckless with me, no one else will either. I mean, I didn't do anything *too* ille—"

"Nope. Don't finish that sentence. I don't want to know anything. Keep it to yourself. Just think of something to save your ass when you speak to Duke and the suits."

My throat dropped to my stomach. "When do I have to speak with Duke?" I asked quietly, not really wanting to hear the answer.

"Now."

Crap.

I'M SUSPENDED. Two weeks. They were still debating whether I should get paid or not. I deserved that anyway, so I wasn't really upset. But being suspended didn't mean I would stop working. The opposite, actually. I researched like crazy for the next few days, buried myself in my work, determined to find any clues connected together, using the information Donatella gave me.

I wouldn't call it information per se. At least not the best information. She gave me an envelope with a piece of paper in it, which had one name.

Victor Baldwin.

A name that had been no help at all. Nothing important had popped up—nothing connected to my case at all. The only information I got from looking him up was that he captained a cruise ship that did popular cruises to The Island.

After spending days and nights trying to get more information from the internet, I sighed and concluded that I had to ask Caspian for help. I hadn't spoken to him after everything that happened since I'd been so busy. Picking up my phone, I tapped on his name and waited.

"What?" Caspian's voice came through the phone, sounding annoyed and tired. Granted, it was like 7 a.m., and he was probably still sleeping when I called.

"Hi, friend, how are you?" I stretched out the last word and smiled, knowing he probably wanted to strangle me for being all hyper so early. Not that he would ever do that, because deep down, he was the biggest teddy bear ever.

"Meadow. Do you know what time it is?" His bed creaked, and he groaned, probably checking the time to see how early it actually was.

"Yes! But I really need your help."

He groaned again. "No, Meadow, I—"

"It's about our case!" I interrupted, hoping that would make him care enough to not be as irritated. I crossed my fingers.

"You're suspended, Meadow."

I pursed my lips. "When has that ever stopped me?" I asked. Long seconds passed by.

"Fine," he finally said.

I punched the air with my fists. Success.

"What time do you want me over?" he asked, getting out of bed, I assumed from all the shuffling in the background.

"Now?" I responded sweetly, making sure it came out as a question rather than a statement. It made it seem sweeter. Silence followed.

"I hate you." Were his last words before he hung up on me.

I jumped up from the bed and did a little happy dance. He was so smart and always had the best ideas when it came to solving cases. I was better at the execution of those ideas.

While I waited for him to come over, I took a quick shower, ate some breakfast, and got all the files and evidence I'd collected so far and brought them down to my living room. I spread them all out on the floor and grabbed my laptop as well, pulling up the article about Victor Baldwin on the screen. I had to get more information on this guy since he was apparently the key to solving this mess of a case.

There hadn't been any more bodies connected to my case since the last one, which was good because it gave me more time to connect all the dots without worrying about another body.

By the time I was done setting up everything, I was confident I had enough information for Caspian to help me tie something together. Now I just had to wait for him to get here. A few seconds later, there was a knock on my front door.

Perfect timing.

I unlocked it, slowly and dramatically opening the door for him.

"Why Meadow," he said, stepping inside, "must you be so dramatic?" He shook his head at me.

I smiled up at him and shrugged. "You know me. Always have to be extra. But what are you wearing?"

He didn't answer.

I waved my hand in front of his face. "Are you there, Caspian? Hello?" I pretended to knock on the side of his head.

He smirked slightly and looked down at his clothes. Black joggers with a pale gray shirt and white sneakers. He rarely dressed down. Not even when he relaxed. I didn't know he owned other articles of clothing besides suits and slacks and button-downs. Oh, and of course, dress shoes.

"Look, I am super tired, and maybe I'm starting to actually take your advice at not looking uptight all the time, whatever that means." He rolled his eyes when my face lit up with glee.

I put my hand over my chest and sniffed. "I am so proud of you, Cas." I patted his shoulder and wiped invisible tears from my eyes.

He shrugged my hand away. "Don't we have work to do? Let's get to that." He sighed.

"Of course, follow me." I led him toward my set up in my living room, and he groaned softly behind me. "I know, I know. But I really think I'm on to something, I just don't know how to connect them. I'm missing something," I explained as I took a seat on the floor.

He sat down next to me and leaned closer to my laptop. "Victor Baldwin?" He grabbed the laptop and placed it on his lap. "Who is that?" He scrolled through the article.

"He's, um, a guy whose name popped up that could somehow help this case."

"Meadow…" He gave me a pointed look, his blue eyes showing disappointment. "Where did you get his name?"

I smiled sheepishly, scratching my head. "Don't worry about that, Caspian. Just know that he is crucial." I shifted to get comfortable and leaned back into my couch. "What I need you to do is research this guy and find out anything important about him that will help our case. Work your magic, because apparently I have none." I chuckled lightly.

"Magic shall be worked." He grinned at me, and we both nodded at each other in agreement and started our work.

I still had the files I took from work, one from 1866 and the other from 2008. I had skimmed over them and was mainly focused on getting the medical examiner's report, which was my mistake. I held the 2008 file and put the others on the floor next to me, then started from the very beginning. Of course, it was similar to our current case, those similarities being the cause of death and the crosses. But one thing the other cases had, which mine didn't, was witness statements.

Skipping to the witness section, I read through the statements in the case of the first pale body found in 2008 to see if anything connected. One thing that stood out was that the victim took a cruise to a place called The Island right before he died. Grabbing a pen from my table in front of me, I circled 'The Island' because this was the first clue connected to Victor Baldwin.

I glanced over to see how Caspian was doing. He was focused, his fingers flying over the keyboard. I smiled softly, glad that I asked him to help. Even though he could be really annoying sometimes, I considered him my best friend. I didn't have many friends, and none I would consider a best friend like I do Caspian. He was it. Turning back to my file, I looked at the other cases in 2008 and the witness statements.

I froze. It seemed like I was reading the same statement in each different case. The witness stated that they saw a man in all black, with a black cross earring dangling from his right ear, and he was at least 6'1". What really threw me off was that the suspect's eyes glowed a vibrant violet, the last thing each witness saw before being knocked out.

I huffed and leaned back into my couch, trying to process everything. Violet eyes? Almost no one had purple eyes, and definitely none that glowed, so I didn't understand. The notes also said they weren't drugged or anything, so why would they say that? Shaking my head to clear all the information I had just dumped in it, I looked to see who the witnesses were. The first witness was an older woman named Mary Taymer.

According to her, she was almost a victim but survived by stabbing the suspect with Jestraetrium. I looked at the word again and tried my best to sound it out. I didn't even know what that was. It sounded like a type of element, but I'd never heard of it. I circled the word to remind myself to research it later.

Whoever conducted the toxicology report for these witnesses must not have done it correctly. *This lady sounds insane.* Thumbing through the rest of the witnesses, there was one name that kept popping up for many cases. I almost dropped the file I was holding.

"Caspian, look!" I basically shoved the file in his face. There was a picture of a man in it and underneath the picture, was a name. Victor Baldwin.

Caspian's eyes grew wide, and he turned my laptop so that I could see what he had pulled up on the screen. The headline read 'Captain

Witnesses Death of Tourists.' The photo attached to the article was of an older-looking man with gray hair, standing in front of a ship—the only photo I'd seen of Victor. During my research, I tried my best to find a picture of him to see what he looked like, but I had no luck.

"Where did you find that article? I could barely find anything on him."

Caspian shrugged and turned my laptop back around. "I guess I'm just that good." He clicked on something else and angled the laptop to me. "If you really want to find out more about him, I just found out where his ship is located."

I grabbed my laptop from his hands and searched through the information he had pulled up. It was a website about Victor and the cruises he conducted for anyone interested in visiting The Island. How people found out about his cruises, I had no idea. I didn't even know about it until I started researching this case.

As I continued to read, I finally saw the location of his ship. In a city called The Harbor, which is only about a thirty-minute drive from the town I lived in, The Angels. Caspian finding this website was a miracle. I didn't know how he did it, but I did know I was grateful and definitely going to pursue this lead.

I turned to Caspian with a huge smile. "Time to go on a road trip?" I asked.

He chuckled and stood up, stretching. "I actually have things planned to do today, sorry."

I frowned and got up to stretch, too. The feeling of my bones popping was actually soothing and felt great. "But I really need your help on this. Please?" I batted my lashes playfully and smiled when he rolled his eyes for the millionth time.

"Not this time, Meadow. I do have a life, you know." He gave me a look and raised his eyebrows. I may have told him one too many times that he didn't have a life because he was always working.

I feigned confusion. "You do?" I tried my best to sound sincere but ended up laughing.

"I do, and now I need to be on my way."

I followed him to the door and opened it. He stepped outside and paused, turning back to me. "I would advise you not to go out researching this little lead we found right now, but knowing you, you'll go anyway. So please, be safe." He pulled me into a hug. He knew me so well.

"You don't have to worry about me, okay?" I patted him on the back reassuringly.

His body relaxed after my statement, and he pulled away, looking me straight in the eyes. "Promise?" His crystal blue eyes widened for emphasis.

I chuckled and tapped his chest with my index finger. "I promise."

He finally looked convinced. "All right, let me know how it goes," he called out as he walked away toward his car. He waved at me once he reached it.

"I will. Be safe driving home!" I watched as he laughed, knowing fully that I was mocking him.

"I will!" He shouted back, his voice high pitched, trying to mock me.

I shook my head, smiling as I went back inside and closed the door, locking it behind me.

Now I needed a plan.

7

"Interesting place," I muttered to myself as I crossed the boardwalk. I finally made it to The Harbor after being stuck in traffic for like an hour, and the place was nothing like I'd imagined. The whole area was vacant, as if no one lived here or had visited in a long time.

There were boats everywhere. Some were little sailboats to relax and enjoy the water close to home, and others were actual cruise ships for nice vacations to many different islands. What stood out as I scanned the scenery and analyzed the boats was that none floated in the middle of the beautiful blue water. All were docked. The scent of fish and other sea creatures filled the air, creating that relaxing seaside feeling.

The area was super clean, and many restaurants bordered the water. But just like the water, they were empty. I passed many storefronts with CLOSED signs on them. Not even a bird made a peep in this part of town. What happened here? I kept walking farther down the boardwalk and looked at the waterfront where the boats were docked to search for the cruise ship in the picture with Victor.

I couldn't see the whole thing in the picture, but part of it was black. I also saw part of the name—the ending of it: *-teros*. The boats and the water and smell all took me back to when I was younger when I would always go sailing with my mom—one of the things she made sure to do every year in my dad's memory. I smiled softly at the memories.

I missed my mom and definitely needed to visit her at some point soon. As I reached the end of the boardwalk, I still didn't see a ship matching the description I saw in the picture. So much for talking to Victor. Scanning the area, I spotted a seafood place that didn't have a CLOSED sign. Instead, it had *Ted's Seafood* plastered on it, and it looked like people were actually in there.

Maybe they had some information I could use. Walking up to the door, I hesitated, taking in a deep breath. *Here goes nothing.* I opened the door, and a briny odor hit my nose. I gagged. I wasn't a fan of seafood, just a fan of seeing them in the water. The restaurant seemed more like a diner, with a rustic feel to it. Bare, dark brown wood everywhere. The bar counter, every table and chair, the whole structure. All wood. I could see the kitchen from the bar area, which was right by the door as soon as I came in.

Everyone stopped what they were doing when I entered the diner. Curse that stupid bell. Not that it mattered because *everyone* meant the only three people in the whole place. The bartender, the cook, and an older woman sitting in the very back, staring out the window.

"Can I help you?"

I turned to the voice and found the bartender looking at me. He was an older man and rugged. His beard was large and long, but nicely trimmed. It matched the dark hair that went past his shoulders.

"Yes, actually. I have a few questions for you, if you don't mind." I made my way over to where he stood at the bar.

As he took his time wiping the inside of a glass, his eyes assessed my attire and eyed my hip, probably looking for a gun. He wouldn't be able to spot it, though. I hid it exceptionally well.

He grunted and picked up another glass, wiping the inside. "You a cop?" he asked, jutting out his chin defensively.

I pressed my lips together and tapped my fingers on the bar counter. "Not today. Just an inquisitive person looking for some answers to connect the dots," I returned. I wasn't getting a good vibe from this man.

He grunted again and scrunched his face up in slight disgust, putting the glass he was wiping down on the counter. He placed his hands down and leaned forward. "Listen here, lady. I can tell you're not from around here based on how you're dressed. It's too professional, and no one here dresses like they're from the government. So, you can take yourself and your questions and leave my place." He stared me down, heat blazing in his eyes.

"Calm down, Ted. This young lady was nothing but nice to you. Don't take your anger toward the government out on her. Shame on you."

Ted, the bartender and owner, averted his gaze from me and looked over my shoulder, his heated stare softening a bit for the speaker. I also turned and saw the older woman staring back at Ted.

"But you know what happens when people like her start snooping in business that doesn't concern them," he retorted, his tone more respectful with her than it was with me. I wondered what he meant by that.

The woman turned her attention to me, ignoring Ted. "What's your name, sweetie?" She smiled softly.

"Meadow," I answered, smiling back. She seemed really nice.

"That's a beautiful name. My name is Mary. I heard you have some questions that need answering. I might have some answers for you." She patted the space in front of herself, inviting me to sit with her. Ted growled a little at her invitation, and I chuckled at his reaction as I made my way over to her. I sat down, and Mary clasped her hands together and leaned on the wooden table. "Now darling, what can I do for you?" She nodded her head at me to speak.

"I am here because of an investigation. A few deaths have occurred, and they all lead back to this town."

Mary nodded and chuckled softly to herself, smoothing her hands across the table. "I knew one day someone was going to come back here asking questions about this. No one ever found out who did it, did they?" she asked, taking in the shocked look on my face.

39

"So you know about the murders?" I asked her, wanting to know more.

"Of course, child. I was almost a victim myself, you know."

It clicked that her name was Mary. As in Mary Taymer from the police report. The one witness in multiple cases. The crazy one.

"I read your statement about that. Can you tell me exactly what happened? Because it seemed kind of…" I trailed off, trying to think of a nice way to say crazy.

She reached across the table and placed her hands over mine. "Darling, I know you want to call me crazy."

I opened my mouth, but she held her hand up, stopping me. "Don't worry, they all think that. They tell me what I'm saying doesn't make sense, but it does if you're aware." She paused and looked down at the table in deep thought. I gave her time to collect her thoughts. She looked back up at me. "It was dark, and I heard a scream. I live just right over there, you know. So I put on some decent clothes and went out to see if anyone needed help. I made it all the way to the end of the boardwalk, and there he was, standing over someone with blood on both of his hands."

"How did you know it was a man and that he had blood on his hands if it was dark?" I interrupted successfully this time.

Her brown eyes widened, and her hands tightened around mine, but not enough to hurt. "I couldn't see anything properly, so I pulled out my phone for brightness, and that's when I saw the blood. When my light hit him, he turned around, and the next thing I knew, a hand was around my throat, choking me. I don't know how he moved so quickly, but I couldn't breathe at all. But that's when I noticed the cross earring in his right ear." She paused again, breathing heavily.

I took my hands out of hers and placed mine on top.

She looked grateful for my small gesture of reassurance and continued. "And his eyes! Oh, the eyes! That was the most frightening part. They weren't normal. They were violet. So that's when I knew. When I knew I had to use the ultimate weapon."

When she spoke of the weapon, I remembered her statement about how she used some type of element.

"You mean, getraum?"

"Jestraetrium, dear. The ultimate weapon. I reached in my pocket with the strength that I could muster, grabbed it, and shoved it in the side of that monster with all my might. Oh lord, the screams he made. It sounded like a large animal dying mixed with nails dragging down a chalkboard. I collapsed when he let me go, and I was coughing really hard and gasping, trying to get air back into my lungs. I didn't wait to see what happened to him after that. I just ran home as fast as I could and prayed I never had to encounter a dark one like that ever again."

I scrunched my eyebrows together. *A dark one?* First violet eyes, now a dark one/monster. She was really out of her mind. "What do you mean, a dark one? And what is Jestraetrium?"

"Whatever you think of when you hear or see the words 'dark one' is what I'm talking about. Jestraetrium is a powerful element, the only thing that can truly kill a dark one. It can be forged into weapons and can only come from one place." She leaned forward, getting as close as she could to me, and whispered, "The Island."

I was so confused. I didn't even know what came to my mind when I thought of a dark one. A dark-skinned man? Someone in dark clothing? I was right about Jestraetrium being an element, but everything else just confused me. Nothing really made sense, and I wasn't sure if anything she told me even helped my case.

I sighed heavily and massaged my forehead, trying to figure out what else I wanted to ask. "Okay, okay. I need some time to process all of this. But I do have a few more questions if that's okay."

Mary nodded at me to continue.

"There's this man who was also a witness in one of the cases. He owns a ship that takes people to The Island. Do you know who he is?" I asked.

Her lips pressed together tightly and she leaned back into her chair, away from the table. She shook her head, and I was about to ask another question, but she kept shaking her head. "No, no, no!" She smacked her hand on the table. "Do *not* trust that man!" She pointed her finger at me, her soft, loving features turning hard, and the anger that flowed from her was very evident. She wasn't done. "That man is the reason these dark ones are roaming this place! Why so many people are dead! He brought them here on that godforsaken boat. That island is cursed, I tell ya! I went there myself! That's where I got the ultimate weapon!"

I tried my best to keep up with what she was saying, writing furiously in my little notepad I kept in my pocket. The weapon came from The Island.

"Mary," I called out to her, hoping she would calm down for this last—maybe last—question.

"I'm sorry. I haven't spoken about this in so many years, and it dredges up so many memories that were suppressed. Go ahead and ask your question."

I smiled at her. "You're very brave for doing this, knowing it would bring up the bad memories. My question is about the ultimate weapon. What did it look like?"

She motioned for my notepad, and I handed it to her along with my pen. She flipped until she reached a blank page and started sketching. I turned my head so I could see what she was drawing. She wasn't the best artist and not close to being done with it, but I could already tell that she was drawing a dagger. I groaned internally, knowing I would have to see Donatella again. This definitely wasn't a coincidence. As she drew, I thought back on everything she told me.

One thing that stuck in my mind was the cross earring. The crosses from the warehouse wall looked similar to the ones engraved on the bodies. I wondered if what she described was the same as the ones I'd come across.

"Mary, could you also draw the earring to the best of your ability?" I asked, and she nodded, still drawing the dagger. At that point, the drawing definitely looked like the daggers I found with Donatella. I should've known that something would come back to her, especially since she knew about my case and exactly what would help me. I knew this day would be eventful.

I'd learned way more than I thought I would, but with this information, I didn't know if Victor was a witness or a suspect. Mary had said some questionable things, especially accusing Victor of bringing the dark ones to this place. Whatever that meant. I was so conflicted.

"Here, I'm done." Mary slid my notepad and pen across the table, and I caught both before they slid to the floor. Bringing my notepad up to my face, I analyzed her drawing. A weird feeling grew inside me. It matched the other crosses I had come across during the investigation. I let out a large breath, feeling a little headache forming. This was way deeper than I thought it would be. I relaxed my face so I didn't seem stressed and smiled at Mary.

"Thank you so much for all of this, Mary. It has really helped me with this investigation. If I need anything else, I know where to find you." I stood up and put my hand out to shake Mary's.

She grabbed my hand and shook it. "Anytime, Meadow. I wish you well with your investigation. And remember—" She lowered her voice and curled her finger at me to bend down. "Do not trust Victor Baldwin. He's not who he says he is. He has followers everywhere, so watch what you say. Also remember, he's bringing the dark ones to and from The Island. *From The Island.* Be careful."

I suppressed the urge to roll my eyes and put a fake smile on my face. "Of course, Mary. Thank you for the warning." I patted her softly on her back, and she patted my hand.

"Safe travels, my dear." She turned back to the window and started humming.

I shook my head as I walked toward the exit. I still thought she might need a little help. I made eye contact with Ted on my way out and nodded at him. He actually nodded back, but his face was still scrunched with distaste.

That was probably just how he was. I left the diner and breathed in the fresh air. Well, as fresh as the air could get over here. That was… intriguing. Very interesting. I opened my eyes and looked at the sky. It was getting darker, but the sky still had a little light to it. I hadn't realized how long I'd been in the diner. What was I going to do with all of this information? I huffed in frustration.

This all needed to connect somehow so that it wasn't so confusing. More boats were docked, filling up all the spaces. Where they came from, I had no idea. I walked toward the boardwalk and made my way to the end, hoping to see Victor's ship. Sure, Mary said to watch out for him, but he was probably harmless.

I got closer to the end and spotted part of a black boat. I walked faster, and more of the ship started showing. Victor's ship. I reached the end and stopped, looking up at the beauty. The entire thing was a pure, shiny black. The only color was the name, *Presbyteros*. It was in a beautiful shade of gold, in cursive. What an odd name.

Looking around, I didn't see Victor—or anyone, actually. Just like it was when I first arrived in The Harbor, it was quiet. I crossed my arms over my chest as the wind picked up a little bit, making it chilly. I shivered and watched the sunset, debating whether I should leave and go home to go over all the information I learned today, or try to find Victor and get his side of the story.

Tapping my foot, I shivered again, blowing air out of my mouth. I twisted my lips to the side, deep in thought. Caspian told me to be safe, and I promised him I would. But going on Victor's ship to find him and ask a few questions regarding the investigation wasn't too bad, right? Pushing back what Mary told me about him, I made up my mind to go on it to find him. I would be quick and safe.

Satisfied with my odds, I took another quick look around to make sure no one was walking on the boardwalk. Once I saw that it was empty, I turned back to the ship and looked for a way onto it. I didn't see the stairs to enter because of the way it was docked. Walking to the right side, I went to the dock's edge and peered on the side. There. The only way to reach the stairs was to either get in the water or walk on the very slim ledge poking out of the ship's side. The sun was one drop away from fully setting, so I didn't really trust going in the water. *Slim ledge it is.*

Making sure my footing was stable, I walked to the edge of the pier and stuck my leg out, leaning to hook my foot on it. I grabbed the top of the closest railing and swung my body across, slamming into the ship's side. The air left my body, and I gasped at the sudden impact. Catching my breath, I grabbed the railing with my other hand and balanced myself, squeezing my foot on the slim part as best as I could. Once I knew I wasn't going to fall, I started moving toward the stairs—one step at a time.

"You got this, Meadow," I muttered, hoping that I didn't fall into the water. I hadn't realized how far the stairs were from my position, and my arm muscles were already straining from hanging on to the railing. I had to hold on tightly, or I would definitely fall in the water. I kept moving. "Don't look down, don't look down." I could swim, but I wasn't a fan of being in the deep water in the dark. That definitely wasn't the right combination. I kept moving and reassuring myself that I wouldn't fall until I finally made it to the stairs.

Grabbing on to one part of the railing, I raised myself up and reached for the next section of the railing, and then climbed until I made it all the way to the deck. I collapsed on the deck and stretched my arms in the air, trying to relax my tight muscles. After a minute of rest, I got up and dusted off my clothes. I expected to see chairs and chandeliers or something fancy, but all I found were lifeboats and life jackets everywhere.

8

Of course. I was at the lowest part of the deck on the ship, basically, so there would be random but essential items down here. There were boxes and statues also crowded down here with the extra lifeboats and jackets. This deck must be used as a storage place. I walked through the crowded deck. It was a little dim, so I had to squint as I looked around, but nothing was interesting on this deck. I found the stairs and made my way up to the next level.

This deck was more exciting and spacious. Elegant golden tables and chairs were strategically placed all over the deck with a beautiful crystal chandelier hanging from the ceiling, glittering even in the dark as it slowly turned. It was super open and not congested on this level, unlike the last one. The railings were high enough to lean on if one wanted to look at the water or the sky.

I went to the railing and felt the night's chill even more on the wide-open deck. It was absolutely stunning, the view. Turning away, I took my time walking past the gold decor, letting my hand pass over the beautiful finishes. Other than the chairs and tables, there was nothing else to see on this level.

As I walked up the stairs, I heard a voice come from the deck above me. I halted. I couldn't really hear what the person was saying or what they sounded like because the voice kept getting farther away. Once I couldn't hear it anymore, I slowly crept up the rest of the stairs. This deck was darker than the one before, the only real source of light coming from the moon that had reached its peak in the sky.

This deck looked like a dance hall; the only thing gracing it was a grand piano. I'd started walking toward the piano when the hairs on the back of my neck stood up as if someone was behind me. I whipped around, bracing myself, but no one was there. I let out a sigh and put a hand over my pounding heart. I had no reason to be afraid, yet I couldn't shake the feeling.

Victor was just another witness, and if he wasn't on this ship, I would just turn back around. Not that I would have to because I definitely heard a voice. I started walking back to the piano and was almost there when a soft whistle filled the air. I paused and listened, waiting to hear the sound again. There was nothing.

Hm.

I looked over my shoulder and breathed as quietly as I could, hoping that it would help me hear better. Nothing happened. I turned back to face the piano and heard it again. It sounded like the wind being blown in different directions on the inside of the ship even though no strong winds were blowing outside. I stood in place and waited for the sound again. After a few long seconds of nothing happening, I took another step. The hairs on the back of my arms and neck rose once again.

My breathing slowed, and I tried not to panic as I felt a strong presence behind me. This time, it felt as if someone was close to me. Their breath warmed the back of my neck, sending my fight or flight instincts into overdrive. I itched to see if someone was actually behind me, but my body wouldn't move. *I'm probably just making things up in my head like I sometimes do,* I tried to convince myself.

It didn't really work.

A hand grabbed my arm, yanking me to the side. I opened my mouth to scream, but a large hand clamped over my mouth, stifling my scream. The person backed up and their body hit the wall, holding me hostage against their chest. My heart was beating too quickly, and it was hard to breathe through the big hand covering half of my face. I screamed into the hand and bit down hard, causing the person to wince and curse.

It sounded like a man.

"Be quiet. He's going to hear you," a deep, accented voice whispered firmly into my ear, sending chills up my spine.

I didn't recognize the voice, yet it sounded so familiar. I shook my head, trying to get the hand off my face, but it didn't work.

"Stop it. If I remove my hand, will you be quiet? This is important," he whispered, slowly loosening his grip on my face.

I nodded quickly, wanting his mint-scented hand off my face. *How dare he.*

He let go, and I looked down, watching as he wiped his hand on his pants. He had two thick, black rings on his long fingers, one on his index finger and the other on his middle finger. His other arm was still wrapped my waist, locking me to his chest. I still had a slight advantage. I opened my mouth to scream, but quickly shut it when he growled.

"Quiet!" he snapped, pulling at my arm. Having a stranger tell me to be quiet and actually yank me triggered my anger instead of fear, and I'd had enough.

I growled back and stomped on his foot, forcing him to let go of me. I butted his face with the back of my head, and he cursed and groaned. I whirled around, raising my knee to his groin. He doubled over, and I started walking backward, trying to see my attacker's face.

It was too dark to see any distinct features, but I could see his eyes as he looked up, clutching his face. They were piercing gray, like a full moon in a clear dark sky. And they totally looked familiar.

"Meadow." His voice was low, but loud enough for me to hear.

I gasped. *It was the guard from the warehouse.* "You!" I whispered fiercely and charged at him, going for his jugular, my hands curled.

He caught both of my arms, stopping me from doing any damage. "Stop trying to attack me. You need to be quiet. He's almost here. I will explain everything after," he whispered back just as fierce—if not more so than before.

I didn't know who he was talking about, but I didn't care. I needed to get off of this ship and away from him. I could talk to Victor at another time.

I yanked my arms out of his grip, but he was too strong. I growled and yanked my arms down again, this time crouched at the same time, and jumped up, slamming my feet against the wall behind him. I threw my body backward, the force making him let me go. I flipped back and landed on both my hands and feet. I looked up in time to see him taking long strides my way. I readied myself to fight. *I don't care how strong he is, I will beat him.* He reached me, and before I could throw a punch, another voice filled the air.

"Did you hear that?" the voice questioned, coming closer to where the guard from the warehouse and I were located.

My eyes widened, and I was yanked backward with a force that knocked the air out of my lungs. We were back in the corner by the piano, his arm wrapped completely around my midriff, locking my arms in place. He made it back to the wall quicker than I could fathom.

"Shh. Don't make a sound."

For some reason, this time, I listened. My heart was racing, and I regretted putting myself in danger. Why couldn't any simple task go right for me?

We waited and stayed in the corner, listening to the footsteps as they got closer.

"I swear I heard a scream down here." The speaker came into view, and I stifled my gasp. It was Victor. His face was exactly the same as in the article. Same low-cut hairstyle with the same clean-shaven beard. He wasn't alone. I couldn't see a face, but the person was in a royal purple cloak, the hood pulled over his or her head. Victor scanned the area, starting with the stairs and ending on where I was standing in the corner with the stalker guard.

Clutching the guard's arm, I was about to speak to reveal myself and explain why I was on the ship so late in the middle of the night, but the guard behind me squeezed my arms, stopping me.

"Don't say a word." His breath fanned my ear as he spoke, so low I almost didn't hear him.

Victor squinted as he walked in my direction. He scratched his jaw. My mind flipped through a dozen flimsy excuses for boarding his ship without permission. The floorboards squeaked beneath his shoes, and the boat rocked gently against the dock. The guy holding me kept us both steady. Victor paused inches away from me, his eyes narrowed. I readied my excuse. Victor hmphed and returned to the cloaked figure.

"I guess I was wrong. Now, as we were discussing, where are you with the replacement?" Victor asked.

"We keep running into problems. The transition isn't completing with some, and with others, they don't have the power we're looking for, so we assign them somewhere else." The cloaked figure's voice was gruff and unnaturally deep. It was like he was trying to mask his real voice.

Victor cursed. "You told me that by this time, you would have a replacement. I give you the people you need, and in return, you give me what I need. Maddox's life depends on this. You know that."

An animalistic growl came from the cloaked figure. He reached his hand out, and Victor floated, choking as he rose.

I covered my mouth before my gasp could escape. The cloaked figure wasn't even touching Victor, yet he was gasping for air, his legs kicking back and forth as he tried to breathe.

"Don't you dare tell me how to do my job! I know what Maddox needs. Your selection has been poor, so the transitions are impossible to complete. Give me a better selection, or your precious Maddox will have your head for incompetence," the cloaked figure roared with such ferocity, I flinched back into the guard's chest instinctively.

Victor nodded quickly, his face beet red from the lack of oxygen, and he fell to the ground, wheezing. What Mary said about not trusting Victor was making a little more sense. The rest of this mess made no sense at all.

"Get up. I'm giving you the next few days to find the perfect

SOULS

replacement that is even better than Dmitri, do you understand?" the
cloaked figure warned Victor as he got up from the floor. Dmitri?
That was who Caspian said he was protecting me from.

Victor nodded vigorously and coughed, rubbing his neck. "But I
thought he was a traitor," Victor said and then flinched when the
cloaked figure growled.

"He's still powerful, and to stop him, we need someone rare like
him."

I felt the guard's chest vibrate as he hissed.

"When I tell you to run, you need to run as fast as you can off the
ship. Do you understand?" he whispered in my ear. "In a minute,
they're going to be able to see us, and it won't be pretty."

I nodded, not really understanding how they couldn't see us in the
first place. I eyed the stairs, adrenaline pumping, ready to sprint like
my life depended on it. Because after what the guard said, it actually
did.

"Traitors don't deserve to live, or people who associate themselves
with them!" A roar come from the cloaked figure, and he turned my
way sharply. A vibrant violet glowed from where his eyes would be
located. My heart dropped, and I was shoved forward hard, causing
me to stumble.

"Run!"

I caught myself on the ground. Something whizzed by my ear,
right where my head was seconds before. The guard stood with his
arms up behind me, clutching a golden handled, blue-bladed dagger in
each hand.

I gasped and scrambled up off the floor, running to the stairs.

He just saved my life.

I was almost to the stairs when I smashed into an invisible force
and flew backward. I landed on my back painfully, gasping for air. My
eyes widened at the cloaked figure, his arms raised as if he was the
cause of me flying back. There was another animalistic snarl to my
right, and my mouth dropped as the guard charged at the cloaked
figure. I jumped up and ran for the stairs again, this time making it.

I ran through the dining hall, pushing chairs out of my way, wincing each time my bruised arms smashed into them. Running down more stairs, I made it to the deck with the lifeboats and jackets and stopped abruptly. No time to walk on the thin side, and the wind had grown too strong. It would probably blow me into the water.

The snarls and growls were getting closer. Time was up.

I took in a deep breath, crossed my arms, and jumped. Someone shouted my name. A force from behind crashed into me, and I screamed as the water turned to wood. I gasped as I patted my body. I was completely dry.

The guard appeared beside me, his eyes glowing the same vibrant violet as the cloaked figure.

I choked on air as I stumbled backward, trying to get away from him. What the hell just happened?

"Where's your car?" His deep voice snapped me out of my fear-filled trance.

I trembled as I pointed to the right, not trusting my voice. He grunted and grabbed me by my waist, crushing me to his chest. The wind whipped at my sore back with considerable force, and it started becoming harder to breathe as the world warped around me. I tried to let out another scream, but nothing escaped. The wind stopped blowing, and it was silent, but I didn't let go of the guard.

"Open your eyes, Meadow."

"No!" I shouted into his chest. I wanted to wake up from this nightmare. It had to be a nightmare. *Had to be.* There was no way any of this was real.

"Meadow." He repeated my name and peeled my arms from around his chest.

I opened my eyes and realized how tightly I was clutching him and moved backward, not wanting to be in his vicinity anymore. I backed into something hard and looked behind me. It was my car. None of this was real. *Wake up!* I repeated to myself.

"Stop. Meadow, stop it." He started snapping his fingers in front of my face.

I held my hand up, palm out. "H-how? How did we get here? I

don't understand..." I trailed off, trying to comprehend. The guard possibly was not...*no*. That wasn't possible.

He gave me an exasperated look, his jaw ticking. "Get in the car," was all he said.

It was still dark, and there were no lights around this area, so I could only see part of his face and his piercing gray eyes.

"No." I crossed my arms, setting my foot down. I heard a shout from down the boardwalk and dropped my arms, eyes growing wide as saucers when I saw the cloaked figure walking down the boardwalk. I yanked my keys out of my pocket, trying my hardest not to drop them. "Let's go." I hopped in the driver's seat. The guard was already in the car before I could push start. I peeled out of the parking lot, not knowing where I was going, but knowing I had to get out of there, pronto.

"Can this thing go any faster?" the guard asked, tapping his fingers so hard on my armrest that he actually put a dent in it.

"Can you please stop destroying my car? And no, it cannot go any faster. I am already going almost fifteen over the speed limit, mister..." I realized I didn't know his name. "Who are you and what is your name anyway?" I asked.

He glanced at me and gave me a lazy smirk, breaking his usual angry expression. "My name is Dmitri."

I almost slammed on the brakes.

"If he catches us, he will kill us," Dmitri warned me, and I stared at him like he had three heads.

"You're like him, aren't you? You're the traitor they were talking about!" I hit my steering wheel a few times, frustrated. Caspian had tried to warn me about him. "Get out of my car right now. All of this nonsense is between you and him, so leave me out of it." I unlocked his door, emphasizing how much I wanted him to get out.

"He's not after me. He's after you."

I slammed my foot on the accelerator.

9

"Why is he after me? I haven't done anything—I don't even know who he is!" I groaned, a headache forming from the information overload.

Dmitri didn't answer.

I glanced at him. He was wearing all black from head to toe. He wore a long-sleeved turtleneck with black jeans, complete with black boots. He had a black stud earring in his left ear, but I couldn't see if there was anything in his right ear. There was silence for a few more minutes until he finally spoke.

"You will understand everything soon, but right now, you need to focus on driving." He pointed to the road.

I rolled my eyes. "Where am I going anyway?" I asked as I sped along the dark highway.

"My safe house. Keep going straight. I'll let you know where to go." He tapped his fingers on his knee, a concentrated look on his face.

"So, how far away is this safe house of yours?"

He stared forward, tapping.

"Is it even really safe? What if someone tries to get in?" I tried again, hoping to get a response out of him or even a little twitch that he heard me. I got nothing. He was totally ignoring me. I huffed and turned my attention back to the road. "Fine. I'll be quiet." I frowned. He was still a stranger, and I still had so many questions that needed answering. He did say that I would get my answers soon, so I guess I could have some patience. I hoped he would keep his word. Sighing, I put my car in cruise control, giving my foot a rest. I was exhausted, and the long distance didn't help at all, but I didn't trust that Dmitri wouldn't pull some trick on me, so I was going to stay behind the wheel.

For the rest of the ride, it was silent. The only time Dmitri spoke was to tell me which direction to go, but nothing more. It was annoying, but I had time to think about places he would get that accent from. Spain? Italy? Greece? I couldn't decide.

When we finally reached the safe house two hours later, my feet were cramped, and I was starving. I almost fell getting out of the car, but a hand reached out and grabbed my arm, saving me from eating dirt. I yanked my arm away. "I don't need your help." I stretched, raising my arms above my head in the air. "I need your answers," I finished and stared up at him, trying to seem intimidating.

He rolled his silvery eyes, turned, and walked to the house.

I looked at the home and blinked, trying to focus. It was a box house. Not your regular pointed roof one, but a modern-day Jetsons, advanced-technology shape. It was painted black, the only color being the windows since they were clear. Despite the monotonous color, it was actually beautiful.

"If you follow me, you'll get your answers." He spoke to me from the middle of the driveway.

I looked around. It was very dark, with a lamp post at the driveway's bottom as the only source of light in the area. There were no other houses close by. The last place I had seen was about ten minutes away. Trees surrounded the area, almost like a mini forest. Shivering in the light breeze, I walked up the few steps in front of the house.

The inside was exactly how I thought it would be. All black. The only other color was gold in a random painting above a couch in the living room and a statue sitting on a little table. I could explore the rest of the house, but I was too tired to do anything but rest. I walked to the black couch and plopped down on it, my body instantly relaxing.

Dmitri knelt over a black chest in the middle of the living room floor and opened it.

"What are you doing?" I asked as he placed the dagger on his black table next to the chest—the same type of dagger I had seen the other day.

"I have to stop Victor from getting more people killed."

I gasped at his unexpected truthfulness. "Victor is the killer? I can have him arrested for that, you know," I pointed out. I could literally bring him in for questioning based on that. Caspian would be thrilled to question a viable suspect.

Dmitri stopped what he was doing and chuckled, a small dimple forming in his left cheek. "Meadow, you could try to arrest Victor, but trust me, you will not succeed. As for the killings, Victor is responsible for their deaths, but he isn't the killer."

I waited for him to continue, but he didn't say anything else. He just went back to browsing through his treasure chest.

"Who is the killer then?"

He paused and looked back up at me, narrowing his eyes. "It doesn't matter, but I can tell you that the bodies you are finding—the ones from your current case—are because of Victor. He may not be the one actually taking the life, but he does bring them to be killed. Which is why I need to stop him before he does it again."

I leaned back into the couch. "So, you're telling me that this case doesn't matter because I can't do anything about it legally, but you're going to do something about it?"

"Exactly."

I sighed and ran a hand down my face. Solving this case was supposed to be the highlight of my career. Agent Saar, the first agent to solve hundred-year-old cold cases. Gave so many families closure. But now that would all be taken away from me because of Victor?

I was too tired for this, but my heart ached because I failed all of those people. What would Caspian think about this information? I had to know more. I studied Dmitri, watching his body language and facial expressions as he continued to search the chest. Was he telling the truth? Should I trust him? I mean, I did let him bring me to his safe house, and I didn't get creepy vibes from him. I still didn't know how to truly felt about him, though.

He reached for the golden statue, and I caught a glimpse of his right ear. Dangling off the lobe was a cross—the same intricate cross I'd seen at the warehouse and on the bodies. What Mary said about the man with the violet eyes and bloody hands with a cross earring in his right ear came to mind.

I sprang from the couch. "Are you sure you're not the one killing all of those innocent people? You match the exact description of the killer that witnesses have seen. That's not a coincidence." I backed up a little faster to the door, keeping my eyes on him. I had to get out of here. There was no way he was exactly how Mary described him and not the killer.

"I am not the killer, Meadow. Do not leave, it's not safe for you out there. Trust me."

"I don't believe you. Plus, I can take care of myself, and I have Caspian."

He stared at me for a long second and threw his head back. The weirdest sound came from his mouth, and his shoulders were shaking. Was he laughing? He could barely smile. I didn't think he could laugh.

I crossed my arms. "What's funny?" I glared at him.

He sat down fully on the floor and raised his legs to his chest, placing one arm on his knees. The corners of his mouth lifted slightly, an almost smile. "Trust me when I tell you Caspian is not on your side. At all."

I scrunched my eyebrows together and dropped my arms. I'd known Caspian for years, and he'd always had my back. Now, this stranger who claimed to know him was trying to tell me how my best friend really was? That pissed me off.

"You don't even know Caspian like that or our relationship. Who are you to say that he doesn't have my back? He has always had my back and always will," I snapped at him, clenching my fists at my sides.

He got up from the floor, and I stood my ground as he walked my way.

Confidence flowed off him as he made his way over to me, his shoulders squared, strides long and sturdy. He stopped toes away from me, forcing me to tilt my head back.

"Stop trying to intimidate me. It's not working." I jammed my finger into his chest.

"If it's not working, then why is your heart rate speeding up?" he asked me softly, making me drop my guard a little.

I couldn't tell him that his dominant presence created the complete opposite of fear in me. I barely knew him. I actually didn't know him at all. I mentally smacked myself, told myself to get it together and focus back on the matter at hand.

"Because you're making assumptions about my best friend. Untrue statements."

His chest rumbled at my statement, and I finally looked him fully in the eyes.

"Caspian is not your best friend. He's not your ally at all."

I snorted. "And you think you are?"

He nodded, his full lips pressing together tightly when I chuckled at him.

"Then why did he say he was protecting me from you if he's not my ally or friend?" His logic made no sense.

"Because he wants to keep you away from the truth. He knows that I have been trying to get you to truly open your eyes again. If you knew the truth, it would destroy his life," he answered, his eyes laser-focused on my face, trying to gauge my reaction. I was so confused.

"All of this is crazy, and I don't want to be a part of it. Thanks for the save and all, but I think I'm good now. Trust me when I say I will solve this case without you." I turned to the door.

"You aren't safe, Meadow. He will come after you no matter where you go."

I opened the front door and paused. "I don't care. I can take care of myself. Bye, Dmitri," I said without turning around. I couldn't trust the word of a stranger I just met, especially about my own life. I walked to my car and looked up when I got in and saw Dmitri standing in the doorway, leaning on the frame, watching me. I rolled my eyes at him, even though he probably couldn't see me from this far, and drove away.

EVEN THOUGH I WAS SUSPENDED, I went to headquarters the next day to speak to Caspian about Dmitri and the information he gave me. How we might not have a case anymore, and about how they knew each other.

He wasn't in his office, so I went to mine and I pulled the notes up on the screen, typing everything I found out yesterday about the case. About the area I observed and its feel, and then about the conversation I had with Mary Taymer, the witness, but I didn't include anything about not trusting Victor. Or the events that occurred after my conversation with Mary.

Caspian was supposed to have his notes typed up, but his page was blank for this week. I shook my head. He'd been slacking. Looking at the time, it had already been a few hours since I got there. Caspian should be in by now. I got up to leave my office, but before I could get to my door, I heard a commotion outside of it.

Yanking my door open, I peered out and jerked backward quickly as one of the employees down the hall ran past me, screaming. I turned to where he came from and saw a crowd of people running in my direction, screaming.

"What's happening?" I stopped one of the front desk employees that was running past close to my office. She stopped and bent over, placing her hands on her knees to catch her breath.

"There's a—" she gulped, out of breath. I repeatedly gestured, trying to get her to hurry up. "There's a man in the lobby. He has Rachel in the air somehow. He was demanding to know where you were. Do you know who he is?"

My heart dropped. This was real.

"No, but thank you for letting me know. I'll handle it."

She nodded and ran off.

I stepped out of my office and walked through the chaos, taking my time. If he wanted me, then he was going to get me. I got closer to the lobby and saw Rachel hovering in the air, her legs kicking back and forth in fear.

Her screams filled the building. A chill shot up my spine when my eyes landed on him. I still couldn't see his face, but his hand was stretched out in the air, just like on the ship.

10

I looked for something to throw, but there was nothing close by or hard enough. Rachel started making noises as if she couldn't breathe, and the cloaked man slowly curled his hand like he had it wrapped around her throat. I couldn't let her go through this.

I readied my feet to bulldoze him and was about to charge at the cloaked man when I heard someone shout my name. I glanced back, and there was Caspian, waving his arms down the hallway in the air, trying to catch my attention. A wave of calm spread through me. I'd missed his face during all of this chaos.

"Caspian!" I ran toward him, pushing people out of the way to reach him. He pulled me into his arms when I reached him, and I squeezed his middle, welcoming his familiar scent and touch.

"What are you doing? Were you really about to try and fight that guy?" Caspian asked, still holding me against his chest.

I laughed, but it came out dry as my fear was still trying to go away. "He has Rachel, and he wanted me for some reason, so I was going to distract him so he would let her go."

He chuckled and pulled me away from his chest and looked at me, eyes filled with worry. "There's nothing you could do to stop him,

Meadow. You need to stop putting yourself in these dangerous situations."

"But did you see how he held Rachel up? It was im—"

Caspian interrupted me by grabbing my arms and spinning around, crushing me to his chest as we slammed into the wall. There was a crash behind me and I glanced back, spotting a desk that was snapped in half, right where we were just standing. I gasped and looked up at Caspian. His eyes narrowed as he quickly looked in the direction the desk came from. More employees ran toward every exit in the building, it seemed, so I pulled on his arm, wanting to get us to safety.

"Come on, Caspian, let's go before we become like that desk over there." I nodded at the mangled desk.

He nodded and grabbed my arm, running in the opposite direction of danger. We ran through the hallways, pushing people out of the way as we went, trying to get as far away from the threat as possible. I tried to figure out where we were going since we were passing up so many exits, but I couldn't figure it out. The hallways stopped looking familiar the longer we ran.

"Caspian, where are we going? I've never been to this part of the building before." I looked around as we slowed down. This area was very dim and slightly congested, and the walls felt like they were closing around us.

"This is a private area that was used for more serious interrogation. Only a few people in the higher ranks know about it. It's not really used much anymore besides for storage mainly." He stopped in front of a door and opened it, turning a light on. He peered inside, then looked back at me, waving me into the room. I walked past him, taking in the large space. I thought it would be a small interrogation room, but it was actually pretty big and spacious. A single table was sitting in the middle of the room with handcuffs attached to it. The light he turned on didn't help much; it was still dim.

"How do you know about this place? Especially if only the higher-ups can know about this?" I asked him as I looked around, trying to familiarize myself with the space.

His eyes lit up and a smile formed on his face that was slightly menacing, and it actually made me a little uncomfortable. I'd never noticed him smile like that before. Dmitri's words about Caspian came to mind, but I quickly pushed them away. I wasn't about to let those words taint how I viewed my friend.

"I have my ways. You're safe here. Stay in here until I come back for you, okay? Don't leave this room, no matter what."

I was confused. "Uh, where are you going? You're just going to leave me here alone? I don't even know my way out."

"I'm going to take care of Rachel and everyone else. I wanted to make sure you were in a safe place first," he answered, walking toward me.

I smiled up at him, cursing myself for doubting him. "Of course, I'm sorry. I'm just really pumped with adrenaline from all of this. Be safe and hurry back please so we can get out of here."

He chuckled and pulled me in for a hug. "Anything for you." He planted a kiss on my forehead and left the room, closing the door behind him.

I sighed and looked around for somewhere to sit. Chairs lined the walls and two more faced each other over the table in the middle of the room. I walked to one of the chairs and paused when I spotted a flower on the seat. I picked it up and sat down, inspecting it. It was a black rose. *This is an odd place to store a flower*, I thought as I placed it on the table in front of me.

I stared down at the cuffs connected to the table, trying to understand why the cloaked man was after me.

Dmitri said I wouldn't be safe anywhere without him, or whatever he said, but I didn't think he was serious. I'd put many criminals away, but I didn't think any of them would get out of prison just to try to get revenge. I tried thinking of anyone that would come after me for payback for any reason at all, but I couldn't think of anyone.

The only person who knew what the cloaked man looked like was Dmitri. I scoffed. I couldn't go back to him, he disrespected Caspian and me. I would have to find out the identity of the cloaked man on my own. Sinking into the chair, I waited for Caspian to come back from his saving spree. There were no clocks in here. I didn't have a watch, and my phone was still in my office, so I had no sense of passing time.

Waiting for what seemed like twenty to thirty minutes made me antsy. Caspian told me to stay in the room, but I couldn't sit around any longer. It was too creepy in here, and I wanted my phone so I could see if I had any messages from Duke about the whole situation. Walking up to the door, I pulled at the handle, but the door didn't budge. What the...? I turned the handle again, but it still didn't move. I kept jiggling the handle and started banging on the door.

"Caspian!" I yelled, trying to get his attention if he was close. Or *anyone's* attention. I wasn't sure if he purposely locked me in here to make sure I stayed or not, but I was definitely not happy either way. I kept banging and yelling, trying to catch anyone's attention, but no one came to the door. I kicked the door and shouted in frustration. I walked around and tried to look for a communication device, but I couldn't find anything.

"Ugh! Where is it?" There was usually a radio or walkie in places like this, but for some reason, nothing was in here. I gave up looking for a device and made my way back to the interrogation table to wait on Caspian. Suddenly, the lights went out, and I froze, my breathing slowing. I ran to the wall and flipped the switch up and down, hoping the lights would turn back on. As I tried to get the lights back on, I started hearing a weird sound, and an odd smell hit my nose.

I inhaled to get a better smell and choked out a cough. It was gas. The scent definitely wasn't fake.

I stumbled through the darkness to the closest chair, grabbed it, and hurried to the door, chucking it as hard as I could. From what I could feel, the chair didn't even dent the door. I kicked the door repeatedly, yelling.

How dare Caspian lock me in this room. Once I got out of here, I was going to give him a piece of my mind.

I wasn't terrified of the dark, but with no way out and the smell of gas, my heart rate was out of the roof. As I tried to calm myself down, something blew in the room, like a gust of wind. I plastered myself against the wall, listening. Once I didn't hear anything else, I slowly got off the wall.

I held my hands out and tried to walk back to the table in the middle of the room. The hairs on the back of my neck stood up. A hand grabbed my wrist, and I screamed. The person caught my other wrist and shoved me against the wall. My breath rushed from my lungs.

"Hush. Whoever put the gas in here is close and wants you dead." Dmitri's voice flowed in my ear, and even though I was upset with him, having a slightly familiar person in here with me calmed me down a little bit, and I pulled him close, crushing him with a grateful hug.

"Please get me out of here," I whispered in his chest, not wanting to let him go. He rubbed my back, and I felt the wind around us go wild, getting louder the more I concentrated on it. Then it stopped.

"Open your eyes, Meadow."

I opened one eye and peered around him, seeing the sky and trees. We were outside. I looked up at him slowly, eyes wide. "What is going on here? I don't understand anything." I spoke, breathing heavily.

He looked down at me, his face serious. "We don't have time right now. Follow me."

I huffed, looking up at the sky for a second before following him. He walked to a black, sleek sports car. I made it to the car and placed my hand on it, sliding it up toward the roof. "Can you unlock—"

An explosion filled the air, and I screamed, ducking down beside the car. I looked up in horror to see the headquarters in flames.

"Caspian!" I screamed toward the building. Dmitri yanked me up by the arm from the ground and pulled me away from the car.

"Let's go, let's go!" he shouted, opening the passenger door and shoving me inside. Dmitri got in the driver's seat and started the car, the roar of the engine snapping me out of my shocked state.

"Wait! I need to see if Caspian is okay! Stop the car!" I yelled as Dmitri weaved between cars, the jerking motion causing me to fly against the passenger window. I hurried and strapped myself in with the seatbelt. "Did you hear me? Dmitri!" I snapped my fingers in his face, trying to catch his attention.

"Caspian is fine." He glanced at me with a severe look on his face.

My brow furrowed in confusion. "How do you know if he's okay or not? The cloaked figure was in the building looking for me, and he went back to help other people get to safety!" I didn't understand why he was acting so nonchalant. He swerved again, and I grabbed on to the dashboard to steady myself. "Dude, can you please slow down? We are far enough away from the explosion and the cloaked man," I informed him, gripping the sides of my seat, trying not to imagine the damage that would happen if we got into an accident at this speed.

"I always drive this fast. You will be okay. Also, I know Caspian is okay because he's the one who created the explosion."

I curled my hands into fists. "How dare you accuse him of trying to kill me!" I moved to shove his arm, but my hand was stuck hovering in the air like something was keeping it suspended. My eyes widened, and I stared at Dmitri, my heartbeat speeding up from … I didn't even know what to call it. I had been trying not to think about all of this weird stuff that had happened since I met Dmitri, but I couldn't ignore it any longer. I had to know the truth. "Dmitri."

He stared me down. He glanced at my arm, and it fell.

"What…are you?" I whispered, my voice almost nonexistent. I wanted to know, but at the same time, I hesitated.

The corners of his mouth lifted, and he gave me a large smile with his teeth. "I was wondering when you would finally ask that question. Especially after everything that has happened." He stopped the car, and I looked out the window. We were at his safe house. "Come on. I'll explain everything to you." He got out of the car and walked over to the passenger side as I unbuckled. He opened my door and offered his hand, and I grabbed it, pulling myself out of the car. We walked to the house, and he opened the door.

"Why don't you lock your doors? Even though it's a safe house, people can still come in. Especially if it's unlocked," I commented as we walked inside.

"Actually, no one can walk in here unless I want them to." He shrugged off his black biker jacket and threw it on the living room couch.

"How not?" I asked and sat down on the couch next to his jacket.

He sat down on the opposite couch, crossing his legs. "Because to the human and non-human eye, this house isn't even here. It's just a plot of land."

"Non-human." I tried to comprehend what he was saying.

"Back to Caspian. You have some questions about him, I presume, based on your reaction to my statement about him." His voice got deeper as he finished his statement.

"Yes, I might have a few questions for you. How did you know Caspian was safe?"

He sighed and folded his hands together. "I told you, he was the reason there was an explosion. He caused it."

I sighed, and Dmitri stared at me, his gray eyes guarded. He continued.

"Did you not find it odd that you were in a room that no one else knew about, in a secluded area, and it was locked?" he questioned.

I shifted uncomfortably. "Of course not. Caspian just wanted to make sure that I stayed safe, as always." I defended him, trying my best to stay calm.

Dmitri leaned forward on his elbows and stared me down, the corners of his mouth lifting. I wanted to smack that smirk across the room.

"Meadow, you do realize that the *exact* place you were in started filling up with gas, and that side of the building exploded. Right?" He quirked his eyebrows and cocked his head to the side, watching my face as it dawned on me what he was trying to say.

I stood abruptly, clenching my fists to my sides. "No. Why would he do that to me?"

Dmitri inhaled and exhaled slowly. He ran his hand through his inky black locks, looking at me through narrowed eyes. "Because he's been trying to kill you for a thousand years."

11

I stared at him for long seconds, probably even a minute after his statement. A smile formed on my face, and it evolved into me giggling, which morphed into a full-blown laugh. I was laughing so hard, I had to clutch my belly and gasp so I wouldn't pass out.

"Wait a minute, *Dmitri*," I emphasized his name, slightly mocking him. "You expect me to accept that ludicrous answer and run with it? Me, my twenty-three-year-old self, by the way, in case you confused your math somehow." I kept laughing, and he just sat there with an irritated look on his face.

"Are you done?" He rolled his eyes when I chuckled at his question. That answered it for him.

"I hate to break it to you, but Caspian has not been trying to kill me, and I am not a thousand years old. I've known Caspian for five years. If he was trying to kill me, wouldn't he have killed me already?"

Dmitri shook his head, sighing. "There's a plan for everything, Meadow. You have to time everything perfectly, and that's what he did. Everything was perfect for him until I got involved. Trust me, he's a patient man."

I rolled my eyes at him, barely listening to the nonsense. "Yeah,

yeah, whatever, man. Do you have an explanation that actually makes sense or not?"

His response never came. His attention was elsewhere, facing in the direction of his kitchen. His eyebrows dipped and his body tensed, hands clenching into fists. I froze as his demeanor changed and glanced in the direction he was looking. A wall blocked my view. He stood up.

"Do you hear something?" I whispered and inched closer to him, just in case anything happened.

He held his hand up, and I shut my mouth, trying to listen. I didn't hear anything. He tilted his head to the side as if he heard something else, and then he disappeared. I gasped and whirled around in a circle, looking for him. There was a crash and someone cursed, so I crept toward the kitchen, trying to make my steps as quiet as possible.

"How did you get in here?" I heard Dmitri demand, and I finally made it to the kitchen entrance, taking in the scene in front of me. Dmitri was standing in the middle of the kitchen by the island, and in front of him was a shorter guy around my height, maybe an inch or two taller than me. He had pretty, copper colored skin and dark curly hair, with a half-eaten sandwich in his hand. His cheeks were stuffed, and I glanced at the ground where a jar of jam lay broken in pieces. *So that's what I heard.*

His eyes widened, and he held his hands up in the air, clutching the sandwich. "Rita phased me through, man. Take it up with her." His words came out muffled from his stuffed face.

Dmitri growled and muttered something under his breath.

Phased? What did he mean?

The guy's eyes turned to me and lit up. "Meadow! Hey, long time no see!" He greeted me with his mouth full, smiling a goofy smile, his cheeks extra large from the sandwich.

I squinted at him in confusion and glanced up at Dmitri. How did this guy know me? I'd never seen him before in my life.

His smile faltered when he saw the look on my face, and his eyes flitted back over to Dmitri, confusion written all over his face.

69

"What's wrong with her?" he whispered to Dmitri as if I wasn't in the same room as them.

Dmitri sighed and glanced back at me, his eyes guarded. "She doesn't have her memories from her actual life. Somehow, they're being suppressed and replaced with a false life, but I haven't found out how yet." He answered softly, trying to speak so I didn't hear, I assumed.

I didn't know what memories he was talking about. He literally made no sense at all. I made a face and was about to speak, but the other guy beat me to it.

"But how? There's no way that could happen unless..." He trailed off, and his eyes widened, looking at me quickly and back at Dmitri.

Dmitri nodded slightly, so subtle that if I'd blinked, I would've missed it.

The guy gasped, his hands flying to his mouth, sandwich still in hand. "No way! That means Caspian succeeded! That brute!"

I was taken aback by his outburst and even more shocked that he mentioned Caspian. I was tired of them talking about me like I wasn't in the room, so I stormed fully into the kitchen, standing between both of them.

"Okay, enough! I am right here, you know. If you have anything to ask me or tell me, just speak to me." I huffed, exasperated.

"She has a point you know, especially since she can't remember everything. All of this probably sounds crazy since she thinks she's human," the strange guy said.

Dmitri glared at him, obviously disgruntled.

I turned and faced the guy, almost eye level. "What do you mean since I *think* I'm human?" I asked. "I *am* human."

He looked over my head when a low growl filled the kitchen, then quickly looked back at me. "Uh, well first off, hi. I'm Dax, since you can't remember. One of Dmitri's so-called friends. I use the term *friend* loosely because he doesn't like anyone, but I consider myself his friend. Right, bud?" He smiled largely, looking at Dmitri.

I didn't turn around, but he was probably frowning at Dax like he did with everyone. I heard a grunt, and Dax chuckled nervously, turning his attention back to me.

"Now, as for the human comment. You aren't human in any way, shape, or form, despite what you believe. And I'm going to stop talking now because Dmitri looks like he's going to rip my head off." He rushed through the rest of his thoughts and disappeared.

I jerked backward and gasped, turning to Dmitri with wide eyes. "Why does everyone keep disappearing! How is that happening?"

Dmitri's hard features softened, and a small smile formed on his face. "We're not disappearing. We're just moving so fast your temporary human eyes can't register the movements," he explained and studied my face.

My shoulders drooped. I was done trying to block everything he was telling me. That required too much energy, and at this point, I was curious about his explanation. "All right. So I'm guessing you're not human either?" I hesitated as I asked, unsure of what to expect. He nodded, and I shook my head slowly, trying to process this.

"Can we go back to the living room and sit? I need to be able to pass out on something that can catch me if needed," I half-joked, and he chuckled, shaking his head at me.

"Of course. Let me grab something quickly, and I'll meet you there."

I nodded and left the kitchen. I looked around on my way to the living room to see if Dax was still here, but I didn't see him. I frowned a little. He seemed really cool and super goofy. He appeared to irritate Dmitri a lot, maybe because he was always running his mouth. I liked it.

I made it to the living room and screamed. A strong breeze hit me and an arm wrapped around my middle protectively.

Dmitri.

He blocked part of my view, but I peered around him at the intruders.

A tall, very pale, blond-haired man with a gun in each hand and a small woman with two blue-bladed daggers stood in the middle of the living room. Their eyes glowed a violet color, and they looked like

71

they were seconds away from killing each other, their growls filling the air.

"Axel, Rita! Put your weapons down!" Dmitri barked. Neither of them moved, their growls getting louder. "Now!" The authority in Dmitri's tone filled the open space, and I shrank behind him, trying to make myself invisible.

Axel and Rita slowly put their weapons down on the table, still staring each other down and very tense, as if they were waiting for the other to make a last-minute move. Once they were both empty handed, Dmitri let me go.

"Whoa, guys, what was that all about?" A voice to my right asked. It was Dax, with another sandwich in his hand.

"Axel here didn't want to come and warn Dmitri about Caspian, so I forced him to come. He got a little pissy," Rita answered, her voice on the deeper side. It contrasted with what I thought her voice would be like. Her slick black hair was in a high ponytail, and she wore a gray jumpsuit with black boots.

Axel scoffed and sat on the couch, a bored look on his face. "I just don't like wasting my time, and warning Dmitri about potential danger was not in my job description." He rolled his forest green eyes.

Dax raised his sandwich to his mouth, covering his smile.

"So why the knives and guns if you guys are here already?" I asked, and all eyes turned to me.

Rita narrowed her eyes at me and hissed angrily, making me take a step back. What was her deal? "Axel was trying to leave, so I was prepared to stop him." Her words came out like hot venom.

"So you were going to stab him with Jestraetrium? Possibly killing him? That's cold, Rita." Dax gasped, feigning shock as he put a hand on his chest, shaking his head.

Rita tsked and sat on the floor. "Ah, all he would get was a little icy burn that would heal in seconds. He would live," she answered nonchalantly, picking at her boots.

"Excuse me, what did you mean warn him about Caspian and danger? What did Caspian do?" I interjected, trying to figure out what was going on and how all of them knew who Caspian was.

Rita glared at me and scoffed, looking over my head. "What's wrong with this chick? Did she get hit over the head with poscaudian?" she asked Dmitri.

I glanced at Dax and mouthed, *What's poscaudian?*

He slid over quietly to where I was standing and whispered in my ear. "It's a memory erasing element."

My mouth formed an 'o' as I understood what Rita was asking.

Dmitri moved from behind and walked in front of me, blocking Rita's view of me. "Caspian got to her before I could, and it was too late," he said, and she laughed dryly, shaking her head.

"Too bad, huh. So is she going to stay like this, or is there a way to get her memories back?" Rita asked in a bored tone.

"I'm still figuring that out, but right now, we need to focus on stopping Victor and Caspian." He walked to the table in the middle of the living room and turned to me, nodding for me to join him.

I walked up next to him and watched Rita's eyebrows dip. Her lip curled when my arm brushed Dmitri's. I stared at her in confusion, and when she made eye contact with me, she looked away quickly, disgust on her face. I looked up at Dmitri then back down at her. *Did she have a thing for Dmitri?* I smiled at the thought and tried my best not to laugh at the fact that she was jealous. That was probably why every time she spoke to me it was with an attitude. I barely knew the guy. I turned my attention back to Dmitri.

"Caspian has caused destruction among humans ever since I left The Comitye. I was the most skilled and powerful in the group, but their ways turned corrupt, so I left." Dmitri paused and looked down at me to see if I was paying attention, and I was. This sounded very interesting. He continued. "The Comitye started going around kidnapping humans and began transitioning them, trying to find a replacement for me. But they have failed many times. Not one was a success."

"That's what they were talking about on the ship. It all makes sense now, kind of," I added, and he nodded his head in confirmation.

"Wait a goddamn minute. You were on a ship with her?" Axel asked, sitting up on the couch from his slouched position.

"We were, and he almost got to her again," Dmitri answered, raising his head slightly at Axel's tone. *He?*

Axel scoffed and threw his hands up in the air. "Then what am I here for if you already know about Caspian's plan?" He stood with an annoyed look on his face. I thought Dmitri was the king of not smiling, but this guy took the throne by a landslide.

"You're here because Caspian already has somewhat of an army that only a few know about. He plans on ambushing Dmitri when he least expects it, so he can take him out for good," Rita answered, standing as well.

"Where did you get that information from?" Dmitri asked, tensing.

Rita pulled out a silver, circular device from her pocket and waved her hand over it. A digital screen popped up in front of her. She held her hands up in the air and moved them outward slowly, expanding the screen. She swiped the screen in the air, and different images popped up and disappeared as she searched for something. "Aha." She tapped on a video.

"Is everything in place?" A terrifyingly monstrous voice asked from the video. Caspian appeared in a purple cloak, looking like the cloaked man from the ship and at the headquarters.

I gasped as everything Dmitri had been saying hit me. Caspian was the cloaked man.

My heart sank.

"Everything is in place, sir. I have a small crew waiting in plain sight in a city called The Valley. Dmitri won't be aware of what's coming," Caspian responded to the speaker. No one else was in the frame, so I didn't see who he was speaking to.

Rita swiped the air, and the whole thing disappeared, right back into the device. "I intercepted it during my rounds. That's when I called Dax and Axel for help. We have to stop him. Dax located the place in The Valley called Lights, Inc., a fake business as a front for where he's keeping his small crew. I'm not sure where he has his actual army, but I'm sure we'll find out soon enough," she informed Dmitri.

He leaned on the table, his face down toward the floor. I still couldn't believe that everything he told me about Caspian was true. How could this be? I didn't even know who he was anymore.

Dmitri punched the table, causing me to jump back, startled. "I thought I had time." He cursed and started pacing back and forth.

"Well, now we have to tell her what we are so she understands everything that's going on," Dax told Dmitri, glancing at me sideways.

I glanced back, eyes wide. "What are you?" I whispered, trying to prepare myself for the answer.

Dmitri stopped pacing and faced me, his eyes locked on mine. "We're vampires, Meadow."

12

M y mouth dropped. I made eye contact with each of them slowly, trying to see if this was all a joke. Every single one of them had the same serious look on their faces. Even Dax.

This wasn't a joke.

"Is this a joke?" I asked anyway. I had to hear it again because one time wasn't cutting it.

"No, it's not a joke. The sooner you get over it, the sooner we can start coming up with a plan to stop Victor and Caspian." Rita was the first to answer, of course, with an attitude. She rolled her eyes after her statement and turned her attention to her nails.

"What Rita is actually trying to say is that yes, it's true that we are vampires, and although you are probably doubting everything we are telling you, we really need you to believe us so we can start planning." Dax's translation made me a little more comfortable with the bomb that had dropped on me.

"I understand. It's just that...vampires are fiction, so it's kind of hard to believe that tales and fables can actually be real."

Dax nodded, but Rita hissed under her breath. Axel still had a bored look on his face, as if he didn't care about anything that happened.

"We can show her something to get her to believe us before we leave," Dax spoke up, looking at everyone. Dmitri nodded and gestured for Dax to go ahead. He smiled and rubbed his hands together excitedly.

"Don't destroy my house, Dax, just show her your fangs or something," Dmitri told him, and Dax frowned, shoulders slumping.

"Fine." Dax turned to me and placed his hands on my shoulders. "Don't be scared, okay?"

I nodded cautiously, not sure what to expect. Dax closed his eyes, and I waited for something to happen. His head started twitching slightly, and he moved his mouth, eyes squeezing shut like he was uncomfortable. His hands squeezed my shoulders, and I winced from his tight grip.

"Dax," I started but quickly shut my mouth when he opened his, saliva dripping down his enlarged canines. I gasped as he opened his eyes, the violet color trapping me in my position.

A throat was cleared after long seconds passed, and Dax blinked, his eyes returning to their normal chocolate color. He closed his mouth and opened it back just as quickly, passing his tongue over his teeth, which were normal again.

I just stared at him. Enlarged teeth? I mean, it wasn't normal, but not impossible. Dax seemed to understand my look and sighed, glancing at Dmitri.

"I got this," Dmitri spoke in a hushed tone, dropping his arms to his sides. "Pay attention, Meadow."

I looked at him, and he jerked his head toward the black table in the middle of the room. There was nothing different about it. "Um, what am I supposed to be…?" My throat dried up, stopping me from finishing my sentence. The table was floating. My eyes widened as it floated higher in the air, and I whipped my head to Dmitri, who was staring at the table. A concentrated stare.

"Are you?" I pointed at the table, not trusting my voice.

He nodded at me, lifting his hand, and I turned in time to see the table land back on the ground.

"Wow," I breathed, placing a hand over my rapidly beating chest. "Vampires, you say? Can all vampires do that?" I asked, wanting to know more. This was amazing. Chuckles filled the air, and I glanced at all of them, confused.

"No, not all of us possess the power of telekinesis. It's different for everyone, and some don't have extra abilities at all," Axel explained, his tone sounding bitter. His face scrunched up and turned his attention to the couch.

"Oh, okay." I took a seat on the couch. *They are all vampires. Caspian is a vampire, and he is trying to make vampires like Dmitri.*

They never told me if I was a vampire. If I wasn't a vampire and I wasn't human, what was I?

"First things first. Caspian does not need to be anywhere near the daggers because he will not hesitate to kill any of us," Dmitri informed everyone.

I raised my hand. It was a respect thing. I didn't like interrupting anyone.

Dmitri nodded at me.

"Why keep him from the daggers specifically and not just any weapon in general?"

"Because the daggers are made out of the element Jestraetrium. The only thing that can *truly* kill a vampire."

My mouth formed into an 'o' shape. Does that mean Donatella... no way, I shook my head. She couldn't be.

"Good thing I happened to be on the ship because somehow Caspian already had the daggers. I made sure to grab them from him," Dmitri told the others as he gave me a sideways glance.

Whoops.

Everyone else had confused looks on their faces.

"How in the world did he have them? Last time I checked, they were locked up securely. The only way for the vault to be discovered and unlocked is by a..." Dax trailed off and slowly turned my way. "Meadow, how did Caspian end up with daggers?" he asked me, accusation seeping through his tone.

I held my hands up. "I didn't give them to him, I swear." They looked like they didn't believe me. I sighed. "The only thing I did was help a criminal named Donatella steal some daggers that look exactly like the ones you guys have now. She said that they were for her boss," I finished, trying to decipher the looks on their faces. I saw confusion, annoyance, shock, but most of all, anger, especially from Dmitri.

"I was there that night, disguised as a guard trying to stop you and Donatella, an—"

"Yeah, and all you were doing was playing mind games on me, confusing me rather than helping me," I interrupted, annoyed at the memory.

He glanced at me and smirked a little, probably thinking of when he smashed my face in the dirt.

"You weren't smirking when Donatella knocked the daylights out of you," I muttered, now knowing all of them could hear me clearly. Snickers filled the air, and I made sure not to look up because I could already feel the heat of Dmitri's glare on my face.

"Anyway, Donatella knows who you really are and took advantage of your abilities, knowing you wouldn't remember who she was." Dmitri shook his head and stared at the ceiling, clearly annoyed. *Abilities? What abilities?*

"You helped Donatella steal the daggers for Caspian? The same daggers made from the only thing that could truly kill us? Geez, Dmitri she really needs her memories back before anyone else decides to take advantage of her. This is getting out of hand!" Axel raised his voice at the end, frustration evident on his face.

"I know. I have a plan in place for that. But right now, let's focus on Caspian. We have the daggers now, not him, so we need to use that to our advantage."

Everyone nodded, and I joined in, even though deep down, I didn't want to hurt Caspian in any way. Maybe I could get through to him and get him to stop this foolishness.

For the rest of the evening, the team mapped out a plan for how to infiltrate the fake business filled with new vampires, and even included me in the planning, informing me about the daggers and how to properly use them. They wanted me to be in the shadows as much as possible so that I wouldn't get hurt in the process.

Dmitri wouldn't let me have a word in about possibly talking to Caspian. He didn't want me near him in any way because he said all Caspian wanted to do was kill me, which I still didn't believe.

Maybe our friendship had changed him, and he would actually listen to me. Whatever happened, I would find a way to talk to Caspian alone.

"I think that's everything. Be back tomorrow morning to go over everything again as a refresher, and then it'll be showtime." Dmitri dismissed us. We all got up, and they walked to the door as I stretched from the long hours of sitting. That didn't seem to bother any of them. Perks of being a vampire, I guess.

"Where do you think you're going?" Dmitri's voice stopped me, and I turned, a confused look forming on my face.

"Uh, home?" I answered. "You literally just said to come back tomorrow morning."

"No, you're not. Caspian knows where you live and will definitely try to attack you there since he didn't finish the job. You're staying here tonight." His tone indicated that what he said was final, and I sighed, not really caring to argue.

"All right, where am I sleeping?" I asked, watching as the last of the team finally left. Lucky them.

Dmitri pointed down the hallway to the stairs. "Up the stairs, first door on the right. It's a guest room. Check the drawers. There should be a change of clothes in there. There is also a bathroom in your room, so you have access to a shower."

I nodded, grateful for his hospitality.

I felt a little awkward with him staring at me so intensely, so I went upstairs to the guest room. As I opened the bedroom door, I turned on the light and pushed the dim option so that it wasn't so bright.

The guest room was more like a master bedroom, and it was amazing. The queen-sized bed sat in the middle of the room, draped with dark gray bedding and light gray pillows. The headboard was a shade lighter than the pale pillows, tufted with dark gray buttons.

Walking into the spacious room, I noticed a dark bookcase in the corner, completely filled with books. I would have to check it out later.

There was a little chest by the bed with a black lamp on it. I turned the main light off and turned the lamp on, creating a pleasantly dark atmosphere with a little light. Comforting. A taller dresser graced the wall opposite the bed, close to a door that led to the bathroom. The bathroom had the same dark gray walls as the bedroom and had a walk-in shower with a spacious tub next to it. I could literally live in this room. Dark colors soothed me.

My loft didn't even feel this comforting. Going back to the tall dresser, I rifled through it to look for something to wear to bed. Dark colored everything—shirts, tanks, and even underwear. I looked at the tag of one of the pairs of underwear and turned a little red. It was my exact size. This was awkward. I was definitely going to have to ask him about this. If I was indeed at least a thousand years old like he claimed, did we have some sort of history? And if we did, what kind of history?

"Are you finding everything you need?"

I jumped, startled at the intrusion of my thoughts. Dmitri stood at the doorway, his arms crossed over his chest, making his biceps bulge. I quickly looked away from his arms and focused on his face, not that it was any better. He was handsome, more in a rugged way than conventional beauty. His dominance added to his attractiveness, making him seem almost irresistible. Not that it swayed me, it was just an observation.

"Um, yes, I am, thank you," I finally answered after a few seconds.

He nodded, narrowing his eyes to analyze me like I had done. "You have a question."

"Yeah, I do. A few," I responded, leaning on the wall next to the dresser. I took a second to process all of my thoughts so I wouldn't stumble over them, and so he could actually understand me.

"Is it true that I'm a thousand years old?" I asked, trying not to cringe at how idiotic that question sounded coming out of my mouth.

"A thousand and more."

"How?" I couldn't understand how that was possible.

He sighed and shifted, adjusting how he was leaning on the doorframe. "As I've said before, you're not human. You may think you're human, and all the memories you have make you believe you are, but trust me, you're not." He paused, staring at the floor, deep in thought. "All I can tell you is that when you get your memories back, everything will finally connect and make sense."

I nodded, trying to understand. "So, my memories, will you be in them?" I asked softly, a little nervous to hear his answer. Rita had to be jealous for an actual reason, and these clothes being my exact size wasn't a coincidence.

He sighed again and straightened, shoving his hands into his pockets. "I will be in quite a few memories, yes," he answered just as softly, as if he was hesitant to give me all of the information.

I inhaled deeply and nodded, processing everything. I went to the bed and sat down, rubbing the soft sheets. "So, we have a history." I peered up at him through my lashes, and he nodded, eyes cautious.

"A long one, yes."

"What kind of history?" I pressed, wanting to get straight to the point.

He looked around the room slowly, eyes landing back on me. "It's getting late. We have a long day tomorrow, so you're going to need all the rest you can get. I'll see you in the morning, okay?" He nodded at me and patted the doorframe as he left.

I scoffed at how he avoided my question and got up from the bed, gathering everything I needed for my shower.

If he thought I would let it go after he totally ignored my question, he was wrong. He should definitely know that if we had a history together. Pushing all the thoughts aside, I took a relaxing shower and prepared myself for bed. Turning off the lamp, I thought about every-thing that was going to happen tomorrow.

If Dmitri knew me well, he knew I would talk to Caspian, and he would try to stop me. I had to make sure he was distracted long enough for me to reach Caspian. Because I would get to him—no matter what.

13

The sun was beating on my back, not helping my mood. We stood outside Dmitri's safe house as he went over the plan for the day.

"There is no way I am staying hidden the whole time. I want to help you guys!" I complained to Dmitri when he told me about my role. I pleaded to Dax with my eyes to help me out.

"Come on, Dmitri. It kind of isn't fair that she has to come to The Valley with us and then stay hidden the whole time. She has a point, you know."

I smiled when Dmitri glared at Dax for taking my side.

He turned his attention back to me, eyes filled with mild annoyance. "If you don't want to stay hidden, then convince me to let you help," he forced out, gritting his teeth. His eyes narrowed as he waited for my response. I was prepared for this.

"Well, I can be a great distraction." I held my hand up before he could interrupt me. He hmphed and crossed his arms. "I can enter the building Caspian is hiding out in first instead of you guys just charging in, fangs blazing."

Dax was the only one who chuckled at my terrible joke, and I gave him a grateful smile. I thought it was pretty funny. "I can act confused, say I got lost or something, then before any of them can even breathe on me, you can appear in front of me and get to work," I finished. It was silent for a few seconds as I watched Dmitri contemplate my terrible proposal.

"As soon as I appear in front of you, I need you to get to a safe place right away. That's final."

I nodded and grinned, happy I was able to contribute in some sort of way. "You got it, boss." I saluted him and chuckled when he muttered under his breath. We all packed up everything we needed for this little mission of ours and hopped into Axel's white jeep.

I tried to get them to pick another vehicle to ride in, but they told me Caspian would be looking for anyone that stood out, so it was better to blend in with the population. I'd never been to The Valley, so I didn't know how far it was. Dmitri was driving, and I sat in the front seat, humming to a random song. I didn't know the song, but I was pretty good at catching on to tunes. A few hours later, we finally made it to our destination.

"Well, that's a pretty building," Dax commented as we all got out of the jeep. He was right, it was indeed pretty. It stood up in the middle of the almost-empty parking lot, around thirty stories high. Tall, but not a skyscraper. A few people exited their cars and entered the building, making it seem pretty ordinary and legit. The building was a beautiful, pristine black.

"Dax." Dmitri snapped his fingers at him, catching his attention. "How many are in the building right now?" he asked, eyes pinned on the building in front of us. Axel and Rita were both on high alert, their bodies tense, ready for anything.

Dax nodded and crouched down on the concrete, placing his palms flat on it. He closed his eyes and bent his head, concentrating. His body twitched every so often, which made me paranoid, not knowing what was going on. Was he in pain?

He suddenly gasped and looked up sharply, his eyes violet. His mouth was puckered as if he'd shoved a bunch of food in it. He groaned and opened his mouth wide, and my jaw almost dropped as I watched his canines shrink back until they were normal sized again. He stopped groaning when his teeth stopped moving and shook his head as if it was a painful process. His eyes turned back to their brown color, and he stood, wiping the dust off his pants.

"I count around fifteen young. I think I felt one more, but I couldn't really get a true feeling. It was as if I was being blocked by something."

"Young?" I asked.

"Newborn vampires. We call them young," Dmitri answered before turning to the others. "It's Caspian. He knows how to block anyone from tracking him." He turned back to me. "Are you ready?" he asked, and I tried my best not to say *aye, aye, Captain*. He probably wouldn't get it, anyway. He didn't seem like the type to have a great sense of humor.

"Of course I'm ready. It's going to be a piece of cake," I answered, trying to hype myself up and not think about how I was literally leading myself to slaughter.

Axel, Rita, Dax, and Dmitri nodded at each other, and I started walking to the front doors. My heart pumped wildly.

I reached the door and grabbed the silver handle, taking in a deep breath. I glanced back at my newly acquainted peers, all of them donning serious looks except for Dax. He gave me a thumbs up along with an encouraging smile. I smiled softly and exhaled, letting my nerves settle so my hands would stop shaking. There was really nothing to worry about, as long as I pressed the distress button on my phone.

Before I could psych myself out and take Dmitri's advice of hiding the whole time, I opened the door and walked in. Cool air grazed my skin. The atmosphere was relaxing, despite who worked in the building. It was friendly and open, the ceilings high, and an actual escalator sat in the area's middle. There was a tall reception desk to my right, with a big sign that read *Lights*.

A lightbulb replaced the dot of the 'i' in the word. Nice. A dirty-blond-haired woman sat at the desk, tapping away at her computer. Small tables littered the area, and a few people were seated at a bunch of them, making conversation with each other. Everyone here seemed pretty normal.

"May I help you?" the woman asked in a high-pitched voice. She had bright purple lipstick on, a contrast to her pearly white teeth. She seemed normal enough to me.

"Hi, yes." I walked over to the desk, placing my hands on it, drumming my fingers as I still looked around. I was trying to take some time to think quickly because I didn't really prepare for the conversation. I didn't expect this place and the people in here to be so...normal.

"Um, do you guys sell lightbulbs?" I mentally slapped myself for asking that dumb question. Duh, they sold light bulbs. The woman smiled politely despite my question. My eyes flickered to her teeth.

They weren't as sharp as I thought they would be, but they were definitely sharper than the average canine. Her eyes followed mine as they went back up to her face, and I smiled a bit to distract her. Hopefully, she didn't suspect anything.

"Yes, we do sell lightbulbs. Have you visited our website to see which one you would like to order?" she asked professionally.

"Um." I glanced at the front entrance, wondering when they were going to come in. Turning back to the woman, I chuckled nervously as she narrowed her eyes slightly, glancing at the front doors herself.

"Are you okay, honey? Expecting anyone?" she asked, and I shook my head quickly.

"No, I'm not. My husband is the one who knows which lightbulb it is, let me jus—"

"No, no, it's okay," she interrupted me when I pulled out my temporary phone. She waved her hand at someone behind me, and I turned, the phone still in hand as two men in black suits across the room started walking my way. "These guys can show you some pictures, and you can see if they look familiar." When she finished, I got a chill up my spine as the men got closer.

Something didn't feel right.

One of them narrowed their eyes and glanced behind me, nodding. I was caught.

I pressed the side of the phone, activating the distress signal Axel programmed for me. It was a silent signal to let them know I was in trouble and to charge in here, guns blazing. I thought it would be silent, but it turns out it wasn't that silent because the men whipped their heads to the front door as soon as I pressed the button, then looked at me, eyes glaring at the device in my hand.

"It's the device in her hand! Grab it!" The woman yelled at the men, and my body went into flight mode. Looking around frantically for an escape, my eyes landed on the moving escalators. I ran in that direction as fast as I could, dodging my attackers. Why I thought I would actually be faster than vampires, I have no idea, but I found out quickly that I wasn't. I skidded to a stop when the men chasing me were suddenly in front of me. My heart was beating fast, and I tried to think of ways to defend myself.

"Hey now, I'm just here for the lightbulbs, and this is my cell phone." I pointed to my phone, giving them my lame excuse. They glanced at each other and then looked back at me, glaring. They opened their mouths, and I watched as their canines started protruding. Both of them groaned slightly. I backed up and kept smashing the button on my phone. Maybe I could throw my phone at one, punch the other, and make a dash for the escalator again. That was a terrible idea. I frantically looked for an escape, but there was no way I was running faster than them.

"Meadow, duck!"

I barely registered what Dmitri yelled, but my body reacted for me, ducking quickly. Something flew over my head, and a loud scream that sounded like nails dragging down a chalkboard ignited in the air. One of the men in black clutched a dagger buried in his chest, his hands wrapped around it as he screamed.

Cringing at the uncomfortable sound, I covered my ears, not moving from my position. The weird thing about the dagger in the man was that there was no blood flow. Around the area where the dagger was located, it started turning blue, spreading across his chest. Dmitri appeared in front of me.

Snarls filled the air as Dmitri grabbed the dagger's handle, shoving it more into the man's chest. Before his partner could do anything, Dmitri pulled out the other dagger and stabbed the second man as well, igniting the chalkboard screams. He shoved it deeper like the first one, but I heard a cracking sound, like bone breaking.

I wanted to throw up. Maybe I should have chosen to stay hidden.

The cracking continued, and I stared in shock as the blue substance spread over both employees' chests, a white color following quickly behind. The process was quick and continued until both of them were covered entirely…in ice?

Two ice sculptures stood in place of the men that stood there a second ago. Dmitri yanked both daggers out of their chests, then turned and stared above me.

Countless footsteps indicated more people coming down, probably to see what happened. There was a yell, and Rita was by my side, an object that looked like a key fob in her hand. She swung her arm to the other side of her body and back down to her hip. The key fob turned into a double-bladed sword, both blades emulating fire. It flickered and moved just like a flame, one blade an orange-red color while the other blade was a mixture of light and dark blue.

It was the most beautiful weapon I had ever seen. Rita yelled and raised her sword over her head, bringing it down to slice the frozen vamps. It was quick and smooth, the two ice sculptures breaking into pieces, scattering on the floor. My jaw dropped.

"Get ready, more are coming now," Axel commented as he joined Rita and Dmitri. I looked over at the receptionist's desk to see the dirty blonde lying unconscious over the desk. Axel grabbed a dagger from Dmitri and quickly jogged over to her, shoving the dagger into her back. I jumped as her body flopped from the force. The blue and white substance fought as it covered her body until she was an ice sculpture, just like her co-workers.

Axel yanked the dagger out and pulled out a gun to shoot the sculpture. I covered my ears as the once woman, now ice sculpture, blasted into many pieces, just like the men before her. Actual goosebumps dotted my skin and my breathing quickened.

"Meadow, get behind the desk!" Dmitri yelled as the footsteps got closer.

Dax reached out and pulled me up with no problem, but I hesitated. "Go!" Dax shoved me away, and I ran to the desk, wiping the ice out of my way as I slid over it. I got on my knees and slowly peeked over, not wanting to miss the fight. The sound of footsteps running filled the room until the owners of the steps appeared.

They were all in purple suits. All of them had straight looks on their faces, each with a furrowed brow. Their eyes glowed the signature violet color, and I had to squint to see if I saw correctly. Their hands looked...odd. I couldn't see exactly what it was, but there was some discoloration. Hisses filled the room as the employees watched my team closely, both parties waiting for the other to make the first move.

One of the females darted her eyes around, taking in the ice scattered across the ground, not melting. Her eyes widened in realization and turned back to my team, a shrill scream filling the air. "They killed our brothers and sister!"

As soon as the words came out of her mouth, the rest of them tensed, then lunged. I gasped, slapping a hand over my mouth. Everything started blurring, I couldn't see what was going on. I only heard the crunching and screeches. An uncomfortable pressure started building up behind my eyes, so I closed them, squeezing them instinctively before reopening them. The pressure was gone, and nothing was blurred anymore. I saw everything clearly.

Rita was screaming as loud as the employees, her double-bladed sword slicing through the air. Bodies were sliced cleanly in half by her sword, blood spraying as she swung. One employee came after her, and she charged at him, passing right through him, and shoved her sword backward. The blue blade exited through the other side of his body. She could phase—now I understood what Dax was talking about.

Dax came into view, and I wish I could've seen my face when I saw what he was doing. Three men were running toward him, and I was anxious for him, hoping he could hold his own. Boy, did he prove me right. He jumped up in the air, lifting his arms as he went, and shoved an arm out in front of him. Sharp sticks flew in that direction, stabbing all three men multiple times.

He landed gracefully on his feet and threw his arm out behind him, green vines wrapping around the legs and arms of the woman who was creeping up. He twisted his arm in the air and lifted the woman as she tried to escape the vines. Then he threw his arms down, slamming her onto the ground. I heard a snap when she connected, and I shuddered, blocking my eyes with my hand.

That was…intense.

Someone yelled, and I looked up in time to see Axel shoot two guys right in the middle of their foreheads. Both of them dropped to the ground, lifeless. He ran to another employee and raised his leg, kicking her right in the chest. She flew backward from the force, crashing into the wall. She screamed and got up, prepared to charge at Axel, but Axel whipped out two different guns and fired at her. Two bullets pierced her forehead. He was really skilled with those guns.

I turned my attention to Dmitri. He was graceful with his fighting, as if he was used to it, so it was nothing to him. The employees couldn't even reach him because when they ran at him, he shot his arms out, lifted them into the air, and clapped his hands together, slamming them into each other. A loud cracking sound filled the air.

I gritted my teeth, trying my best not to flinch. Every time I heard a snap or a crack, I almost *felt* what was happening to them. I was so caught up with the fighting, I almost forgot about my own personal agenda—to go find Caspian and persuade him to stop all of this nonsense.

Dmitri's back was facing me, so it was a perfect time to bolt. Getting up to a crouched position, I grabbed on to the desk's side and scouted the area one last time. Once I was totally sure that the coast was clear, I ran to the escalator.

I ducked when one of the employees crashed into the wall beside me and continued running, not wanting to get caught by my team. I reached the escalator and paused, glancing behind me to make sure I was still in the clear. No one was looking my way, so I hurried and jumped onto the moving steps.

"Meadow!" Dmitri shouted, and I glanced back at him. The anger on his face almost made me want to go back down to safety. *Almost.* Another employee attacked him, distracting him. I made it to the top and ran to the elevator, smashing the button to go up. The doors opened and I threw myself inside, rapidly pressing the top floor button. That was the only place Caspian would be.

The elevator jolted to a stop, and the doors opened, revealing a spacious office with long, clear windows surrounding it. The room held a small desk with a comfy looking black chair behind it, and a laptop sitting in its middle.

I stepped out of the elevator slowly and spotted a purple lip-shaped couch in the corner. Interesting. There was nothing else in the office besides a flatscreen tv hanging on the wall to my left. And Caspian. He stood with his back to me, his hands clasped behind him. There was another door to his right, with an exit sign above it.

He was wearing a purple cloak with a hood that I'd seen him in, back when I didn't know it was him. I cleared my throat so my voice wouldn't come across with fear in it. His head moved, the only sign I saw that he actually heard me.

"Caspian," I whispered. My voice already betrayed me.

His shoulders tensed, and he slowly turned around, his blue eyes wide. Was it shock?

"Meadow, how did you get in here?" He seemed surprised. For some reason, I didn't believe his tone. I could hear behind the facade that he'd probably always used on me.

I crossed my arms and narrowed my eyes at him. "Why are you trying to kill me?" I asked, getting straight to the point.

His face morphed into a...sinister one? "Who said I was trying to kill you?" he asked sweetly.

I almost gagged from how fake he sounded. "Dmitri," I answered, his name making Caspian halt his steps.

He tilted his head to the side and narrowed his eyes into slits. "I am not trying to ki—"

"Meadow!" Dmitri shouted, interrupting Caspian, and appeared next to me, eyes wild and searching. Once he saw that I wasn't harmed in any way, he slowly turned, facing Caspian.

I moved and stood next to Dmitri, tired of him always standing in my way like a shield. I wasn't looking at Dmitri, but I could tell he was probably glaring, based on the smug look on Caspian's face.

"Caspian," Dmitri growled as his body tensed.

Caspian's smirk turned into a huge smile. "You seem stressed, Dmitri. Are you okay?" Caspian taunted, pacing in small circles with his hands clasped in front of him.

Dmitri took a small step forward, fists clenched. "Stay away from her. She knows nothing anymore, therefore she's not a threat. So why are you doing this?" Dmitri asked, his breathing getting deeper as he got angrier.

Caspian tsked and pulled at his cloak. Was he nervous? "Dmitri, I am not a fool. I know her memories are gone for *now*. Just like I also know that you are trying to find a way to restore her memories. Because of that, I have to eliminate her."

I gasped quietly at his statement, my heart dropping. The corners of my eyes stung, and I blinked rapidly, not wanting the tears to fall for him. It hurt, but I would rather channel the anger that was building up. I pointed my finger at Caspian. "You lied to me?" I questioned angrily, my face scrunching up with fury and hurt.

He chuckled lightly, which stung even more. "Of course, I did. You didn't really think I cared about you, right?" He raised an eyebrow, and all I saw was red.

I lunged at him but was stopped by an arm wrapping around my waist, pulling me back. "Let me go! I'm going to destroy him!" I screamed, arms outstretched, and hands curled into claws at Caspian. I couldn't believe him. I valued my friendships dearly, like family, and the fact that he had tossed me aside like trash and wanted to end my life made me want to break down. I didn't understand how he could hate me so much.

"Meadow, stop fighting me. You are in no way equipped to fight him. He *will* kill you," Dmitri whispered in my ear.

I kept trying to get out of his grasp anyway, with no luck, of course.

"Stop it! Look at his hands. He's starving," Dmitri whispered fiercely and so low I almost missed it.

I looked at Caspian's hands and stopped moving. I realized why Caspian kept moving around, agitated and twitchy. His hands looked normal at first glance, but once Dmitri brought it to my attention, I saw the purple streaks in his veins, covering the outer part of his hands, disappearing up his cloak sleeves.

I couldn't see his neck because his cloak covered it, but if I could, the veins in his neck would probably be purple as well. I was in slight awe from actually seeing that up close. Dmitri moved me behind him and blocked my view of Caspian. I almost growled in frustration.

"Give it up, Caspian. It's over," Dmitri told him in a steady voice.

Caspian laughed and stopped pacing. He squared his shoulders, and I moved to Dmitri's side. "I am *not* going anywhere." His eyes dared Dmitri to challenge him. Caspian wasn't going down without a fight, and there was nowhere to escape without Caspian catching me.

Good job, Meadow, what a position to put yourself in, huh?

"If you won't come willingly, I will have to kill you," Dmitri warned him.

Caspian laughed again, rubbing his chin between his fingers. "Bring it on, Dmitri," Caspian growled and lunged at him. Dmitri shoved me out of the way.

Caspian was throwing jabs at Dmitri, missing every time. Dmitri elegantly jumped and slammed his foot into the side of Caspian's head, sending him into the glass window. I flinched. That had to hurt. But the impact didn't seem to bother him as he picked himself up from the floor. The glass surprisingly didn't shatter from the force.

"Oh, you want to play? Let's play!" Caspian lifted his arms sharply, and a noise to my right caught my attention. My jaw dropped as the laptop hovered in the air. Caspian had abilities like Dmitri.

Of course he did. He was the one who held Rachel and Victor up in the air. I wondered if she was okay. Wait—how did he take me to the interrogation room at the same time? Getting out of my thoughts, I watched as Caspian jerked his arm back and clenched his fist, hurling the laptop Dmitri's way.

14

Dmitri teleported out of the way. He appeared behind Caspian and wrapped his arm around his neck in a choke-hold. The laptop crashed to the floor. The only other sounds in the room were my heavy breathing and Caspian's gasps for air.

"I'm not letting go until you confirm that you will come willingly," Dmitri growled. He grabbed his left wrist with the right hand, tightening his hold. Caspian stood there with a stubborn look on his face, unflinching. But a quick look of panic crossed his face. He was uncomfortable, but didn't want to look weak.

"Caspian, do it, or I will have to put you down," Dmitri warned when Caspian made no move to agree.

Caspian's jaw ticked, and after a few seconds of silence, he finally tapped Dmitri's arm, indicating he agreed.

Dmitri slowly let him go and walked around, facing him. "Grab what you need and come with me quietly. You know where you're going, and you won't be out for a long time."

Caspian scoffed, walking past Dmitri to get to his desk.

Dmitri angled his body to follow Caspian as he walked, and I glanced at his waist, eyeing the dagger. The anger I felt inside only grew as I thought about what I could do with it. Before I could talk myself out of it, I grabbed the dagger.

"Monster!" I raised my arm to stab Caspian in the chest. His hand flickered before my arm could come down, and the dagger was now in his hand. His other hand shot out, I heard a crash, and Dmitri groaned.

Caspian tsked, grabbed my shoulder, and shoved the dagger into my stomach. The initial pain I experienced when the dagger sliced cleanly through my abdomen was a type of pain that I had never experienced before. I couldn't comprehend what I was feeling. My throat started closing up. I couldn't breathe, and I gagged from the uncomfortable sensation of thin liquid sliding up my throat. But nothing came out of my mouth.

My hands flew to the dagger still inside of me. I stared in awe as the blue substance crawled up my chest, followed by a white substance. A chill settled directly in the middle of my chest. I blinked as my vision started to blur, and I looked up to see that Caspian was gone, and Dmitri replaced him. His arms were jerking forward toward the elevator.

He stopped and turned to me, eyes wild, and his lips were moving. I couldn't hear anything coming out of his mouth. Why did he seem to be freaking out? Caspian was gone, so we were both safe, right? Dmitri started clapping in my face.

What is he doing? I suddenly got tired, so I closed my eyes so I could sleep. There was another clap, and my eyes snapped open. *What is his problem?* I just wanted to take a quick nap. He looked like he was shouting something. Only part of it reached my ears.

He grabbed my shoulders. "... don't touch it! Open your eyes! Stay with me!" Don't touch what?

I looked down. The ornate handle of the dagger protruded from my abdomen. It finally clicked. A weird sound came out of nowhere, and I looked around frantically for the source.

"Meadow! Stop screaming!" Dmitri yelled.

That was me? I couldn't breathe. I clutched my throat and stared at Dmitri wide-eyed. My lids got heavy, and I really wanted to take a nap. So I closed my eyes, and darkness surrounded me, all-consuming.

After what felt like a minute later, I opened my eyes and took in my surroundings, confused. How did I end up in my loft? I was just with Dmitri at...I looked down and saw that I was lying on my couch. Weird. I sat up and blinked, rubbing my eyes. Bad habit, I know. When I opened my eyes again, Dmitri was standing in front of me, his back toward me.

"Oh, thank god. What happened? One minute we're in that building with Caspian, and the next minute, we're in my loft? How did we get here?" I asked him, stretching out my limbs. I waited for him to answer, but he didn't say anything. He didn't even move. He looked...frozen?

"Dmitri?" I called out his name, and he suddenly started moving, but not toward me. I was about to speak again, but he beat me to it.

"You really don't remember me?" he asked, but his back was still facing me. I scrunched my brows in confusion.

"What are you talking about? I know who you are now," I responded. Why wasn't he facing me? I walked closer to him and reached out to grab his shoulder, but my hand went right through it. What the...what was this? He stepped forward, and I looked over his shoulder to see what had his attention and choked on a gasp.

It was me. But how? I looked back and forth between the other me and Dmitri. The outfit I was wearing looked familiar.

I squinted. It was the outfit from the other day when I woke up in bed in my work clothes...was it a dream? This *had* to be a dream.

I started walking to my other self to try and figure out what was going on. Everything around me began to move quickly before I reached myself, as if someone clicked the fast forward button.

"What is happening?!" I screamed into the air. I closed my eyes and covered my ears as the wind howled around me. Where did this wind even come from? I waited until everything seemed to stop moving, removed my hands from my ears, and slowly peeled my eyes open, taking in the scenery.

I was on a beach of some kind, water surrounding the area. The water seemed to go on forever, making me assume I was on an island. How did I get there, though? Was this another dream? My dreams were never this vivid. The sun was setting, creating a beautiful pink-orange hue in the sky. I heard a yell and turned to my right. Dmitri, Dax, Rita, Axel, and...Caspian? They ran along the beach. There was also another female with them, but I didn't know who she was. She had long, inky black hair that flowed down her back, tied in a ponytail, her skin a beautiful dark chestnut color. All of them waved their arms, screaming as they ran. I couldn't hear clearly. Walking a little closer, I tried to catch what they were saying.

"Stop!"

"Don't do it!"

"No, please don't!"

I turned to see what or who they were running after. It was a woman with dark auburn hair, dressed in a black, long-sleeved robe that buttoned all the way to her feet. It was hard to see who it was from my position, but I didn't want to expose myself.

The woman raised her arms, the black fabric spreading out like wings. She didn't seem to be aware of the group running toward her. Her eyes turned a liquid gold color, and she jumped up in the air. She hovered as the wind tousled her long hair.

I watched in awe as her auburn hair started turning black, and she raised her arms again, a smoky black and purple trail following her movements. The colored smoke wrapped around her body protectively, and the sky darkened, thunder making its presence known.

All of them kept shouting, and before anything else happened, everything started moving in fast forward like before. I started losing consciousness, and the last words I heard from the dream left my blood cold.

"Meadow! Don't do it!"

Me? Was that really me? How?

I blacked out.

I was swimming, but I wasn't in water. It was hot, dry, and black everywhere.

"Will she be okay if you take it out?" I heard someone ask. It sounded like Dax.

"Who cares," someone else muttered. Rita. Of course.

"I'm not sure, but we can't just leave it in there."

Mom? Was that my mom? What was she doing? *I haven't seen her in a while, I need to say hi.* I tried to move, but nothing happened. Something shifted in my lower abdomen, and icy fire shot up my chest, making it hard for me to breathe. But that wasn't the worst part. The worst part was in my abdomen. A burning sensation started off like a fire but turned into what I thought frostbite would feel like. I let out a bloodcurdling scream.

"Hold her down!" a voice yelled. Hands pushed my shoulders down, and more hands held my legs still. I didn't feel myself move, so I didn't know why they were locking me down in place.

"Why does she keep whispering that?" Someone asked, and another person sighed. I tried to figure out who was speaking, but I couldn't get past the darkness, the water, to let them know that I was in so much pain.

"You need to wake her up right now." That was Dmitri.

"Kid, I know what I'm doing. This is my daughter."

I stirred. That was definitely my mom. I tried to speak, but my lips were sealed shut, unmoving.

"Be still, Meadow. I'm almost done," my mom whispered in my ear. Nothing happened, but it was quiet again. The pain from my abdomen was gone. There was tugging on my belly, but other than that, I didn't feel anything.

"Okay, she's good. *Wake.*"

The word was whispered in my ear, and the pressure in my chest slowly started going away. I moved my lips, and they actually parted for me. My eyelids were super heavy, making my eyeballs roll from how hard I was trying to open them.

I paused, waiting for the feeling to go away. When the pressure seemed to be gone, I tried to open my eyes again. I squinted from the light that shone directly in my eyes.

"Oops, sorry."

The light went away, and I blinked a couple of times as I stared at the ceiling. A familiar face came into view, soft brown eyes warm and inviting.

"Mom!" I shot up and grabbed her, crushing her into a hug. She chuckled and wrapped her arms around me, hugging me back just as hard. I inhaled the sugar-cookie scent she always wore and it comforted me.

She pulled back and wiped a tear from her eye, helping me sit up on the couch.

"Don't ever scare me like that again, you hear me?" She warned but had a huge smile of relief on her face.

I smiled back and sank into the couch, exhausted. "I won't, mom." I laughed lightly and looked down. My whole abdomen was wrapped in gauze, and I was wearing a sports bra and sweatpants. "Who changed my clothes, and what exactly happened? I only remember pieces." I stretched, wincing at how sore I was.

She blew out a breath and got up from the floor, looking over my head. "I changed your clothes, but I'm not sure what happened. Dmitri, could you explain to her what exactly happened? You can give her more details than I would be able to."

I turned around to see Dmitri and Dax standing behind the couch. Dax had a worried look on his face, and Dmitri had his typical stoic expression. He nodded at my mom, and she patted my knee and left the room.

Dax looked back and forth between Dmitri and me and let out an awkward chuckle. "Uh, yeah, I'm gonna go tracking with the rest of them," he muttered to Dmitri and gave me a reassuring smile as he walked backward toward the door.

Once he was gone, the tension in the room rose like heat. I slowly raised my eyes to him, regretting my decision immediately. He was glaring at me with such intensity, I was surprised I didn't disintegrate right there on the spot.

He made his way around the couch and stopped when he was standing directly in front of me. I twisted my lips to the side and glanced down before looking back up, staring him down. My stomach turned from knowing he was totally furious with me, but I made sure not to let it show in my eyes or face.

"Why, Meadow?" He finally spoke, his deep voice thick with his accent. It wasn't usually so noticeable, but it got thicker when he was emotional in any kind of way. I sighed and tried not to roll my eyes.

"Because I wanted to." I crossed my arms over my chest, challenging him.

He sighed, rubbing his forehead with his thumb and index finger. He looked around and sat in the rocking chair across from where I was sitting, a hand cupping the side of his face. He stared at me and didn't say a word, his gray eyes piercing. He looked a little worn out.

"Look, I know you're trying to protect me for whatever reason, but I don't do well with strangers trying to tell me what to do. I can take care of myself," I finally said after he said nothing to my response. He leaned back in the chair, closing his eyes. He mumbled something, but it was too low for me to hear.

"What are you saying?" I asked, getting frustrated.

"I'm not a stranger," he mumbled again, but this time loud enough for me to hear.

"That's what you tell me, but how am I supposed to know that?" I threw my arms up in the air. "I believe we had some sort of connection, but I like information. Some evidence would be nice, at least."

"You will know soon when I figure out a way to get your memories back."

"And when will that be? Because I'm tired of waiting for my lost memories to come back." I rolled my eyes, leaning back into the couch.

He pressed his lips into a thin line. "Patience is key," he responded, eyes still closed. He was relaxed as if he wanted to sleep. This wasn't something to have patience for. I wanted to know *now*.

I settled back into the couch, softly rubbing the gauze where my wound was located. Dmitri didn't even explain what happened like he was supposed to. "So, what happened in the office? You still didn't tell me anything. I only remember bits and pieces."

He sighed heavily and groaned softly. "You decided to do something idiotic and go after the person who is trying to kill you, and almost died when he stabbed you with the dagger." His eyes snapped open, and his face darkened at the memory. "You're lucky your mom knows how to heal."

I quickly perked up at the mention of my mom. "Wait," I started, shaking my head. "How did you even find my mom? Does she know about you guys?" I sat up slowly, careful not to shift the gauze too much. There was no way she didn't know if she somehow healed me from what the dagger did to me. And how did he even know my mom and where I used to live?

He sighed. His eyes raised to mine, and the look there gave me my answer before he even responded. She did know. He nodded, barely, but enough to confirm. I huffed. How did she know about all of this, but never told me a thing?

"Before you leave and go off on Maze, remember that whatever she has done was to protect you. Don't be too mad at her." He got up and walked to where I was sitting.

I stood up next to him, not sure how I really felt. "How could I not be mad? This is my life we're talking about, you know. I just want to understand. That's it. I'm so tired of this guessing game." My face scrunched up, and the sides of my eyes tingled. My chest squeezed, and I took in a deep breath, willing my tears not to fall. I couldn't break down in front of him. I *wouldn't*.

Dmitri walked closer to me, his hand curled into a fist at his side. He unclenched it and moved it up, seemingly hesitant.

I discreetly wiped the side of my eyes before tears could fall and turned so Dmitri wouldn't see my face.

He did the unexpected and wrapped his arms around me, pulling me into his chest.

I grabbed the front of his shirt and buried my face in it, finding comfort in his embrace.

"Talk to your mom, Meadow. I know it's frustrating not knowing everything, but trust me, you'll get your answers in due time," he said softly, slowly rubbing my back. He pulled away, holding me at arm's length.

I nodded, thinking about taking his advice. A small smile graced his face, and he patted my shoulder as he walked past me. Not thinking, I reached out and grabbed his arm, stopping him. I didn't want him to go. Something about his presence made me feel comfortable and safe. His face softened at my worried one.

"I have to go tracking, but I will be back tomorrow sometime. Okay?" he reassured me, and I tilted my head.

"What's tracking?" I asked. Dax mentioned it earlier, but it didn't register. The corners of Dmitri's mouth twitched as he raised his shirt's sleeves, revealing violet streaks going through his veins, disappearing under his sleeves. My eyes widened as I understood.

"You're hungry. Got it."

"Yes. I'm going to join the others, and while I'm out, I'm going to continue looking for a way to restore your memories." He reached out, and the tips of his fingers grazed my cheek, making my heart rate go up. So innocent, yet it felt more intimate than the hug. There was a connection between us that felt so natural and right. It made me want to know more about our history.

"All right. Be safe and have fun, I guess?" I didn't know if that was the right term to use.

He smirked a little and nodded, then left through the front door.

I rubbed my forehead. I needed to relax. I went back to the soft blue couch and spread out on it, cuddling the colorful pillow. It smelled like my childhood, the same smell my mom had worn for as long as I could remember.

"Meadow? Are you all right?"

I sat up sharply, wincing at the pain that shot through my abdomen.

"Are you in pain, honey?" Mom asked, trying to catch my attention. She came and sat down next to me, placing her hand over my gauze.

I smiled softly at her tenderness and nodded. "I'm fine, mom. Just a little pain, but I'll be okay." I patted her leg to reassure her.

She smiled and smoothed down my hair. "Don't worry. The pain should be gone in a couple of hours, and you'll be good as new. And honey, I know you're upset about something. I can't help fix it if I don't know the problem."

I raised my brows at the first part of her statement. A stab wound healed in a couple of hours? At this point, nothing was impossible I guess. I sighed, leaning into her hand. "So much has happened in the past week that has completely changed my life, and I am stressed to the max." I paused, taking in a deep breath. I turned to her, looking straight into her chocolate orbs. "And I just found out that you are aware of all these..." I tried to find a word to describe them. "...creatures with their different abilities, yet you have never told me about any of this. It's like the life I have lived is a lie." I studied her face as she absorbed everything I just told her. Her face was calm, and she had her thinking face on.

"Meadow, you have to understand. I did that for your safety."

"Why does everyone think I need protection? What happened for me to need it?"

She sighed and shifted, moving the couch a little as she did. "It would be too much to explain, and you wouldn't understand since you don't have the memories of your true life." She held her hand up when I raised my head up to speak. "A lot has happened in your life that prompted me to make sure that you were protected at all times. Which included not telling you about who you really are."

I stared at her, almost glaring. None of what she said made any sense or clarified anything Dmitri already told me.

"Dmitri told me that I wasn't human. Is that true?" I held my breath for the answer. I already believed, but I wanted her to confirm.

She slowly nodded.

I let out a breath and passed a hand over my face. "If I am not human, then what am I?" I whispered.

She twisted her lips, glancing at the ceiling.

I crossed my arms. I knew what that face meant. "I'm guessing you can't tell me that either, huh?"

She opened her mouth to speak but was interrupted by her pager. She gave me an apologetic look and picked it up, her face getting serious. "The hospital needs me right now. Can we continue this conver-

KAHILAH HARRY

sation another time, please?" she asked, and I nodded. She got up and planted a kiss on my forehead. "I love you, Meadow."

"Yeah, yeah, I love you too, Mom," I mumbled, and she squeezed my shoulder on her way past me. I stayed where I was until she left the house and I listened for her car to start. Once she was gone entirely, I got up from the couch, thinking hard about getting the answers I wanted.

When I was younger, my mom always kept a chest in her bedroom closet that I was absolutely forbidden to touch. Only once I tried to open it with no luck. I saw a side of my mom I had never seen before, and I was grounded for a month after that. The recent events made me question whether the chest had something to do with who I really was.

At the top of the stairs, I turned left and opened her bedroom door. Her warm scent hit my nostrils, and I didn't hesitate, going directly into her walk-in closet. There was a mini dresser in the middle of the closet, and I scanned the room for the chest, passing over her designer heels, dresses, and pants until my gaze landed on something black peeking out from under the sneaker section.

I went over and got on my knees, pushing up the shelf filled with shoes.

Bingo.

The chest looked exactly the same as it did all those years ago. Completely black with gold accents. There was a keyhole in the middle of it. I grabbed the sides and yanked it upward, trying to get it open.

No luck there. I looked around the closet for a key, but found nothing. I got back on my knees and huffed. Maybe the whole thing was actually a decoration my mom just didn't want me to touch because she treasured it so dearly. Sighing, I placed my hands over the top of the chest and grazed the keyhole with my thumb, trying to see if it was an actual hole or not. Something unlocked, and I removed my hands from the chest, paranoid at what just happened. The top slowly started opening.

"Um, okay?" I whispered to myself. Maybe applying pressure was the way to open it? Either way, it opened fully, and I peered inside. It was very organized; each section was filled with something different. I reached into the chest and picked up a beautiful silver necklace with a sapphire pendant.

It looked identical to the necklace around my own neck. I never took it off, not even when I showered. I looked to see what else was in the section and pulled out two more necklaces that looked the same as the ones I held and wore around my neck. I was confused by this because when I was younger, my mom told me my necklace was a gift from my dad. Which was why I never took it off. Maybe he gave her a bunch as well, even though I didn't know why she would need so many different sizes.

There were more in the chest, and the smallest one seemed small enough to fit around a newborn's neck. Not trying to dwell on it too much longer, I put all of the necklaces back and started searching for something that would actually help me find out who I was. After about five minutes, I didn't find anything that helped me, or that seemed important. It was just a bunch of junk.

Huffing, I sat and crossed my legs, thinking hard as I scanned the chest. I thought about the warehouse's vault and how I didn't notice it before until I really started looking. It made me think about a secret compartment. Pulling the chest closer to me, I felt along the inside to see if there was a soft spot or button for a hidden section. There was nothing.

Sighing, I closed the chest and was about to push it back in the corner where I found it, but had a last-minute idea. Turning the chest around, I passed my hand over the back of it, feeling for any gaps. My hand reached the middle of it and stopped when I heard a hissing noise. I leaned forward to listen and felt a little bit of air coming from the center. I grinned, sensing a great victory.

I pushed the middle of the back, and the hissing got louder until a flap sprung out like a latch. I pulled on it until a larger tray slid out, revealing a cluster of envelopes. Now, that was more like it. I grabbed all of the envelopes and spread them out on the closet floor. Every single envelope was a beautiful gold color with blue accents. I went through a few. They were all letters, and all opened.

That made it easier to read without my mom realizing that I went through her stuff. I counted roughly eighty letters. Hopefully, my mom would be out for the rest of the day at the hospital so I could have time to finish all of the letters. This was going to take a while to get through. Opening the first letter, I let out a breathy laugh.

The handwriting was exquisite, like it was written in the 17th century or close to it. The ink was faded, but luckily, I was still able to read it. Getting comfortable, I started reading. A few letters in, I recognized some names. There was a lot of talk about a woman named Feina and keeping her safe.

Sounds like me right now. I chuckled. There was also talk about a dark, evil man that the writer was warning the reader of the letter—probably my mom—to watch out for. As I continued reading, I learned that the evil guy's name was Legend. That was a pretty cool name. As I read more, I found out that Legend turned good, making me feel better about liking his name.

The letters I was reading were sent by the same person, someone named Augustus. He was some type of scientist, I wasn't sure of what exactly. I went through about fifty letters before the sender changed. The second batch I read was from a priest named Aloysius. I had never, ever heard that name before, making me believe that these letters were indeed written a very long time ago. But then again, maybe not, because some of these letters spoke about recent events.

How old was my mom then, if some of the letters were possibly written hundreds of years ago? She wouldn't tell me what I was so I didn't think she would tell me what she was...if she wasn't human. The only thing I knew was that she was some type of healer, which made sense since she was a surgeon at the hospital. Getting out of those thoughts, I took my time and read the rest of the letters, until I got to the last one.

It had some instructions, but the rest of it was schematics of some kind of temple—a huge temple. After an hour or so of reading the long letters, I was no closer to finding out who I was. Groaning, I leaned back into the dresser. There had to be something I could use from these letters. I didn't want it to be a wasted effort.

Wait.

I sat up quickly. Grabbing a few letters, I went back through them. Augustus, the scientist, put an address in one of the letters for if my mom ever needed help with anything.

Ha, got it. It was located in what he called The Lucky. I knew where that was, and it was only a few hours away. I was going to check it out since no one else would tell me anything.

I was going to find some information on my own.

15

The location was set up in the car's GPS. The trip would take about five and a half hours to my destination. That was fine with me, and it'd be worth it. I hoped this scientist could provide me with some answers or at least clues to help me understand anything at this point. After setting my music up with my favorite songs on repeat, I started out on the highway as the sun was setting. I turned up the volume, belting out my vocals. With the sun casting its beautiful colors and the phenomenal singing, I started thinking optimistically about my life. Maybe whatever I was wasn't so bad, and the adjustment to that life would be swift. Despite being negative sometimes about the whole situation, deep down, I was actually thrilled about the thought of a new life with new experiences. I was caught up in my thoughts for a while before I noticed it.

A dark gray shadow in the air, following me. It was dark outside already as the sun had set, and the only reason I noticed it was because the color was slightly lighter than the dark sky. At first, I thought it was just some type of fog, but then I realized it was with me for every stop and turn. I sped up, thinking that I would get some distance and get away from it. No such luck. It was still there like it was latched on to the car somehow.

I tried not to panic as my heart started beating faster. I reached toward the GPS, but stopped abruptly. I was going to find alternate routes so I could get away from the creepy shadow, but my course wasn't on there anymore. There was just a loading screen, the blue circle continuous. I pressed the screen to see if it would change, but nothing happened. I clicked all of the buttons around the screen, but that didn't work either.

"Ugh!" I slammed my hands on the steering wheel. Why now of all times did the GPS decide to malfunction? The highway was almost empty, the only other car on the road miles ahead of me, lights almost disappearing. I gripped the steering wheel and glanced in my rearview mirror again. I'd actually put some distance between the car and the shadow.

"Yes!" I did a happy dance as I widened my lead until the shadow was basically gone. I sighed and relaxed, shaking my head. *What was that?* I didn't want to think about anything...supernatural, so I turned my music back on and turned my attention back to the road.

I smashed my brakes and screamed, gasping as the seatbelt slammed into my chest. The shadow was in front of me, but then quickly disappeared. It was too dark to see anything properly, even with my headlights, so I just took a deep breath and started driving slowly. I heard a screech, and my eyes widened when I spotted the shadow a reasonable distance ahead of me. I slowed down to an almost stop, checking my mirrors to make sure no cars were coming, and the shadow started creeping closer.

As I watched, it stretched, and two smoky arms emerged in the front. I kept driving the slowest I possibly could, ready for any moment to swerve past it. My plan was thwarted when the shadow expanded, filling up almost the entire road. It continued to float my way faster, and began to form hands from the arms. The hands stretched out my way, and I realized what was about to happen. It was going to crash into the car with me inside of it.

"Oh my god, oh my god, oh my god." I fumbled with my seatbelt. *I need to get out of here.* I sped up until I got close to the shadow, and the arms stretched even more. I unbuckled my seatbelt quickly, threw my door open, and flung myself out of the car.

My feet touched the ground, and I rolled, protecting my face with my arms. Surprisingly, I didn't sprain anything, but my arms were definitely scratched up. A loud crash filled the air, and I looked up in horror as the shadow exploded straight into my car through the front windshield and came out the back, glass flying everywhere. I slowly got up, wiping dust off my clothes.

The shadow didn't stop there. Grabbing the bumper, it lifted the back and flipped the car in the air. My mouth dropped. The car flipped twice and landed on the hood, the vehicle flattening from the force. My mom was going to absolutely kill me. That was her favorite car. A loud roar came from the shadow, and it turned my way, making me freeze in place.

A scream was on my lips, but I didn't want to let it out. I couldn't let whatever that was know that I was absolutely terrified. It roared even louder, and I screamed, forgetting about being tough. There were no other cars on the road, so no one could help me. It was either run down the long stretch of open road or hide in the woods behind me. I chose the woods.

Not knowing how I would get help, I ran into the woods anyway, pushing the branches out of my way. A soul-cringing screech filled the air, and I glanced back. The shadow morphed back into a blob and flew upward to the sky. It was going to get a bird's eye view, not good. Running even faster, I weaved between the trees and looked for somewhere to hide, squinting through the dark.

The moon disappeared between the trees, making it almost impossible to see anything. I stopped running at a thick tree, catching my breath. I didn't see the shadow above me, and trees were too tall with thick leaves, blocking most of the sky. I couldn't continue like this, not without being able to see properly.

I closed my eyes and took in a few breaths, wishing I could see clearly, and started thinking of a way to conceal myself from the shadow. A gust of wind whistled through the trees, and my eyes snapped open. As I scanned the area for the culprit, I held on to the tree. I blinked a few times and squinted.

Letting go of the tree, I turned in a half circle. It was still dark—nothing changed—but I could see the forest clearly. The gust of wind got stronger, almost blowing me off my feet, and I spotted the shadow, weaving through the trees to my right. I gasped and kept my back pressed against the tree, trying to make myself smaller. As I contemplated what my next move would be, I saw what looked like a hole in the ground a few feet away from me.

Perfect.

I dashed away from the tree. Screeching filled the air, and I dodged a tree, glancing back to see the shadow coming after me. I was almost to the hole, but I needed to distract the shadow so it wouldn't follow me. Shrugging off my jacket as I ran, I threw it up high, hoping it caught on a branch, and skidded to a stop when I reached the hole. Peering over, it looked like it was once used as a trap from the spikes on the side. There were none at the bottom, and it looked deep enough for me to fit inside. Good enough for me. I crouched down and jumped in when it was clear.

Dirt flew everywhere and in my mouth, making me spit and claw at my face to get it off and out of my mouth. Breathing hard, I looked around. I was surrounded by dirt. It was better than whatever that was up there. A screech tore through the air, an angry one. I guess it found my decoy.

I looked up, and I could finally see the moon shining directly on me. Crap, that thing could pass over and see me from how bright the moon was shining. Before I could look for something to shield myself with, something grabbed my arm and yanked me backward. A large scream ripped from my throat, and I struggled against whatever had me trapped.

"Shh, shh. It's me, Meadow, it's me," a voice whispered fiercely in my ear. All the stress and fear went away as soon as I registered who it was.

"Oh my gosh, Dax!" I whispered, relief evident in my voice. I'd never been so happy in my life to see someone. "How are you here?

How did you know?" I asked as he stepped into the light. He was wearing all black, his shirt standing out with a red skull on it. For the first time since I met him, he donned a serious look on his face.

"I'll tell you later. Right now I have to get rid of this Umbra," he whispered.

I mouthed 'Umbra' to myself, trying to pronounce it like he did. *What did it mean?* The screeching intensified above us, making me shrink into the dirt even more, trying to hide from the moonlight.

"Your scream alerted it to where you are. Not an exact location, but it will eventually find you and try to kill you."

I shuddered at his honesty.

"But I won't let that happen, of course. I'll help you get rid of it." He glanced back at me and gave me his signature smile. I smiled back, grateful for his presence. He started walking forward, standing directly in the moonlight. His head tilted to the side.

"Okay, it's almost time. I'm going to need you to grab onto my shoulders." He told me. Placing my hands on his shoulders, he reached back and patted them, securing them both on his shoulders. "You're going to need both hands because you could fall from what I'm about to do." He warned, patting my hands again.

"What are you about t—" my scream was lost in the wind as Dax jumped in the air quickly, making me lose my breath as well. He landed next to the hole, and I let go of his shoulders, trying to catch my breath. The world spun in a circle, and the trees started disappearing, the sky coming in my main line of vision.

"Whoa!" Dax grabbed my arm and yanked me forward, saving me from falling back into the hole. "Are you good?"

I stretched my arms out at my sides, making sure I was balanced. Once the world stopped spinning, I nodded and slowed my breathing back to normal. "I'm good, sorry. You just caught me off guard with the jumping," I finally answered, out of breath.

He chuckled and glanced around. "Sorry about that. I forgot that you don't have your memories, so you're not used to the speed anymore." He looked around again, and I inched closer to him. It was eerily quiet. The shadow was nowhere to be found.

"Um, is it normal for the shadow to just leave, you know, from boredom or something?" I whispered to Dax, hoping that was the case.

He shook his head and pressed a finger to his lips, quietly walking away from the hole. I followed behind him just as quietly, with no clue as to where we were going. He weaved through the trees speedily, and I had to catch his arm and hold on to it when he started going faster. He didn't slow down, the trees starting to blur.

"Dax, where are we going?" I whispered. He stopped, and I bent down, catching my breath. I was so winded, I just wanted to go home at this point.

"I needed us to get as far away from the hole as possible in a short amount of time, so I could set everything up." He lifted his shirt, revealing a fanny pack. He unzipped it and took out two vials, one filled with a blue liquid, the other filled with a purple liquid.

"What are those for?" I asked as he closed his eyes. He didn't answer me, and his lips started moving quickly like he was reciting something. His eyes snapped open, and he took the corks off both of them, spilling the liquids on the ground. I gasped as the colors moved on the ground, worming its way into a perfect circle around both of us, creating a magenta color.

A terrible screech filled the air, and I flinched. It was so loud, I almost had to cover my ears. Dax looked around, his face getting serious. Strong winds blew the trees, leaves snapping off branches from the force. My hair blew in the wind, making me regret not putting it back into a ponytail when I had time.

"Back up just a little bit, Meadow," Dax whispered, and I stepped back, making sure I was still in the circle. I slowed my breathing so that I could calm down and hear my surroundings better. "Here we go." Dax's eyes were frantic, making me a little anxious. The screech filled the air again, this time so loud, I had to cover my ears. A ringing sound filled my head and gave me a slight headache. The shadow was a few feet away, hovering in the air, unmoving.

I inched closer to Dax, not sure what to expect. "What is it doing?" I whispered, keeping my eyes on the shadow.

"It's scoping out the area, trying to see what the best way would be to attack us," he answered, searching in his fanny pack.

"Then why aren't we running?"

"Because it can't get to us," he explained, still searching.

Another screech filled the air, and a small yelp left my lips. The shadow raced our way with so much speed, I started backing up, not sure I trusted what Dax said about it not being able to get to us. The shadow roared, and I covered my face, waiting for impact. There was a crash, but I felt nothing.

Opening my eyes, I dropped my arms, and my mouth followed. The shadow was being blocked by some invisible barrier. I looked down and saw that the magenta circle was glowing. Dax was grinning at the shadow, standing in front of it, unflinching. Whatever he did was working.

"How is this possible?" I didn't see anything in front or around us, only a little ripple when the shadow hit the barrier, trying to get through.

"The two potions, mixed together, create a forcefield for whoever is standing in the circle." He explained, pulling a pouch out of his fanny pack. "Ha! Found it!" Dax parted the circle with his foot, the magenta color disappearing. The only things there now were the dirt and grass. "Now, this will make it disappear. All you have to do is throw the powder at it."

The circle turned magenta again around me. He took a step forward, but he was yanked to the side before he could take another.

I gasped as Dax hit a tree, the small pouch leaving his hand. The shadow turned its attention to Dax, slowly making its way to him.

"Dax, throw me the pouch!" I yelled at him, and he jumped up. He hurried and grabbed it from the ground, tossing it my way. I caught it and dumped the powder in my hand and stepped outside the barrier, exposing myself.

The Umbra faced me and screeched, expanding as it prepared to engulf me. I tossed the yellow powder in the air, every single particle clinging to the shadow.

"Cover your ears, Meadow!" Dax shouted, and I slapped my

hands over my ears. The screech was deafening. The shadow exploded, and the screeching stopped, gray particles dropping to the ground. I dropped my arms and stared at Dax with wide eyes, my mouth open.

"Pretty cool, huh?" Dax asked, grinning like a birthday kid with his cake as he walked my way.

I nodded and placed a hand over my racing heart. My poor heart was going through it today.

"Come on. Let's get out of here." Dax beckoned, and I followed him through the woods until we reached the highway. On the edge of the road sat a black Rubicon, blending in with the night. I couldn't even admire it or get my brain to form any questions right now, I was so drained. I hopped in the passenger's seat and buckled up, getting comfortable.

Dax got in the driver's seat and started the car, driving away from the woods. It was quiet during the first few minutes of the drive as I tried to form questions to ask. I think Dax was giving me some space to process, and I was grateful for that.

"Do you know where you're going?" I asked, realizing I never told him where I was going, yet he was driving confidently.

"I do. You're going to see Augustus, the scientist," he answered, glancing at me.

My mouth was slightly open, I was confused. "How do you know? And how did you know where I was?" I asked, furrowing my brow.

He sighed and twisted his lip, seemed to be thinking about how to answer my questions. "Well, I went tracking with Rita and Axel, and Dmitri came later. I was done before everyone else, so I decided to come back and see how you were doing. I heard you talking to yourself about Augustus, and then you left in a car. So I followed you," he explained, and I closed my mouth, slowly shaking my head.

"I guess that makes sense. Thank you for helping me." I playfully punched his arm, and he laughed, shaking his head at me.

"Don't worry about it. What are friends for?" He wiggled his eyebrows, making me burst out in loud laughs. Him saying that made me think of another question.

"So, when I get my memories back, will you be in them?" I asked, gauging his reaction.

He smiled softly and nodded. "I will definitely be in a lot of them because we are the best of friends. We've been through a lot together, and we're basically inseparable." He sounded proud, and I smiled. No wonder we seemed to click so easily.

"Okay, I think that's all the questions I have for now. My brain can't possibly process anything else at the moment." I sighed into the seat. We both were quiet, and he turned on some music. Classical, very relaxing. I stared out of the window and thought about the questions I planned on asking Augustus.

The main one that lingered was *who am I?*

16

"Wake up, Meadow. We're here." Dax's voice flowed through my ears.

I opened my eyes slowly, squinting at my surroundings. I was in the vehicle with Dax in the driver's seat, a worried look on his face. Everything rushed back as soon as I shook off the sleepy state I was in.

"You okay? We don't have to go in if you're not comfortable."

I shook my head, unbuckling my seatbelt. "I'm fine, just a little shaken up from the Umbra, but I need this."

He nodded at me, turning off the jeep. As I stepped out of the vehicle, I stretched as I scoped out the area. It was still dark, but a building in the middle of the field stood out.

It was six stories high, small and rectangular, with a small triangle shape at the very top. The only light I saw was on what looked like the sixth floor, and the light was flickering like a candle.

"Is this where he is really located? This place is in the middle of nowhere," I whispered to Dax as we walked to the building.

"Yeah, he likes to conduct experiments—dangerous ones—so he needed a place to do that," Dax explained.

Interesting.

We made it to the building and stepped inside, a cold draft hitting us right away. I shivered and rubbed my arms as we walked through the foyer.

I thought the building was an office of some sort, but the inside was like a house. It was dark on this floor, but I could still see part of what looked like two red couches to my left and a massive bookcase filled with books to my right.

"Come on. He's always on the sixth floor," Dax told me, and I followed him, taking the spiral stairs in front of us. So I was right about the light on the sixth floor. I quietly congratulated myself on accurately guessing that. We walked up all six flights of stairs until we made it to a large door, the only entry on the floor.

"Can't he invest in an elevator?" I complained, reaching down to rub my sore calves. Dax gave me a side glance and smiled, shaking his head. I shook my head back at him.

There were two old but well-polished knobs on the door, and Dax turned both of them and let go. The door split in half, revealing an expansive office. As I stepped in, I realized it was more like a lab than an office.

More like half lab, half office. There was a massive black and white painting of an older man with glasses on, donning a serious look. He had a large, long beard, and his hair looked like it went past his shoulders, down his back. There were plush lounge chairs littered around the room, and bookcases stuffed with books covered every inch of the office walls.

Massive volumes. Not one book looked like it was smaller than 700 pages. The only space without a bookcase was a table with a maroon, silky tablecloth on the back wall. On the tablecloth sat different sized flasks and tubes, each filled with different colored liquids. On a separate shelf above the table were additional items, weapons it looked like as I got closer.

All of them were in square glass cases to protect them or show them off, I wasn't sure which one. What stood out to me was that all of the weapons were a beautiful teal color, like the daggers. Golden flecks dotted each weapon differently, also like the daggers. What were these weapons? I reached up to touch the glass case, but a deep, accented voice stopped me.

"I wouldn't do that if I were you," the voice warned. He sounded British, maybe Irish? I wasn't good at figuring out accents. I turned around slowly, and the beaded curtains by one of the bookcases, which I'd thought were only decoration, parted to reveal the old man from the painting.

He was wearing a long golden robe that covered his feet. The robe had sleeves that reached his hands, wide and trailing down, almost reaching the ground. Blue accents were sewn on the robe, most of the blue color on the sleeves' ends. The robe wasn't the thing that stood out the most, though.

His hair was a beautiful teal color and curly, going all the way down his back just like I thought. His magenta beard reached down to the middle of his robe. His left eye matched the teal of his hair, and his right eye the magenta of his beard. The colors went perfectly with his brown skin. He had reading glasses perched on his nose with golden circular frames. I'd never met someone as colorful as he was. I liked it a lot.

"Hello there, Meadow. Since you were about to touch glass laced with a paralytic, I can only assume that your memories are no longer in that little brain of yours." Augustus spoke, making me like his style less. *Little* brain?

"How do you know who I am?" I walked toward him slowly.

Dax appeared by my side, crossing his arms over his chest.

Augustus' eyes flickered to Dax and then back to me. "I know of everyone in this realm, miss. Whether they are aware of who I am or not. It is my job." He yanked gently at the sides of his glasses, and the frames split down the middle. He brought them back together around his neck, and the frames lost their shape, making the lenses disappear. The glasses weren't there anymore. It was now a golden necklace. I glanced at Dax to see if he witnessed what I saw, but the look on his face told me that he was used to it. I was the only one surprised. It was a neat trick.

"It's just science, deary. No need for the astounded look on your face," Augustus chastised, and I furrowed my brow. Who did this man think he was? Before I could say anything smart back, he turned his attention to Dax. "Ah, hello, young man. I see you defeated the Umbra since you are standing in my presence." He started walking to the tables with colored liquids.

"I did, no thanks to you. A little warning that he was coming would've been nice," Dax said icily. His tone shocked me. I'd never heard Dax even remotely get mad. He didn't seem to like this man, and I was starting to see why.

Augustus chuckled and faced us again, a humorous look on his face. "Young man, I look out for only myself. He came to me with an offer I couldn't turn down, so of course I helped him." He smiled, and I swear his teeth glittered from how shiny white they were.

"I thought you were supposed to be good. I read the letters you sent to my mom," I spoke up, seeing that Dax was getting really upset. I wanted him to be calm so he wouldn't do anything to the man that might be the key to me getting my memories back. Augustus may be old, but I felt like he could probably do some real damage if he wanted to. He raised an eyebrow and tilted his head.

"Your mother?" he asked, a confused look on his face.

"Yes, my mom? Maze? I thought you knew everyone in your little realm."

His face relaxed, and a small smile formed. "Ah, yes. Maze, beautiful woman. I am what you call an opportunist. Whatever benefits me, I take it. That is the only way to survive in this world, especially for someone like me." He smiled again, but it seemed fake, not really reaching his eyes like his last smile.

"Do you know Caspian?" I asked since he seemed to know everyone.

He shrugged, turning back to his flasks. "Not really. We only made a one-time deal, which is why I knew he would attack you tonight." His casual admission made me gasp.

"That was Caspian?" I gritted my teeth. "How is that possible?" I curled my fists, my fingers digging hard into my palms. How was he always one step ahead?

"It was because he wa—" Dax started.

"Uh, uh. Let the expert explain, please." Augustus basically sneered at Dax before turning back to me. "What attacked you tonight was an Umbra. It is a shadow that vampires can project and send anywhere they desire. Only those with extensive training know how to properly project." He paused and turned, grabbing something from a drawer on his right, and turned back around. In his hand was a small cloth bag, just like the one Dax had earlier. "The only way to stop an Umbra is with this powder that I created. Saeclum is what I call it." He tipped the bag, and the yellow powder spilled out onto his hand.

"Wait, you created that?" I asked, in awe.

"That is what I just said. I create most of the potions, powders, and elements that the creatures of my realm use." He looked at Dax for confirmation. He rolled his eyes and nodded at Augustus, confirming. Augustus smiled in triumph and marched past us toward the lounge chairs. He gestured to the space in front of him. "Join me. I am sure you didn't travel all this way to speak about the Umbra."

I paused, glancing at Dax. He didn't look like he wanted to move at all. I started walking toward the chairs first, and Dax slowly followed behind me. I sat in the long chair in front of Augustus, sinking into the lush fabric. For a vampire, Dax walked extremely slow, and I waited until he was finally sitting before I asked my first question.

"Since you seem to know who I am, that means you know *what* I am, correct?" I fiddled with my thumbs as I thought about how tired I was of asking the same question.

Augustus sat back into his chair and folded his hands. "That is indeed correct, Meadow," he said simply. Of course, he was the type that answered only the questions asked, not insinuated.

"What am I?" I asked more directly.

"Ah. That, my dear, is not for me to answer. That is something you must find out on your own," he answered.

How was I supposed to find out if no one would tell me?

"Your memories were taken away for a reason. Now you must journey to restore them. The journey is what helps your memories come back. It will be worth it."

I stared at Augustus as if he had three heads. "A journey? You're telling me that I have to complete something just to get the memories that were taken away from me, back?" I asked in disbelief.

"That is correct, my dear. Repeating what I told you will not change that fact," Augustus said with a smug look on his face.

I curled my hands into fists and pressed them against my sides. Heat rushed to my face. I came here to get answers, and all I got was a cocky scientist with an ego the size of The Lone Star, who just wanted to play games. I sat back and rested my head in my hand, hiding the fact that I was clenching my teeth in anger.

Dax gave me a side glance, his face twisted in pure disgust as well. "All right, Augustus. Enough with these games. What does she have to do to get her memories back?" Dax asked, authority seeping through his tone. He folded his hands together, narrowing his eyes.

Augustus stared back just as fierce, then looked back and forth at us for a few seconds. He sighed and uncrossed his legs, patting his knees. "Fine. Since you are no fun, I guess I can speed this along and give you the information you so desire." He flicked his wrist and turned his face toward the ceiling. "The only person who can help you restore your memories is a man named Aloysius."

Dax jumped up from the chair. "You said no more games! Aloysius is nothing more than a fable. Give us some real information."

My eyes widened at his outburst.

"Sit down, young man, and let me finish." Augustus held his hand up, and Dax sat back down, still disgruntled. "Aloysius is far from a fable. Only those who cannot properly reach him believe that. But he is real, and he is my brother."

Dax wore a surprised look on his face that turned skeptical.

"Aloysius has been around as long as I have plus more. You must journey to find him. You can only find him on the highest peak of the highest mountain." Augustus paused, making sure I was still paying attention. "This journey will not be an easy one. You will need a team of people you trust to take the journey with you. It cannot be completed alone," he finished, getting up from his chair.

I stood as well, so many questions running through my head. "What do I do once I find him?" I asked, wanting to know more.

Augustus chuckled as he walked to his beaded curtain. "*If* you make it to my brother, you will not have to do anything. He will know who you are and the reason for your visit. All you need to do is make it to the peak and be in his presence, and your memories will be restored."

Just be in his brother's presence, and that was it for my memories to come back? It seemed too easy.

"There is one more thing, Meadow. Follow me." He beckoned, and I followed him, curious but cautious. Why was he so willing to help me? He paused and looked at Dax. "You stay here."

Dax rolled his eyes but stayed in place as I followed Augustus through the multicolored bead curtain to a back office that was basically a mini version of the room we just left.

There was a small brown desk on the wall in front of us and three bookcases filled with books to our right. Different shaped flasks and vials filled with different colored liquids crowded on the desk, just like in the other room. A maroon chair that looked very soft sat randomly in the middle of the space. Augustus sat in the chair and reached behind him, pulling out another chair...from the desk? The chair seemed to come out of nowhere, but I was too busy wondering what more Augustus needed to show me.

"Have a seat." He gestured to the chair he just pulled out.

I looked at the chair and then back to him, shaking my head. "I'd rather stand, thanks."

He shrugged and crossed his legs. "Suit yourself." He reached behind him to the desk again and grabbed a vial filled with red liquid. He popped the cork off and poured the liquid directly in the middle of his hand, steam rising from the same spot on his palm. He turned it to the floor, but nothing was there anymore. The liquid was gone. He smiled and pressed his hands together, slowly putting one finger over the other, one at a time.

"Now, I didn't want to tell you this part in front of your moody friend out there, since I assume he will be embarking on this journey with you," he started, a small smile forming on his face like something was funny. I waited for him to continue. "Are you absolutely sure that you want to embark on this journey to get your memories back?"

Was I sure? I made a face. My best friend of five years had tried to kill me. I wanted to be able to defend myself for the next time he attacked.

Swallowing the lump in my throat, I nodded. "Of course, I do. Did you not listen to anything I said out there?" I pointed behind me.

He held his hand up. "I did. I only ask because some rules come with taking this journey. Getting your memories back is not a small task." He cleared his throat and gestured to the chair again, his face getting serious. "You might want to sit down for this next part."

I rolled my eyes and sat down in the chair, wishing he'd hurry up. The longer I was here, the longer I was delayed getting my memories back. I was tired of being in the dark, and Dmitri was taking too long to find a way.

"There is only one way to reach the top of the mountain for my brother to restore your memories. A *price* must be paid."

"Okay? I'll clean out my savings, take out a loan, whatever it takes."

Augustus burst out laughing, clutching his middle. I scowled, irritated. He calmed down and wiped an invisible tear from the side of his eye. "Humans." He scoffed. "Not a monetary price. You'll know when the time comes."

"Human? I thought you said I wasn't human."

"You aren't, but you *are* in your human form, so as of now, you're one of them." He waved his hand dismissively, and my nostrils flared. What did he mean I'd know when the time came? How would I know?

Augustus shook his head and stood, tsking. He walked up to me slowly. "That is a beautiful necklace. I will place my hand over the pendant so that the potion I poured on my hand can enter it. It will give you the protection you need for your journey." He finished and stared me down.

I stood up and backed away slightly. "How do I know you're not actually trying to sabotage it?" I asked him, narrowing my eyes. Based on how he'd spoken, he only seemed to care about himself.

"I've seen you at your full potential. You are one of the most powerful beings I've come across, and I would love to see you up against Caspian. I enjoy sitting on the sidelines watching everything unfurl. Such great entertainment." A wide smile spread across his face, and he actually seemed genuine.

"Fine. Go ahead."

He reached forward and hovered his hand over the pendant. It slowly left its place on my neck and rose, red particles leaving his hand and landing right on the sapphire, changing the icy blue color to a brilliant, deep purple. I watched my necklace hover off my neck, the purple fading and original sapphire color showing again. *What kind of science is this?* I'd never seen anything like it.

Augustus dropped his hand and smiled. "Safe travels, my dear. Tell no one of this conversation. If you do, the pendant will not protect you on this journey." His eyes narrowed as he warned me.

I waved my hand in the air. "Yeah, yeah, I got it. Goodbye." I walked past him and through the beaded curtain, breathing in deeply. I didn't realize how stuffy I felt in that small space until I was out of there. Dax was pacing back and forth in front of the lounge chairs, and his head snapped up when I came through the curtains.

He rushed over to me. "Are you okay? What did he do? What did he say?" Dax grilled me with questions before I could even speak.

"Hold on." I held my hand up, chuckling. "Let's get out of here first and then I will tell you everything." I grabbed his arm as I started walking. He smiled and nodded, and we made our way out of the building as quickly as we could. As quickly as I could, at least.

Once we were back in the jeep and on the road, I began to speak.

"He didn't say much of anything of importance. He just repeated to me what I had to do to get my memories back, and how to make it up the mountain." I tried to keep my voice even.

Dax glanced at me, slightly narrowing his eyes in suspicion. "Are you sure that's all?"

It took all my willpower not to tell him everything, but I had to keep my word.

"The only other thing he did was something to my pendant to protect me on the journey, according to him."

Dax glanced sharply at my necklace, narrowing his eyes. As he continued to stare, his eyes glowed violet. He hmphed when he was done, turning his attention back to the road.

"Was that the thing he wanted to give you?"

"Yes, Dax. He didn't give me anything else. That was it." I sighed, ready to change the subject. All I could think about were the requirements for the journey. He said I'd know when the time came. How would I know when the price would be paid? What was the cost?

"Okay, okay. I'm just making sure he's not putting you in any danger. He likes to pull tricks and put people in danger without them even being aware of it," he explained.

I nodded to show him I was paying attention.

Everything he was telling me made sense, and I appreciated him wanting to make sure I was safe. But I really couldn't stop thinking about Augustus' warning. What if I was putting someone in danger by taking this journey? I didn't want to put anyone's life in danger, but I also couldn't continue the life I was used to anymore. I wasn't human. I didn't just want my memories. I *needed* them.

I glanced over at Dax, smiling a little because of his concentrated yet happy face as he focused on the road. I'd known him for like two days—well, two days for me—yet I felt like I'd known him forever. I trusted him. And I didn't want anything to happen to him.

Dax looked my way, catching me staring, and smiled. "What are you thinking about?" he asked, splitting his attention between the road and me, trying to gauge my mood from my face.

"About how I am grateful that we met, and about this journey," I answered truthfully, resting my arm on the side of the door, head in hand.

"Oh, you don't have to worry about that. I am so on it. We're on our way to Dmitri's safe house so I can tell him everything and get his help."

I groaned when he finished. Not Dmitri. He would literally ruin this with his attitude.

"Do we have to get Dmitri's help?" I asked, making a face at Dax.

"Uh, yes! He's the only one who knows where the mountain is because he's traveled there himself before. He never gave us many details about the journey, though..." He trailed off at the end, glancing at me.

"He has? For what?" I asked, curious about that little detail. Did Augustus give him the same ultimatum? If so, what was the price?

17

After my little on and off four-hour nap on the way back, we reached Dmitri's safe house. He was there, working out in the middle of the living room. I paused abruptly as soon as my eyes landed on him, catching my jaw before it hit the ground. Dmitri was shirtless, doing crunches on the floor with a mat underneath him.

I usually try my best not to ogle anyone, especially Dmitri, but I had no choice. His bronze body was immaculately chiseled. Arms were my weakness, and his were enticing, each groove perfectly sculpting his tan muscles. Each time he leaned back and lifted himself up, he huffed from exertion, and the muscles on his abdomen literally rippled. Each muscle with a mind of its own. Sweat dripped down his back muscles and arms, making him shine.

A throat cleared softly, and I whipped my head to Dax. He had a sly smirk on his face, and I shut my mouth quickly, realizing what I was doing. I cleared my own throat and licked my lips in slight embarrassment from getting caught checking him out. When I cleared my throat, Dmitri paused mid-crunch, turning half of his body around to face Dax and me. I tried my best not to focus on his bare chest and concentrated on his eyes instead, which had a slightly annoyed look in them.

He made a noise somewhere between a heavy sigh and a groan as he got up from the mat. I glanced at his back again, and squinted. Two black symmetrical lines were on his back. He turned and grabbed a rag from the table next to him, and then wiped his face, dragging the cloth to the back of his neck.

I was tempted to ask him to turn back around, but that would be weird. But I'd swear I saw two large scars etched into his skin, stretching down to his back dimples. His silver eyes formed into slits, giving us both a once over.

"What do you want?" His deep voice was rough from the lack of talking.

I glanced at Dax, unsure where to start. Dax nodded his head slightly, letting me know that he got it. He started explaining everything to Dmitri, and I let out a sigh of relief. I usually let no one intimidate me, but Dmitri was on another level.

He was alluring yet dangerous. He hadn't even done anything I remembered for me to believe that he was dangerous, but the dominance that flowed from him gave me that feeling. As Dax explained everything to him, I watched Dmitri's facial expressions, trying to figure out what he was thinking or feeling. For the most part, he had his signature stern frown on his face.

The only time it changed was when Dax mentioned Aloysius not being a myth. His eyebrows raised at that one and again when Dax told him about Augustus placing something in my pendant to protect me. His eyes flicked toward me, mainly my pendant, with a curious look. When Dax was finished with the story, Dmitri's face was back to where it began, hard.

"Can you help us get to the mountain?" Dax asked.

Dmitri growled. "Absolutely not."

Dax flinched, and I frowned. I expected him to not help, but his response was more aggressive than either of us were prepared for.

"Why not?" I stepped forward, a little closer to him. "Dax told me—"

"What did you tell her?" Dmitri interrupted me and glared at Dax.

"Hey, hey, hold up now. I didn't tell her anything about *that*, so calm down. All I told her was that you have traveled to the mountain before, so you know how to get there." Dax crossed his arms over his chest, staring Dmitri down.

I shook my head and collapsed on the couch, mentally and physically drained. "So, after everything, dragging me from my life, altering it by dropping all of these bombs, you won't even help me get my memories back? The main thing you said you were trying to do yourself?" I questioned him, my shoulders slumping.

"My main focus is on stopping Victor and Caspian," he said plainly, passing a hand through his hair.

I furrowed my brow. "What was the whole point of exposing me to this life if my memories weren't a priority?" I could've been stress free, living my life simply.

He rolled his eyes at the question. "Because Caspian was trying to kill you. So it was better for you to be aware of it than to be in the dark. I was tired of having to swoop in and save you," he finished, starting to pace. It took me a second to gather my thoughts. Augustus said not to mention it to anyone, but I couldn't think of any other way to convince Dmitri to help me.

"A price must be paid," I mumbled under my breath, my voice almost inaudible.

Dmitri stopped pacing and narrowed his eyes at me, tilting his head. "What did you just say?" he demanded, taking a step toward me.

"You went on this journey yourself, correct?" I asked, and he nodded. "Then, you know the consequences..." I trailed off at the end of my sentence for dramatic effect. I stared him right in the eyes, slowly getting up. I walked toward him and only stopped when I was right in front of him.

"Wait, what consequences, Meadow? What are you talking about?" Dax spoke up, sounding confused. I didn't say anything, continuing my stare off with Dmitri. His eyes dared me to tell Dax, and mine told him I had no problem completing that request—but at what cost.

He clenched his jaw, eyes filled with rage. "Dax, leave us," Dmitri told him through gritted teeth, still staring me down.

Dax scoffed, and I saw him from my peripheral, looking at me to help him out. But I kept my eyes locked on Dmitri. I wanted to have this conversation. Once Dax saw that neither of us were budging, he mumbled under his breath and stomped away, slamming the door behind him. I shifted my legs, crossing my arms over my chest, and waited for Dmitri to say something.

"He gave you the same warning." Dmitri finally spoke, his words coming out like a statement, not a question.

I nodded, eyes caressing his face for more answers. "Why did you go to the mountain?" I asked, narrowing my eyes when he clenched his jaw, breathing heavily out of his nose in frustration. I waited for him to say something, but he just stood there. "Stop being a coward and just tell me." I lifted my head in a challenge. His eyes rolled to the ceiling, nostrils flaring. I wish it rolled to the back of his head and stayed there.

"I knew he would do something like this," he mumbled under his breath, but loud enough for me to hear.

"What do you mean?" I asked, trying to catch his eyes to bring his attention back to me.

"Augustus knew giving you that ultimatum would force me to tell you things you're not prepared to find out in this state," he answered, his voice low as if he didn't want to really explain anything to me.

I was perplexed, and it took me a second to register what he was saying. "So, the warning isn't real?" I asked, the pressure from the stress leaving my chest in the hope that it was fake. For the first time since I met him, Dmitri looked nervous and wouldn't look me in the eyes. My heart started racing. It *was* real.

My eyebrows dipped as I tried to calm myself down so I could rationally think about all of this, but it was hard.

"Dax," Dmitri called out, and Dax was back inside in a flash. Dmitri still didn't look me in the eye and turned his attention to Dax. "I want to help, but I can't," he told him, making his face scrunch up in confusion.

133

"But why?" he asked, stealing the question right out of my head.

Dmitri sighed and started tapping his foot. "As I said before, I have to stop Victor and Caspian." Dax opened his mouth to speak, but Dmitri held a hand up. "It's not as simple as you think it is. Caspian and Victor are making more young to create an army. They're doing it in the name of Maddox, so they're not going to stop."

Maddox? That name sounded familiar.

"Who's Maddox?" I interrupted, wanting to understand everything.

"Maddox is a myth. Like a god to some creatures, so it makes it easier for them to spread evil," Dmitri explained. Surprisingly, with no attitude. It finally clicked why the name sounded familiar. It was in the letters from Aloysius addressed to my mom. He spoke of Maddox, but as if he were a real being, not a myth. Maybe Aloysius was one of those who believed.

"But what does that you have to with you helping us? Can't you do both? This wouldn't even take long." Dax tried to reason with Dmitri.

He kneaded his forehead with his fingers, blowing out a breath. "Your journey will be a week, so a little long. And it's too late for me to help you. I already left Victor bait, so wherever I go, he will know where I am."

Dax gasped, and I looked at him, confused. What did that mean? Was that a bad thing? "Dmitri—"

"Don't give me a speech, Dax," Dmitri said lowly, almost a growl.

I looked back and forth at them, trying to figure out what was going on.

"But you know what happened last time you baited Caspian." Dax raised his voice, placing his hands on his hips. He had a distressed look on his face and was staring at Dmitri with hard eyes.

"Last time I wasn't prepared. Now I am."

"Prepared for what? What happened last time?" I interjected, waving my arms in the air to catch the attention of both of them. They stared at me blankly, then glanced at each other. "Okay, well, since you guys obviously don't want to answer that, let's get back to the subject." I turned my attention to Dmitri. "Can't you help me journey to the mountain and just lure Victor there?" I asked, getting impatient.

Dmitri opened his mouth to speak, then closed it, tilting his head in thought. "That would be a good idea if it weren't for the fact that me luring Victor means I'm luring Caspian as well. I would be putting you in extreme danger," Dmitri explained, his face softening—just a little.

Aw, he cares about whether I'm in danger or not, I said sarcastically in my head.

"Well, wouldn't that be even better for you to get them in one place and then do whatever with them?" I asked, throwing my hands in the air.

Dmitri kneaded his forehead again and blew air out of his nose. "I'm not going to do just anything to them. I'm going to *kill* them," Dmitri said.

My eyes darted to Dax, trying to see his reaction. He pressed his lips together and nodded in agreement. I raised my eyebrows and blew out a large breath. I was going to have to get used to hearing them talk about killing like it was nothing. I guess in their world, that was normal.

"Okay, forget about protecting me. Dax will be there to help you. If Axel and Rita help too, we should be fine," I explained, nodding at my idea.

He shook his head, passing the cloth over his bare chest as he stretched.

I crossed my arms over my chest and tapped my foot. "If you don't help me, I'll go by myself. I don't care how long it takes me. Trust me, I *will* find answers." I was tired of dancing around this conversation. It was like he was purposely shutting me down to prolong the conversation. As if he didn't want me to get my memories back on my own.

Dmitri smirked at me and scoffed. "You wouldn't."

I gave him a look and chuckled in his face. "Try me," I whispered fiercely. He shrugged, and I rolled my eyes, turning around. I walked past Dax, and he raised his eyebrows at me. I gave him a little smile and opened the front door.

"Stop." Dmitri's voice stopped me from walking out the door. I shut the door and listened to his breathing as it got shorter with each inhale. He growled in frustration, and I turned around to see him passing a hand down his face. "All right. I will help you. But we have to go by my rules. I will definitely need Rita and Axel to help us." Dmitri glanced at Dax, who nodded and pulled out a cell phone. Dmitri turned his attention back to me. "You're going to need to mentally prepare yourself tonight for the journey. It's going to be rough, and you're not going to get a lot of sleep during the week of the journey."

I nodded. I'd planned on doing that anyway based on what Augustus told me. "I understand. What do you need me to do now?" I asked, sitting on the couch.

He sat on the arm of the other couch and stared straight ahead. His eyes slowly landed on me. "What I need you to do is relax and stay here. Dax will retrieve clothing and whatever else you'll need for the journey." He finished and stood up from the couch, glancing around. "I need to freshen up and get prepared. Will you be okay down here by yourself?" He glanced at Dax, who was still on the phone with his back turned.

"Well, I won't completely be alone." I smiled at him, and he nodded.

"Snacks are in the pantry in the kitchen if you're hungry." He nodded at me and left the living room, his steps the only prominent noise in the whole house.

I couldn't hear Dax speaking, yet it seemed like he was having a full-blown conversation. I relaxed into the couch. I heard a sigh and turned to see that Dax was off of the phone, looking deep in thought.

"What's the verdict?" I asked, making him jump a bit.

"Axel is excited for the adventure, of course, mainly for the fights that might happen. He always wants to fight something. Rita was more hesitant when she found out it was to help you, but I got her on board." He smiled largely at me when I made a face at the Rita comment.

"I am surprised you were able to get Rita onboard. Thank you so much for everything. You've been so supportive. It's actually helping me through this confusing patch." I told him sincerely, making his face light up.

He walked my way, and I stood. He pulled me into a hug, squeezing me tightly.

"Anything for you, Meadow." He squeezed me one more time before letting go. "I have to run an errand before this trip, so you'll be alone for a little while. Will you be okay?" He asked, a worried look in his eyes.

"Oh yeah. I'll find something to occupy my time, don't worry." I gave him a pretty convincing smile.

He smiled back, gave me a quick peck on the cheek, and left through the front door.

I turned the television on and flipped through the channels, looking for something to watch so the time could pass by quickly. As I browsed, I saw a fire on one of the channels, and I flipped back to one of the news channels. It was about the explosion that happened at my job. They were reporting a gas leak, and I scoffed, changing the channel. Of course, they wouldn't tell that public the truth about someone purposely leaking gas into one of their interrogation rooms and lighting the place on fire. I flipped through the channels until I landed on one about home renovations. As I relaxed, my mind started wandering. Dmitri hadn't explained a lot about the journey, or how we were getting to the mountain, but I guessed he'd let us know later tonight or tomorrow before we left. Since it was going to be tough, I could only assume the worst. Especially since Victor and Caspian would be following us. Would there be another fight like the one at the fake business? What would the temperature be like? The main thought that stayed on my mind was the price that needed to be paid. Why did Augustus have to be so vague?

18

I didn't realize I fell asleep until it felt like an earthquake was happening in my sleep. It was Dax, shaking me awake, and apparently it was the next day already. I grabbed some clothes from a large black backpack that looked like it was supposed to be used for hiking. Everything I needed was in the bag. I made my way upstairs to shower and tried not to think too hard about the events that were going to occur today.

I took a quick shower and dressed in black camouflage pants with a long-sleeved black shirt, as recommended by Dax. By the time I was back downstairs, Rita and Axel had joined Dax and Dmitri in the living room. Breakfast was on the table, and I hurried and ate, not really tasting my food. I didn't want to waste any more time than I had to.

Rita, Axel, and Dax all had identical bags to mine on their backs. Dmitri was fiddling with the straps on his, and I didn't have my backpack on yet because it was pretty heavy. I would wait until we were about to leave to put it on.

A small smile formed on my face. Today was the day. The beginning of the journey that would lead me to what I'd wanted since I found out I wasn't human.

My memories.

It took all of me not to dwell on Augustus' words about a price being paid for me to take this journey. It would only make me sick to the stomach.

"So, what happens now?" I asked, breaking the silence in the room. They all looked at Dmitri, who slowly raised his head.

"Now, we make sure we have everything we will need for the journey."

I nodded. We seemed to be pretty equipped for this journey. They all patted themselves, and I went to my own pack, making sure that it was ready.

"Everyone, follow me outside."

We followed Dmitri to his backyard, which was more like his own personal forest. Standing in the middle of the greenery, we waited for Dmitri's next order.

"Bring your bags closer to mine to form a little circle to mirror how we are standing," Dmitri told us, and we followed his instructions quickly. I didn't know what we were doing in the woods, and by the looks on everyone else's faces, they didn't either.

"What are we doing exactly, Dmitri?" Rita asked. She hadn't said anything about the journey the entire time she'd been here.

Dmitri looked at her and raised his brows. "We're going to the mountain. Through a portal."

I almost gasped out loud. *Portal?* I really needed those memories back.

"Wait, are you telling me that you actually have Lanuae Magicae powder?" Dax asked excitedly.

Dmitri smiled. "Yes, I do." He looked at me. "It'll take us to a hidden part of our home world, Beauty. Everyone grab the top of your packs. It's going to get a little bumpy."

We all grabbed our packs, heeding his warning. Dmitri tilted the black pouch, blue powder falling out and landing in the little space between all of our packs. Blue smoke slowly rose from the powder in the middle of our packs, hovering in that one spot. I waited for something to happen, but nothing did. Dmitri's eyes were closed, and he seemed to be concentrating. I was going to ask what he was waiting for but decided not to break his concentration. After a few more seconds, his eyes snapped open, and he looked at the blue smoke before eyeing everyone.

"*Beauty.*"

The word came out as a whisper. The blue smoke moved, slowly spreading out on the ground, swirling at our feet. My hand on my pack started moving, and I realized that all of our packs were moving as if something was making them vibrate. Suddenly, the blue smoke shot up in the air into a cloud above us. It slammed back down to the ground, blue smoke flying up and hitting us all in the face. The smell was familiar, like a bouquet of flowers, giving me a warm feeling inside.

It twirled around us and grew thicker. The smoke rose, and I started getting a little anxious when it got so thick I couldn't see the trees anymore. The rumbling continued and intensified to the point where we were all clutching our packs, trying to keep our balance.

"Hold on tightly!" Dmitri yelled, but the rest of his sentence got lost in the wind that came out of nowhere. My hair whipped around my face, and the smoke thickened until I couldn't see anyone, just blue smoke everywhere. I gripped my pack so hard my knuckles turned white, but I didn't care. I wasn't letting go. The ground disappeared, and I was completely surrounded by the blue smoke. The only things I could see were my clothes and my pack.

The wind picked up even more, stinging my eyes. It started becoming harder to breathe, and I closed my eyes, inhaling deeply. I felt as if I was being thrown around as the wind picked up even though I was planted in one spot. I refused to open my eyes again and waited for the wind to stop pushing me around. A few more long seconds went by before the wind completely stopped. I was no longer being whipped around. Before, the wind had roared. Now all I heard was...blades of grass moving?

19

I slowly opened my eyes and squinted at the bright sun. As I looked around, I noticed that the blue smoke was gone. No trace of it remained. Axel and Rita were looking around, their jaws dropped. Dax hopped up and down on his toes, excitement evident on his face. Then there was Dmitri, standing a few feet away, scouting the area. We were completely surrounded by grass.

Each blade had a different colored flower attached to it. It stood tall, up to my waist, and I couldn't see the ground. The plants caressed my hands with a soft touch like a feather, and they didn't make me itch like regular grass. Green, blue, purple, pink, and yellow going on for miles. Like a meadow.

There was nothing else in the area except for the mountain. I covered my mouth and my eyes widened as I took in the massive structure.

It was expansive, with the same flowers from the field peppering the entire mountain. It was so high, it disappeared into the clouds. From where I was standing, it looked like it might take us a while to reach it, but I was okay with that. I was in another world. I breathed in the fresh scent of flowers and hugged myself from how giddy I was feeling. My life was about to change. I was about to finally understand everything and be a part of a world that seemed to have endless opportunities.

"I haven't seen anything like this before in my entire existence," Axel said out loud in awe as he turned his attention to the beautiful mountain. We all nodded in agreement, except for Dmitri, of course, since he'd been there before. He scoffed, and I frowned at him, not wanting him to ruin this for us.

"It's just a facade. Don't believe or fall for anything here. It's meant to keep you trapped and end your life," he warned, furrowing his brow.

I sighed. "Why do you always have to be a party pooper? At least let us enjoy the scenery before we have to worry about staying safe," I chastised him, putting my hands on my hips.

His eyes darkened. "You can enjoy the scenery when we're at the top of the mountain, safe and sound and not chopped up in pieces, scattered across the mountain," he retorted.

I scoffed and turned my attention back to the mountain.

"Grab your bags, let's go. It's going to take us a few hours to get to the mountain. Follow me and watch your step. In this place, anything can happen."

The rest of the team responded right away and picked up their packs, following Dmitri. I grabbed my pack and dipped a little to help get it on my back, and then jogged to catch up with the rest of them.

"This is such a beautiful place, I hate that he always has to be a mood killer."

I glanced to the side and saw that Dax had joined me, commenting on what I was thinking. "Right! Why is he like that?" I asked, lowering my voice when I noticed how close we were to him.

Dax scratched his neck and eyed Dmitri, a little hesitant to answer my question. "I couldn't tell you even if I wanted to. That's something else that only he can really tell you. Not even we fully know why he is the way he is," Dax whispered, still eyeing Dmitri. If he could hear what we were talking about, he made no indication of it.

"Understandable," I responded as we continued to walk, taking in the scenery. The sun was high in the sky, beating on us, and sweat dripped down my back. We had barely begun the journey, and my body was already showing signs of fatigue. Getting my mind off of how tired I was already, I turned my attention back to Dax. "Do you know anything about this place at all?" I asked him in a low voice. I kept an eye on Dmitri to see if he would make any movements showing that he was eavesdropping.

"According to the books I've read and the whispers, no one makes it off the mountain alive," he whispered, and my eyes widened as he nodded, smiling.

"Why are you smiling?" I muttered fiercely.

"Meadow, it's okay. Those are just rumors, and the book is also based on rumors, which is how they form theories. So we should be good." He tried to reassure me with a smile. It helped only a little bit.

"*Should?* How do you know that we will actually be good?"

He glanced around before moving closer to me. "Because Dmitri made it off the mountain alive," Dax said, eyes growing into large saucers. He glanced at Dmitri and then back at me. "He's the only one in history to do it."

I looked up at Dmitri in awe at this new information. *Maybe that's the reason he is the way he is.* It made me more grateful that he was doing this for me, risking his life again to make sure I got my memories back. But it also made me feel uneasy. Dax said no one made it off the mountain alive. Was that the price that needed to be paid, and I just brought everyone to their deaths?

"Pretty spooky, huh? He al—" Dax's shouts filled the air, and I yelled out his name, throwing my arm to grab his hand as he dropped into the ground, but missed. Dmitri was by my side in a flash, just in time to catch Dax's hand, keeping him from falling all the way down in the hole that appeared out of nowhere. Dax was panting and swinging his legs, a panicked look on his face.

"Whatever you do, don't look down. I'm going to slowly pull you up. Don't make a sound," Dmitri whispered fiercely to Dax, and he nodded, closing his mouth. Rita and Axel were by my side, worry etched on both of their faces. I peered over the edge and saw nothing but darkness. The hole didn't seem to have a bottom. One that I could see anyway. Dmitri started slowly pulling Dax up, and he was almost out of the hole when something orange dropped on his shoulder. He yelled and swiped at his shoulder.

"No!" Dmitri hissed, eyes widening. He was yanked down, and he let out a sharp breath from the force and gripped the edge of the hole to stop from falling in with Dax. Rita reached out to help Dmitri, but before she could, he shook his head fiercely.

"Don't. With both of us pulling, it will rip Dax apart."

"Ow! Dmitri, what is that?" Dax yelled, glancing down frantically below him. Dmitri didn't answer and yanked Dax upwards, trying to get him out of the hole, but something pulled Dax right back down. I leaned a little closer to the hole to see what it was and squinted to help me see better.

"Oh my..." I whispered to myself, gasping, wild eyes turning to Dmitri. Orange tentacles wormed their way up the hole slowly.

"It burns! Dmitri, it burns!" Dax cried out, pain twisting his features. My heart clenched in fear for him as he kicked his legs, and I saw what was holding him down. A flash of orange was wrapped around his ankle, preventing Dmitri from bringing him to safety. Dmitri kept trying to pull Dax up, but he couldn't. He was actually straining, and I swear I saw a drop of sweat roll down his face. Maybe I had imagined it.

"Dmitri!" Dax screamed, and I flinched at the sound.

"Axel! The gun!" Dmitri snapped, looking around for him. I didn't turn around to see if Axel was getting the gun, but I heard something drop to the ground.

"Axel, *now!*" Dmitri yelled when he didn't get the gun right away. I heard rustling, and then someone breathing next to me. It was Axel with a double-barreled pistol in his hand.

"Scoot." Was all he said to me, and I stood up, backing away just a little bit to give him some room. Dmitri let go of the edge and propped himself up on the heels of his feet, planting them. He grabbed Dax's arm with his other hand so that both were gripping him, and turned to Axel, his silver eyes piercing.

"Do it now," Dmitri told him, getting a nod from Axel. He raised his arms, cocked the gun, and aimed into the hole. He tilted his head to the side and waited. Shots filled the air, and an ear-splitting screech came from the hole, forcing me to cover my ears. Dmitri yanked his arms back, and Dax came flying out of the hole, landing on his back.

The screeches continued, and Axel kept shooting until the screeches ceased. My eyes flew to Dax, who clutched his leg and frantically pulled up his pants, revealing his skin. We all gasped except for Dmitri. Dax's once brown leg was now a moss green color from the middle of his leg down to his ankle. The wound was bubbling, and I gritted my teeth at how gross it looked.

"What is that?" Dax yelled, hovering his hand over it. He had a distraught look on his face and was panting heavily. I wasn't sure if it was from the exertion or the pain, but he was starting to sweat. My heart pounded in my ears, and I stared at Dmitri, waiting for him to do something. Would Dax die? Was it poisonous? He hadn't explained anything and was just standing there, staring at Dax's leg.

"Dmitri, do something!" I yelled, throwing an arm up in the air. He raised a finger at me, and I gave him a look, still wondering why he was just standing there.

He looked as if he was thinking hard about something and then suddenly tossed his pack to the ground, moving quicker than my eyes could keep up with. He was at Dax's side before I could register what he was doing. He had a black pouch in his hand and dumped blue powder in his palm. He looked up at all of us and focused his attention on Axel. "You're going to want to hold him down." He turned back to Dax. "This is going to hurt like hell. Ready?"

Dax nodded vigorously, probably wanting to get it over with already. He was still clutching his leg, and sweat dripped down his face.

Axel hurried over to Dax, crouching behind him. I glanced at Rita, and she just had a straight face, making it hard to tell what emotion she was feeling. A hiss made me turn my attention back to Dax, in time to see Dmitri coating his leg with the blue powder. Dax's jaw ticked from how hard he was clenching his teeth, and his arms strained against Axel's, holding him in place. Dmitri finished sprinkling the rest of the powder on his leg, and the wound started festering even more, grotesque bubbles growing and shrinking at an alarming rate.

Some popped, making the wound look like melting mold. I didn't even know what melting mold looked like, but I would assume it looked like Dax's leg. Disgusting. The wound changed from a green color to eggplant purple, and I swear I could hear the hissing of bubbles forming and popping. Dax began to scream, and Dmitri held his leg down so that the powder could fully dissolve.

"Axel, make sure he's secure. This next step will be intense," Dmitri warned him, and Dax's eyes widened.

"Intense? This isn't intense?" Dax panted, blinking rapidly as sweat rolled into his eyes. Dmitri dug in his pack and pulled out a hunting knife. I covered my mouth, and Dax's eyes grew, and he started shaking his head. "Oh, no, no, no. I'm good, it's all good. I will heal, just give me a second." Dax tried to reason with Dmitri, but it didn't work. Dmitri looked up at Axel, and he nodded, hooking his arms underneath Dax's to secure him. I gritted my teeth in anticipation as Dmitri grabbed his leg, positioning it in front of himself. He slid the knife slowly into Dax's swollen, bubbly skin. Dax screamed. My heart rate sped up as he thrashed wildly in Axel's arms, trying to get out of his grip. He was kicking his leg, trying to get Dmitri to let go, but that didn't work.

His screams grew louder, and then turned into an inhuman sound. He started panting heavier and narrowed his eyes at Dmitri, a growl escaping his throat. My mouth dropped open as his eyes changed to a vibrant violet. He growled again, and his canines started growing, liquid dripping down his teeth. He snapped at Dmitri, harsh growls filling the air, but Dmitri didn't budge. Dax thrashed around again, wildly, and Axel tightened his arms, a strained look on his face.

Dmitri continued sliding the knife in Dax's skin, slowly carving and slicing off the now dark purple skin. It looked dead. Dark, red liquid dripped down Dax's leg from the slicing, and pink flesh was now exposed where the dead skin used to be. It took all I had in me not to puke. Blood didn't make me queasy, but the smell of rotten flesh made my stomach turn.

"I'm almost done. Just one more," Dmitri reassured Dax, pausing his slicing. Some of his hair was falling in his face, a few curls dropping right in front of his eyes, yet it didn't seem to bother him. Dmitri resumed. When he stuck the knife back in Dax's leg, he went wild and screamed. The ground shook, making me tense in place. Dax's yells intensified, and snapping sounds filled the air, making me wildly look around to find the source of the sound.

I screamed as thick green and brown vines shot up in the air, twisting around each other. I had to jump out of the way of the vines and turned to see Dax still screaming, his eyes glowing intensely violet. This had to be his doing. My breathing grew jagged, and I clutched the straps of my pack, ready to bolt to safety at any minute. I didn't want to be collateral damage from Dax's pain.

Dmitri glanced up, a flash of emotion passing over his face when he saw all the vines. I wasn't sure what it was, but when he made eye contact with me, his eyes widened briefly, and he quickly carved the rest of the skin off, tossing it to the side like he did with the rest of the dead skin.

"Dax! You're good! Drop the vines!" Dmitri yelled, shaking Dax to get him out of his painful stupor.

Dax gasped loudly, inhaling deeply, and closed his eyes. He stopped thrashing. His eyes snapped back open a second later, and they were back to its natural brown color. The vines dropped to the ground, disappearing like they were never there. Dax patted Axel's arms, and Axel slowly let go, stretching out his arms. Dax stood slowly, and Dmitri helped him up, making sure he was steady.

"I think I'm good now," Dax croaked, breaking into a coughing fit. He cleared his throat and brought his hand up to it, rubbing softly. His voice was probably hoarse from all the screaming. Dmitri let him go, and Dax adjusted the pack on his back, wincing a little when he put pressure on his wounded leg.

"You will be okay. If I hadn't cut off the skin, it would've seeped into your veins, and the poison would've killed you," Dmitri explained.

Dax managed a strained smile, giving Dmitri a thumbs up.

I exhaled and placed a hand over my chest. If this was only the beginning of the journey and we hadn't even made it to the mountain yet, what more was waiting for us on the actual mountain?

I shivered and turned my worried eyes to Dax, who was checking out his wound, a huge smile on his face. Only Dax would smile in a situation like this one. Me on the other hand, I was trying to stop myself from worrying about one of them dying and how close Dax came to death. Was this it? Did he come close to paying the price? Was that what Augustus was talking about? I couldn't stop wringing my hands together.

"Hey, you're okay. Breathe in and out deeply three times for me." Dmitri murmured in my ear, and I followed his directions without looking at him. I could feel his body heat on my left side, and his presence alone helped me for some reason. My heart calmed down, and my head was a little clearer than before. Slowly, I looked up at him and was locked on his gray eyes.

His eyes were hard yet soft at the same time. I tilted my head a little bit. Was he worried about me? Once he saw that I was calmer, he glanced at the sky.

"We need to get going. It'll be dark soon, and we need to reach the mountain before nightfall." Dmitri picked up his pack, slinging it on his back as he started walking. I adjusted my own heavy pack and hurried to catch up. I didn't want to be the next one in a random hole. Instead of walking behind him, I decided to walk next to him to make it easier on myself. And now maybe he would slow down to my pace so that I wouldn't have to almost jog to keep up with him the entire time.

We walked through the colorful field for the next two hours. About thirty minutes into the two-hour walk, I grumbled to myself about how fast he was walking and that not even my long legs could keep up with his for much longer.

He slowed down after my grumbling, much to my surprise. I

forgot he had super hearing or something. I thanked him under my breath to see if he could hear me, and without turning my way, his head slightly nodded. So he *could* hear me, which meant he probably heard my earlier conversation with Dax. Good, maybe he'd give me some answers.

An hour passed by. My shirt was drenched in sweat, it was that hot. But the good thing was there were no bugs to bite at me, which was a little weird. The only sound of a bug I'd heard the whole time was from a cicada. My legs burned, and my throat was starting to close up from the dry air. The longer we walked, the worse it got, so I peeked up to see what kind of mood Dmitri was in. He seemed to be deep in thought, so I assumed that meant he was in a mellow mood.

"Pst." I looked in my peripheral to see if he reacted. His face didn't change, and his steps didn't falter. "Pssst." I tried to catch his attention again, and this time his jaw clenched.

"What do you want, Meadow?" he asked in a bored tone, not even bothering to look my way.

"My throat is dry. Did you bring any water for the human?" I joked, trying my best to look at him and walk at the same time without tripping on air. It was working so far. He raised a brow at me and narrowed his eyes, as usual.

"You're not human, but yes, I have water. Why didn't you bring any for yourself?" he asked, grabbing something from his left side. He stuck his arm out with a black canteen in his hand, ready for the taking.

I eagerly grabbed it, chugging the water and sighing as it soothed my raw throat. Once I was done, I gave it back to him and he put it back in the side of his bag. "I thought you brought everything that was needed. You didn't tell me I had to carry anything extra. And at the moment, I *am* human," I finally answered, staring straight ahead. I didn't go through some magical transformation after finding out I wasn't human, so I assumed that whatever I was would manifest when I got my memories back.

He didn't say anything to my response, and we continued to walk for another hour.

149

The sun dipped lower in the sky as time passed, and it looked like we were almost to the mountain. I couldn't see if there was a way to actually get on the mountain or not. Maybe when we got a little closer, I would be able to see something. My stomach fluttered with nervousness. *So close.* I was so close. Once we hit the mountain, that was when the real journey would begin.

I breathed in and out slowly and started humming softly to get my mind off of everything. I didn't want to stress prematurely. The sun started disappearing quicker, and the sky turned into a beautiful pink and orange mix. I glanced at Dmitri, and my brows dipped when I registered the look on his face. His eyes were darting back and forth quickly across the field, and I scanned the area with him, trying to see what he was looking for—or at. I didn't see anything. I glanced back up at him, and a panicked look passed over his face for a second, then it was gone.

If I'd blinked, I probably would've missed it. I tensed, eyes darting left and right when he slowed down. He wouldn't even slow down for me unless I asked. Whatever he was seeing had to be serious. I slowed down and inched closer to him, careful not to trip.

"Do you guys hear that?" Dax asked from behind me, and I glanced back at him. He had a similar look of panic that passed over Dmitri's face a second ago. I listened for anything but heard nothing.

"I heard it too," Rita whispered.

Dmitri came to a full stop, causing me to bump into his shoulder. I opened my mouth to say sorry, but the words never came out because Dmitri stuck his arm out, pushing me behind him. He was tensed as if something was after him, so I grabbed his arm and peeked around him to see. The only sound I heard was my breathing.

"It's getting closer. What's the plan?" Axel asked, placing a hand around the holster on his waist as he eyed the field.

Dmitri didn't answer, but it looked as if he was thinking hard. He looked at the darkening sky and then at me, eyes narrowed.

Suddenly, a loud screech followed by hissing filled the air, making me yelp and clutch Dmitri's arm in slight fear. *What the hell was that?*

I'd never heard anything like that before and it definitely wasn't any creature I'd encountered with this group.

"What in the world was that?" I asked out loud, trying to control the fear in my voice. Whatever it was, I was hoping we would be able to outrun it. The creature screeched and hissed again. This time, the sound so forceful, I saw sound waves move in the air.

"We go now!" Dmitri snapped and started walking quickly, glancing back to see if I was following. I jogged after him, stumbling over my feet as I tried to keep up with him. Another screech reached my ears, and I heard rustling in the field this time, prompting Dmitri to put an arm out, stopping me.

"On my back," he almost growled, a serious look on his face. He took his pack off his back and put it on his chest. "Meadow, *now!*"

The next screech that was belted vibrated the air so hard that we were all pushed back a little bit from the force.

"You're taking too long. Let me help you." Before Rita even finished her sentence, I was launched into the air, igniting the loudest scream from me. Reaching out, I clutched Dmitri's shoulders when I landed, my legs and arms automatically locking themselves around his waist and neck. His arms wrapped around my legs, holding them in place, and then he took off running.

I squinted at the force of the wind and buried my face in his shoulder when it became hard to breathe. I couldn't see anything clearly anyway. Everything was a blur of colors. I squeezed my eyes shut and heard Dmitri yell "jump," prompting me to tighten my arms and legs around his body so I wouldn't fall off. The wind was hitting the side of my face forcefully at this angle and continued until I couldn't feel it anymore.

Dmitri stopped running. He actually stopped moving altogether. "You can get down now, Meadow," Dmitri spoke, his voice echoing as he patted my leg. Echo? I opened my eyes and peeled myself off his back, blinking a few times to get my eyes adjusted. It was dark, and I couldn't really tell where we were.

"Where are we?" I asked, my voice echoing as well.

"We're on the mountain, in a cave," Dax spoke.

I nodded, still looking around. Made sense now why it was so dark and why our voices echoed.

"This is where we'll stay for the night. It is the safest place at the moment. The creature below will be in the area until the sun comes up," Dmitri explained, and I shuddered, not wanting to think about what would've happened if we stayed down there a second longer.

I let out a sigh and looked out the cave's mouth into the darkness. The only source of light for us was the moonlight and the stars twinkling in the sky. It was a beautiful sight that I rarely got to see in The Angels. Something shiny on the ground outside of the cave caught my eye, and I squinted to see it. A gem? A necklace? Squinting didn't help. "What is that on the ground outside?" I pointed to it.

Axel gasped, throwing his pack on the ground. "That's mine." He started walking to get it, but Rita and Dax's protests stalled him for a second.

"Axel, wouldn't it be smarter for you to just get it in the morning?" Rita asked, a worried look on her face. Rita, worried? What was she concerned about?

"Yeah, man. I have to agree with Rita on this one. Just wait until daybreak." Dax chimed in, a similar look on his face. I looked at all of them, confused. What was wrong with him going outside to get the gem or necklace? I didn't see a problem with it, mostly since the creature that was chasing us was in the field. Maybe they just didn't want to risk anything happening to him.

Axel shook his head. "Sorry, guys. This is really important to me. I can't risk not having it on me." He shrugged. He took his time walking to the mouth of the cave and crouched when he got there, letting out a breath. He glanced back at Dmitri, who gave me a quick glance before nodding at Axel. *Why are we looking at each other?* I watched Axel stretch his arm out the cave to retrieve his fallen object.

Why he didn't just walk out there like a normal person, I had no idea, but I guessed he wanted to be extra safe. When his arm left the cave and came in contact with the outside air, his skin started changing. Purple flecks flew off the skin on his arm and fingers. Small steam wisps rose from the purple.

"What the...?" I gasped to myself, squinting to see what caused it. Was something falling from the sky? Was he in pain? He didn't really seem to be in pain. He was just grunting as he reached. I stared at Dmitri and Axel with my mouth agape, trying to figure out what was happening.

Axel grabbed the object and jerked his arm back sharply, standing up. He walked back into the cave to where we stood, shaking his arm.

"Are you okay? What happened?" I rushed and grabbed his arm. I searched for burns, but it was perfectly smooth like nothing happened. "But, I just saw..." I pointed to the mouth of the cave, picturing exactly what happened in my head.

Axel chuckled and shrugged. "I'm all good. Perks of having fast healing." He winked at me, tossing his head back to get the blond pieces of hair out of his eyes.

"Will that happen to me too?" I asked, eyes widening as I thought about my skin burning.

They all laughed at my question. *What was so funny?*

"Not at all, Meadow. You have nothing to worry about," Dax said, chuckling.

I chuckled dryly with him, my heart rate returning to normal. *Hallelujah.* I glanced at Axel, watching as he caressed his palm. "What is it that you lost?" I asked, curious about what was so important.

A small smile appeared on his face, and he opened his hand, revealing a golden necklace with a sun attached to the chain. It was pretty, but nothing that didn't look replaceable. Maybe it had a deeper significance to him that I didn't understand.

I nodded and let go of his arm, yanking the straps of my bag off my shoulders. None of this made sense, but I wasn't even going to try to process it anymore. My pack dropped to the ground, and I rolled my shoulders, rubbing them the best I could to relieve the stress. More thumps filled the cave as the others put their packs on the ground as well. Dax was the first to get totally comfortable, sitting down on the cave floor and stretching his legs. It was dim in the cave, but the moon shone bright enough for us to see a little bit.

"Everyone get some rest. In this particular part of the world, the sun rises and sets every five hours, so that's how long we have to rest. Once the sun is up, we will be up as well to cover as much distance as we can," Dmitri explained.

We all nodded, and Dmitri nodded back, his attention turning to his pack. I guess that was it. I walked to one of the cave walls, dragging my pack with me and sat it against the wall, sinking to the ground myself. Exhaustion spread throughout my body, and a yawn forced itself out of my mouth.

Through the blurry vision caused by my yawn, I saw the others taking sleeping bags out of their packs. I dug through mine as well, and indeed, there was a moss green package the size of a deck of cards. I inspected it to find the button. It was on the other side of the square, and a hissing sound came out when I pressed it.

Placing it on the ground, I stepped back as it grew into a full-sized sleeping bag, large enough to fit three grown men. After taking off my boots, I climbed into the sleeping bag, embracing the warmth it gave me from the chilly night. I snuggled deeper and pressed the button next to my head for the pillows to pop up. That was much better than the stone-cold cave floor. I closed my eyes and tried to relax my mind and not stress about the journey like I had been doing, even though I told myself this morning that I wasn't going to worry.

I couldn't help it. All the information dumped on me in such a short period of time was so much, I was surprised I didn't just shut down. It was *so* much. Last week, I would've never in ten million years thought I would be traveling to a different world through a portal, with vampires, to get back memories that would prove I wasn't human. Oh, and let's not forget my best friend of so many years was also an evil vampire who wanted to kill me for who knows what reason, with a sidekick who was killing people, changing some into vampires, and taking them to an island.

I didn't even know if I got that story down correctly, but any normal person would've broken down by that point. I think I'd made it so far because deep down, I knew the life I was living couldn't be all it had to offer. I was destined to be more than an agent on a sucky salary. Honestly, I probably would've hopped on board any train that showed me there was more to my life.

This was why it was kind of easy to convince me of supernatural elements being real, despite all my questioning. And my life was about to get even more enjoyable. I just had to wait five more hours.

2 0

I woke after a few hours and felt all right. The sleeping bag was better than I expected, though. I sat up and stretched, eyeing the entrance of the cave. The sun was rising, some of the rays spilling into the cave. Dmitri was in the same spot he was in last night, sitting at the cave's mouth with his legs pulled up to his chest. He had a black pouch in his hand and was tossing it up in the air, crushing it in his hand every time it landed.

I planned on joining him to ask why he wasn't getting any rest himself, but I decided not to, seeing as I was still a little tired, and he looked deep in thought. Kicking my sleeping bag off, I pressed the button on the side, and the entire thing shrank back into a small square. I put it in my pack, grabbing some jerky I spotted before I zipped it all the way up.

By the time I was done eating and washing it down with some water, the rest of the team were getting out of their sleeping bags. Seeing that made me think about vampires and their need for sleep or lack thereof. So they did need it? I put it in the back of my mind to remember to ask them about it another time.

I stood and stretched, getting my body ready for a long day. I grabbed my pack by the top strap and semi dragged it with me as I walked over to Dmitri. I stood next to him, and he didn't even look up, still staring straight ahead at the field. Lifting my pack up a little bit, trying not to think about the strain it put on my arm, I dropped it with a loud crash on the cave floor. Dmitri's shoulders raised and dropped dramatically, slowly lifting his head to stare at me.

"So, what's the plan for the day?" I ignored the glare on his face. He shook his head and stood, towering over me. I crossed my arms and tilted my head, waiting for an answer. He grabbed his pack after our little stare down, positioned it on his back, and glanced at the others, who were starting to walk our way.

"Today is the day the real journey starts. I will reveal the path for us to travel on." He looked around at all of us and nodded to himself when he saw that we were all ready. "Follow me." He walked out of the cave, and I heaved my pack on my back, following closely behind him. I squinted as the bright sun hit my eyes and slowed when I saw the field. It looked even more beautiful from this height, showing much more than green grass with flowers. I could actually see how the flowers accentuated the field. Every time the wind blew across the field, the flowers formed into a random shape.

It was constantly moving, making the field even more breathtaking. I walked carefully to the edge, in awe of the beauty, and whistled. The ground was so far from where I stood. I didn't even want to think about how we got on the mountain, glad that I kept my eyes shut.

Dmitri continued walking once I stepped away from the edge, and I followed him onto a plain gray path, the only part of the mountain that didn't have flowers on it. It was a comfortably wide path, enough for all of us to fit side by side. As I continued to walk up the mountain, it got a little steep. I had to jog so that I didn't fall backward.

"Where are we going, Dmitri? What happened to showing us the path?" I asked, panting from my jog. I had thought I was in great shape until I met my current acquaintances.

"We're here." He stopped walking, and I stopped as well, looking around. I didn't see anything different from where we started. The mountain was still littered with flowers in this area. The only difference was that we were a little higher than before.

"What's here?" Rita asked, walking up beside me. Dax and Axel also stepped up, both with confused expressions on their faces.

"This is the spot that will help reveal the path for us," Dmitri responded, digging around in his pocket. He pulled out the black pouch he'd been messing with earlier and stared at the ground. He bent down and grabbed a rock, turning his back to us. Still crouched, he drew a line on the hard ground, and a dented line appeared. How, since the ground was solid rock, I had no idea. Once he was done, he tossed the rock to the side and stood back up, dusting off his pants. He tilted the black pouch, blue powder spilling into his hand.

"The powder that led us here is sitting in my hand. It will also be the powder that reveals the path to help us make it to the top of the mountain. Once I dump the powder on the ground and it reveals a path, there is no turning back. We can't leave until either we make it to the top... or we die." The last part came out dark enough to send chills up my spine. "If even one of you guys aren't okay with this, we will turn back now." He eyed all of us, mainly Rita, for a reaction.

I shifted, eyes darting at all of them. My chest tightened as I thought about the price. Should I tell them about the price to be paid for me to successfully get my memories back? Would it even affect them? Would they be upset with me? I opened my mouth to speak, but Dax beat me to it.

"No one is backing out. We are in this together," Dax spoke for everyone, confidently looking at the others to see if they agreed. They both nodded in agreement with Dax, and when he looked at me, I tried to smile confidently, but I could feel it wavering. Dmitri nodded and turned his back to us again. I sighed in relief.

Blue powder fell from his hand and crawled on the ground to the line he created. Once his hand was empty, the rest of the powder made its way to the line, until there was just a blue line in place of the original.

"Back up, it's going to get a little dusty," Dmitri warned, and we all backed up a few steps. Blue dust shot up about ten feet into the air, creating a wall of smoke in front of us. It floated in the air for a few seconds and then started falling down quickly, like a soft drizzle.

"Dmitri, wha—" I gasped, taking a small step forward, keeping my eyes on the scene in front of me. Where we were currently standing was sunny and the colorful field visible, but in front of me, it was very different. Rain poured down, the drops pattering against the ground. In the middle of the earth, a thick, yellow line glowed.

"All right, guys. The yellow line is the path we follow. Whenever the line disappears, that means some type of trap is near, and we need to be cautious. The path will appear again after five seconds, so if we miss it for any reason, that's tough luck for us. We need to always be paying attention to the path." He gave us all a hard stare, probably to make sure that we were paying attention. "Meadow, be sure to protect yourself from the natural elements, like rain or snow. The weather can change at any moment, so you have to be prepared for that. We will help the best we can, but sometimes we won't be able to," he finished, stuffing the black pouch into his pocket.

I inhaled deeply and nodded, eyeing the scene in front of me. The rain looked a little intimidating, and my heart rate sped up. This was the official realest step I was about to take for this journey. "I understand. Let's get to it," I responded.

Dmitri nodded, leading the way into the pouring rain. I followed him and hesitated for a moment at the line, glancing at my current surroundings and everyone else one last time.

Lightning crackled in the sky on the other side, lighting it up, and thunder roared immediately after, making me jump. My eyes met Dmitri's, catching him staring at me. The rain flattened his hair so curls spilled over his eyes, and he nodded at me, prompting me to step into the rainy, dark world. As soon as my foot landed on the ground, the wind pushed me, causing me to fly to the side, landing on my back. My pack luckily took most of the force. I coughed hard and swiped my hair out of my face, squinting to see through the pouring rain. A hand pulled me up and helped me get my hair out of my face.

"Are you okay?" Dax asked, eyes darting across my face, inspecting it for any damage.

"I'm good, I'm good." I wiped my eyes and adjusted the pack on my back. "I think my pack might be a little wounded, though." I laughed airily, still trying to catch my breath. The worry in his eyes dimmed a little at my statement, and I threw in a smile as the cherry on top.

Before he could say anything else, lightning lit up the sky again, actually giving us enough light to see our surroundings a little better. The first thing I noticed was that the mountain no longer had beautiful flowers. It was bare and dark, almost as black as obsidian. Dmitri was standing, looking in the direction of where the field used to be. I walked over. The field was completely gone and replaced by piles of rock molded together, forming spike-like structures.

"Where is the field? What happened to everything?" I asked, wiping my face.

"This is where the journey actually begins. It's meant to scare you away and be complicated, but don't worry, it gets sunny here sometimes," Dmitri answered, pulling his hair back into a ponytail. That was a good idea since the rain didn't know how to leave my hair alone, but I didn't have anything to pull my hair back with.

Rubbing my hands together to warm them up from the chills the wind was bringing with the rain, I happened to notice that the yellow path expanded, no longer just a thick line. It was wide enough for multiple people to stand on it, side by side, and fit. I tried to see where it ended, but it went on for miles, disappearing over the mountain where my eyes couldn't reach.

"This is going to be a long day," Dmitri muttered under his breath.

I gladly followed him down the path, hoping the rain would stop soon. I loved the rain, but not when I was in it. It was pretty dark, despite the sun being in the sky. It was blocked by a dark storm cloud from what I could make out. I hoped it moved out of the way soon.

As I walked, I had to continually swipe my hair out of my face, which was becoming annoying. I also had to pay close attention to where I was walking because the path had narrowed. I stayed close to Dmitri, not wanting the wind to blow me off the mountain or something. I almost laughed at that image out loud. As we trudged through the never-ending rain, I did slip a few times, much to my chagrin.

Lightning crackled in the sky, lighting it up so brightly, I thought the clouds had stopped blocking the sun for a second. There was a loud snap to my right, and sparks flew our way, making me hop and skip to avoid getting hit by one.

"Whoa..." I breathed when the sparks stopped flying and it was dark again. Sometimes I glanced behind me to make sure that the rest of the group was still following. They were.

After a couple of hours, it was still pouring rain. I was thoroughly soaked and starting to shiver in the cold air, and I didn't like that.

My mouth opened to ask Dmitri if we could take a little break, when the yellow path started blinking. My eyebrows bunched together, and I slowly walked as I inspected the ground. I looked up at Dmitri, and his back was tensed up, his walking slowed down as well. The yellow line completely disappeared. Collective gasps filled the air, and my eyes darted around quickly, expecting something to jump out from around the corner and scare us. The yellow path reappeared.

"We need to speed up now. Prepare yourselves," Dmitri told us, glancing over his shoulder to make sure we were all still there.

"What's going to happen?" I whispered as I walked faster.

"I'm not sure exactly. It was different for me. I don't think the same thing happens in the same order for travelers, but I could be wrong." Dmitri whispered, slowing his pace to match mine, even though I was walking as fast as I could to keep up. So many emotions passed over his face, but the main one was stress. He looked so stressed, and I was the cause of it. Not because the journey was to retrieve my memories, but because I was a liability. I slowed everyone down.

Another half hour passed, and we'd made it up another steep part of the mountain when the rain let up to a light drizzle. As soon as I started wondering if Dmitri's little theory of the path disappearing was actually accurate, a loud groan filled the air, echoing off the rocks.

The rain slowed and then completely stopped. The silence that fell was deafening. A soft groan came from in front of Dmitri, and my eyes widened in fear as he abruptly stopped walking, tilting his head to listen for the sound again.

"This isn't good," he whispered to himself, silver eyes filled with confusion. His eyes were glued to the rocks in front of us. "I remember this one."

Another groan echoed off the mountain, making my eyes dart quickly to the piles of rock on the other side.

"Meadow, take this." Dmitri grabbed something from his pack's side pocket and placed it in the palm of my hand. It was a lighter.

I looked at him quizzically. "What is it?" I asked, inspecting it. It was red with a black dragon on it.

"A weapon you used to use during battle. One of your favorites. Flip the cap open only when danger comes your way," he explained.

I nodded, grazing the black dragon etched on the side of it with my thumb. I was in a battle?

"Dmitri, what exactly is coming?" Rita tied her hair into a ponytail, ready to fight.

"Prodigium Ignis, the fire creatures," he answered in a hushed tone, eyes casing the area.

Dax let out a whistle, and his smile grew, eyes twinkling in excitement.

"Here we go," Axel said in almost a whisper as a gust of wind blew over us.

I took this as my cue to prepare myself, so I shrugged my pack off to give me better mobility, placing it by the boulder that sat behind us. Creatures started running on the rocks in our direction—black, scaly creatures with orange grooves tattooed into their bodies, glowing like lava. They had no eyes, and when their mouths opened to snarl, I could see the inside clearly, pure lava simmering like they were gargling it. Their mouths seemed glued until they actually opened it, black gooey substance stretching, making me want to gag. Where did these creatures even come from? I tried to spot where they'd appeared, but I didn't see a starting point.

They seemed to form from the rocks themselves somehow. One of the faster creatures made it to our side and leaped into the air at Rita, long talons extending from its hands. Rita yelled and jumped in the air as well, twirling her weapon in front of her, slicing the creature in half. She landed back on the ground, two chunks of blackened flesh dropping to the ground behind her, oozing an orange substance.

I let out an *ew* softly as the orange substance turned into black goo, solidifying into the mountain.

"Don't let them touch your skin for any longer than five seconds, it will burn!" Dmitri yelled out as he punched a creature.

"Got it!" Dax yelled back as he leaped into the air and kicked a creature in the face.

I grounded myself and put my thumb on the lighter's cap, ready for a creature to come my way, yet none did. My heartbeat thundered in my ears.

Axel grabbed one by the throat when it leaped in the air and slammed it into the ground, shooting it three times in the skull. Black and orange skin flew in his face, but it didn't seem to bother him at all as he wiped it off with his forearm.

The feeling of wanting to gag was prominent, yet I held back, knowing that if I gagged, I would definitely throw up. I heard Dax yell excitedly, and I turned my attention to him as three creatures sprinted his way. He rose in the air atop a pillar of rocks as he raised his arms, controlling the pace. A creature launched itself at him and reared its head back to spit a ball of black goo at him. Dax exclaimed and threw an arm out, a rock colliding with the ball.

He raised both arms, making more pillars appear, and ran across them expertly, launching himself into the air. Dax turned, faced the thing following him, and yelled, lifting his arms and clapping his hands together. The beast was crushed between two flat rocks. As he landed, the two other creatures tried to attack him, but Dmitri appeared out of nowhere, grabbing both by the neck and smashing them into the ground. There was a sickening crunch that made me cringe as black and orange oozed from them as well.

"Thanks, man," Dax said as he stepped down from his pillars.

Dmitri nodded and patted him on the back encouragingly. All of the others were breathing hard, eyes darting around to make sure they were all good so far. Dmitri's eyes landed on me, and I gave him a thumbs up, showing I was fine. He nodded.

We prepared ourselves for the next wave. The fire creatures came in waves, and each time the team sliced, shot, and crushed each of them. One of the creatures slowed when it made its way to our side, head turned my way. It ran at me, its growls filling the air, and my breathing picked up. I flipped the cap up, and the lighter rumbled in my hand. It shot a few feet in the air and expanded, turning into a black staff with pure fire pulsing around it. I leaped up and grabbed it, slicing the creature. The smell of charcoal filled my nose.

I felt at one with the staff, a certain familiarity that gave me newfound courage. I was ready to take these creatures on. I charged at them and stabbed and sliced, leaping up to catch the ones that tried to attack my team from behind.

Out of nowhere, I was hit in the chest, and my staff fell from my hand as I hit the ground, pain igniting in my side. I sucked in a breath and clutched my chest, trying to get up. I came face to face with a fire creature.

It took its time, walking slowly as it sniffed me. It looked smaller than the other creatures and just as ugly, but it was still bigger than me. Its hot breath fanned over my face as it panted. It didn't have eyes. The only things on its face were two large holes that expanded and contracted rapidly. Its skin was scalier up close, the orange grooves glowing bright and swimming within itself quickly. I realized it was moving to its own heartbeat. I tried not to breathe, hoping it wouldn't notice me and would just walk away. That proved to be more challenging than I thought.

When it became too hard to hold in my breath, I slowly exhaled, as low as possible, without alerting the creature. It didn't work. The creature snarled, its mouth opening, and black goo flew all around me.

The creature swiped at me. I barely dodged in time, and I dove arms first through the narrow space between its legs. The rough ground scraped my hands and arms. On the other side, I snatched up my staff, prepared to destroy it, but more creatures swarmed around me.

"Meadow!" Dmitri yelled and appeared in front of me.

A squelching sound reached my ears, making me shudder. He yanked his arm backward, and his hand dripped with black and orange goo as he squeezed it tightly. The creature fell and melted into the ground. I shoved my staff into more of the creatures, but it wasn't enough. They kept coming. I let out a slow breath, clutching my staff with both hands, the heat radiating off of it flowed through my veins. It filled me up, and I closed my eyes as the pressure grew in my chest, traveling to my head. I had to let go. My eyes snapped open. The scream that left my mouth echoed, and I slammed my staff into the ground, fire leaving the staff to engulf the fire creatures. As I screamed, the wind whipped at me, helping carry my voice to the origin of the fire creatures. Once the pressure was gone from my chest and head, I closed my mouth, my body going limp from exertion, and I slumped to my knees. Sweat rolled down my face, and I heard whispers from my team.

"Mutatio." The word rolled off my tongue naturally, and my staff became the lighter once again.

"Whoa. How the hell did she do that? I thought this was her human form. There's no way she should've been able to wield that staff." Axel was the first to speak, and I got up from the ground. I looked up, and they were all staring at me in awe. Dmitri was the only one who had a soft smile on his face.

"It seems the closer we get to retrieving her memories, the more her true self comes forth. It was just a theory I had, which is why I gave her the staff. Seems I was right," Dmitri hummed in satisfaction.

I smiled at his explanation. That was insane. It was like I had no control over myself while fighting. Like my body knew what to do. I gave the lighter one more glance before pocketing it. Now I could adequately defend myself.

"Let's get going, guys. It's getting dark, and we need to find a place to rest." Dmitri grabbed his pack and started walking. I grabbed mine and followed him, my mood boosted from the fight. I was giddy and itching for another. We quickly found a cave and got settled. The sound of packs dropping to the ground echoed off the walls, and I heard some water dripping deeper in the cave.

Dax let out a tired yell, collapsing to the ground. "Ah, I am so worn out. I don't think I've exerted this much energy in years. That was actually really fun," he said, fatigue evident in his voice.

"Dax, that was not fun at all. We could've died out there, and for what? I'm not looking forward to what's coming next," Rita grumbled, sinking to the ground beside Dax, who rolled his eyes.

"You're always a buzzkill. You know you wouldn't ever pass up an opportunity like this." A yawn escaped Dax's mouth after his statement, and he smacked his lips during the process.

"I have to agree with Dax here," Axel chimed in, dropping onto the other side of Dax and stretching out his limbs. "This was the most fun I've had in years." He clicked his tongue at Rita, earning himself a middle finger from her. He chuckled and blew her a kiss, and she turned red.

I agreed with Dax as well. That was really fun. I smiled at their playfulness, even though it made me a little sad. That was the type of relationship I once had with Caspian. But not anymore. I slid down to the cave floor, trying not to think of it much or else I would stay in this sucky mood.

"Guys, remember we only have five hours to sleep and regain strength for more fighting tomorrow. We may not have to fight, but we always have to be prepared," Dmitri reminded us.

Everyone murmured in agreement and started rummaging around in their packs for their sleeping bags. I dug mine out as well, expanding it. This time, I kept an eye on Dmitri while I got ready for bed to see what he did this time. He sat down at the mouth of the cave again.

Why does he do that? Was he trying to be on the lookout even though the caves were supposed to be safe? Was he not able to fall asleep? Did he get sleep in between watching outside the cave? So many more questions ran through my mind and wouldn't stop. I needed some answers. Pushing my thoughts aside, I got into my sleeping bag and laid down as if I were going to sleep like the others. I waited until everyone was asleep before peering over at Dmitri.

He was still at the entrance, in the same position. I quietly got out of my sleeping bag and picked it up, dragging it with me to where he was sitting. I gently placed it next to him and got comfortable inside of it again, this time sitting up. There was no moon in the sky tonight, so there wasn't any light shining to see clearly. But he still had a frown on his face, probably not happy that I was beside him.

"Now is not the time, Meadow. You need to get some sleep like the others," he finally spoke, staring straight ahead.

"What about you? Don't you need some rest as well?" I countered, scooting closer to him so that I wouldn't have to speak loudly.

"I'm not tired," he responded simply.

I crossed my arms over my chest. "Well, neither am I. Looks like we're both going to be sitting here, staring at the sky." I shuffled a little bit to get comfortable.

His jaw ticked, and he inhaled deeply. "*Please* go to sleep." He tried to tell me nicely, but I didn't pay him any mind. I was on a mission for answers and wasn't going to sleep until I got some.

"I want to know why you're sitting at the mouth of the cave like you were at the last one," I spoke in almost a whisper.

He finally looked at me, a look of mild surprise on his face. "You saw me?" He asked, eyes scanning my face.

"Yes. I was going to say something to you then, but you looked like you didn't want to be bothered and I was tired, so I decided not to."

He grunted, staring straight ahead again. A few minutes of silence passed, and I contemplated whether or not to ask him another question. I mean, the worst that could happen was that he wouldn't answer, which I expected anyway.

"Why are you always frowning?" I blurted the question, clenching my teeth in anticipation as I watched his reaction.

His body tensed for a second before relaxing again. He turned his head to me, eyes piercing mine. He laughed dryly and shook his head, staring at his lap. I didn't rush him, giving him time to gather his thoughts. He looked lost in them, different emotions passing on his face. A few more seconds went by, and he finally sighed, looking up and staring ahead. "My life used to be amazing. My childhood was filled with so much love and happiness. I wouldn't have asked for it to be any other way." He leaned on his legs that he had pulled up to his chest. "It was almost perfect. My life didn't start going downhill until I was fifteen, an adult in everyone's eyes. My parents were killed, and suddenly, I was orphaned, with no sense of direction in life."

I gasped softly. His eyes were filled with pain, and I was beginning to regret being so nosy and almost forcing him to answer my questions. "I am so sorry about your parents," I said softly, looking down awkwardly at my hands, not knowing what to do in this situation.

"It was a very long time ago," he responded. His accent reminded me I had never asked him where he was from. Since he was already telling me about himself, I didn't think asking him where he was from was too bad, right?

"If you don't mind me asking, where are you from? I've been trying to figure it out, but can't quite put my finger on it." I asked him.

He seemed to relax at my question. "I am originally from Gralatia, a country between Greece and Turkey, but I was mostly raised in Macedonia."

"That makes sense," I replied, getting lost in my own thoughts. We were silent for a little bit, but it was a comfortable silence. I tried to think of him as a little kid growing up in Greece, but it was hard. I needed pictures to visualize.

"Would you like me to continue the story, or is that good enough for you?" Dmitri asked, looking me directly in my eyes.

"I would like you to continue the story, please, if you don't mind," I answered, and he smiled softly.

"As I said, I was young and had no sense of direction. I didn't know what to do with my life. I felt like I had no purpose. So, I decided to join the army, thinking it would help me find my purpose. How, I have no idea. I was just so sure it would help me." He paused, looking down at his hands, fiddling with his thumbs. "Joining was one of the worst decisions I've ever made. We were treated like slaves. We weren't shown any respect, and I started losing more of myself, not that I had much to begin with. People I made friendships with died right in front of me." His voice got softer the more he spoke, so I placed my hand over his to comfort him.

That was the only thing I knew how to do in sad situations. A hug, a gentle touch, anything to let the other person know that I was there for them. To my surprise, he gave me a grateful smile and placed his other hand on top of mine, sandwiching my hand between both of his.

"What happened after the war? What did you do?" I asked as a prompt so that he wouldn't just stop talking about it. This was already way more than I thought he would tell me, and I didn't want the moment to leave just yet.

"After the war, I was even more lost than I was before joining it. I didn't know where to go from there until someone approached me to join a group. A brotherhood called *The Comitye.*" He paused again and looked at me, a strange look in his eyes. I didn't know what emotion that was and had a feeling I didn't really want to know either. "The Comitye was advertised as a brotherhood where everyone helped each other out and grew together. I jumped on it so quickly. The idea of being surrounded by people who would help lift my spirits sounded better than winning the lottery." He chuckled dryly and shook his head, his cheek expanding as he pressed his tongue against it. "At first, it seemed legit, and I thought I was helping people...until I realized what was really going on."

My eyes were wide as I ate this story up. He has been through so much. No wonder he was the way he was. I saw him as a trooper for surviving.

"What was happening? Was it that bad?" I wanted him to finish the story.

He twisted his lips and glanced around the cave, seeing that the others were still sleeping. I glanced back myself to make sure that no one else was up. I wanted this to be exclusive to just me and him.

He continued, "I was being used to create an army, along with many others. We were changing humans into young, and what we didn't know was that anyone who didn't complete the transition was being killed. After discovering what they were doing, I became defiant and started going against everything they stood for. Instead of killing people, I started saving them. Once The Comitye found out what I was doing, I was punished. Tortured because I was saving innocent

169

people. After months, I finally escaped with the help of Axel and Dax. I wouldn't have been able to get out without them. I am forever indebted to them for saving my life."

I poked my bottom lip out, looking back at the sleeping forms. I didn't know they all knew each other for that long. "So, that's the reason why you frown all the time." I mocked myself, now understanding.

"I tried to find happiness again. Some light at the end of the tunnel, but it was hard to make connections with anyone. I even lost my best friend because I didn't want anyone in danger of being pursued by The Comitye because of me." He sighed after finishing his sentence, sliding his legs down.

My hand fell from his, and I put it back in my lap. I noticed his breathing was heavier than usual and looked at his chest as it rose and fell. The fact that he was still here, trying to help people and use his abilities for good, warmed my heart.

"Now do you think it's a good time for you to sleep? Because I do," he commented casually, making me laugh softly.

"I guess it is. Will you be getting any sleep?" I asked, finally looking at his face.

He shrugged. "We'll see." He turned his head lazily, giving me a crooked smile.

I shook my head, laughing, and got up to drag my sleeping bag back to its original spot. Sliding back into it, I got comfortable and gave Dmitri one last glance before trying to sleep. I couldn't stop thinking about Dmitri and his story. I wondered if I already knew this story, and telling me again was weird for him.

But the way he was telling me, it didn't seem like something he was repeating. He rarely spoke about this, I decided, and was grateful that he shared it with me. I stared at the cave ceiling, different thoughts flying through my mind. What if I had gone through something like that, but because I didn't have those memories, it wasn't affecting how I was as a person? Was I always bubbly and happy, or was I more like Dmitri, reserved and frowning all the time?

What if... getting my memories back wasn't a good thing?

21

The sun was shining bright in the red-inked sky on this new day, beating on my exposed skin. A total contrast to the rainy weather we experienced the day before. I expected it to be as hectic as the day before, but nothing happened for the first three hours. Not a growl or snarl, or even a little hiss. Those hours were slow, the entire time being spent on the lookout for the path blinking and making sure no one was sneaking up on us. They reminded me of Caspian and Victor being able to track us because of something Dmitri did. I wasn't entirely sure what he did because he didn't explain it well enough for me.

Dmitri hadn't even given me as much as a glance so far. The only good thing that had happened was that I was able to get a little bath in that morning from the spring I found inside the cave. The water was pretty warm, and I only needed a few minutes to get clean. I changed into a brown long-sleeved shirt and black cargo pants that I found at the bottom of my pack.

"When is the next trap coming, Dmitri?" I asked, kicking a few rocks that crossed my path. I waited and listened out for his response, but it never came. I didn't know why he was ignoring me, but it was starting to piss me off. We had the best talk last night, and I thought that would change his behavior toward me, at least. But I guess not. I huffed loudly, hoping to catch his attention that way, but that didn't work. Someone chuckled next to me and I turned to see Dax, a huge smile on his face.

"What's up with you today?" he asked, eyes darting across my face to gauge my mood. "You were so happy and excited at the beginning of the trip, and now you look like you want to rip someone's head off."

"It's about my memories," I answered, keeping my voice low.

"What about them? Are you getting really nervous about getting them back?" He had a concerned look on his face.

"No, it's not that. I mean, it was for a while, but now it's more than that." I paused to gather my thoughts, my eyes trained in front of me to make sure I didn't collide into Dmitri. "Last night, when I was trying to sleep, I was thinking about my memories and what exactly I will remember and what will be different or the same."

"That doesn't seem too bad to me," Dax commented when I paused, and I gave him a side glance.

"Well, that's not all. More thoughts crossed my mind, like how will I be once I get my memories back? Will I change if I remember all the bad and traumatizing things that happened to me, if there are any? What if none of my memories are good, and I'm stuck wishing I never got them back?" I rattled off, my voice getting higher as more questions rolled off my tongue. Another thing I was thinking but didn't say out loud was if I could live with one of my friends dying so I could remember who I was. What if someone dying was the price to pay? I couldn't live with myself if something happened to one of them.

"Whoa, whoa, whoa. For one, you need to slow down. Two, take in a few breaths and don't focus on anything that just came out of your mouth." He smiled encouragingly.

I took his advice, and it calmed me down a little bit. Only a little. The sun was so hot against my skin, and I could feel a headache coming on, which wasn't helping me much.

"What happened for you to think about all of this?" he asked, glancing at Dmitri. Why was he looking at Dmitri? Did he know that we talked for a while last night? Had he been only pretending to sleep?

I made sure not to be obvious about seeing him do that and looked back at my feet.

"Nothing, really. Just thoughts," I said, not wanting him to know much.

"Well, here's what I can tell you. Stop stressing. There's no need to. Trust me when I tell you that you are definitely the same person, if not even more wonderful. Don't focus on the negative. Find something positive to think about that will overshadow that. Everything in your life wasn't all dandy, like any person ever, but you did pretty well for yourself. You have nothing to worry about," he reassured me, and I wanted to hug him for his kind words. He was always so positive. I wondered about his backstory.

"Thank you, Dax. You are so kind. That really helps. I will try to think positive thoughts. Just give me a few more minutes," I told him with a smile.

"No rush. Whatever caused you to think about that, try not to let it become a distraction." He glanced at Dmitri again, and this time my eyes followed, staying on him a little longer than I wanted to.

I just nodded, not wanting to make eye contact with him. If I did, it would only confirm that he knew Dmitri was the reason for my negative thoughts. While I was trying to get my positive vibe back, the wind started blowing, feeling great on my boiling skin.

As we continued to walk, the wind picked up, whipping my hair around my face. I yanked my hair back, trying to get it out of my face, but it didn't matter. The wind continued to pick up, blowing so hard it started smacking my face. "Ugh! What is happening?" I complained, ducking my head to stop the abuse on my face. I peeked up a little, and it looked like even Dmitri was having a hard time.

"Everyone, be careful and watch out for the path blinking. I have a feeling something is about to happen," Dmitri shouted over the roaring wind.

I put my head back down and gasped, my steps faltering as the path started blinking, and then entirely disappeared. "Guys! The line is go—" The rest of my sentence never left my mouth because my scream replaced it. I was snatched backward. By what? I have no idea, but somehow I was in the air, getting further away from the group with no way down.

I think my name was yelled, but the wind was smashing itself into my ears. I couldn't even tell who yelled it. I continued to scream and claw at the air, and Dmitri threw his pack on the ground and blurred as he ran.

My eyes couldn't keep up with him until he leaped in the air, disappearing and appearing in front of me. I leaned toward him, straining against the force. He grabbed my hand and yanked me into his chest, and I held on to him for dear life. We fell as gravity took over, and another scream escaped my mouth. The air shifted around me, everything disappeared for a split second, and then it all appeared again when we hit the ground.

The impact forced a breath out of the both of us, Dmitri taking the brunt of it. It didn't seem to affect him, and he wrapped his arms around me protectively. He jumped up, steadying me.

"Wha…what the *hell* just happened?" I looked around wildly. There was a loud snap. Dmitri pushed me behind him, shoulders tensed as his head whipped back and forth, searching. The others were looking around as well, in defensive stances. I looked down—the yellow path was back. It must've reappeared when I was yanked by who knows what.

That was the craziest feeling ever. My heart was still beating quickly. I'd never experienced something so frightening yet thrilling at the same time. The wind was still blowing strongly, and the ground suddenly started moving. A gasp left my mouth as the rocks on the ground rattled. I turned, and my jaw dropped as the top of the mountain, what I could see of it, start turning colors, to pure white.

"Guys, look!" I yelled, pointing at where the color of the sky started changing.

They all followed my finger, and Dmitri hissed. The sky changed from red to a dark purple, creating an eerie atmosphere. The white color blanketed the mountain, and my eyes followed as it reached the ground. A wind chill blew past me, and the white kept going past where I was standing, covering the entire mountain. I turned in a circle, taking in the change of scenery.

The entire mountain was covered in snow. I'd never seen snow in person before. The snow left a cold spot in the middle of my hand as it melted, causing me to shiver even more. My breath came out frosted.

"Let's go." Dimitri's voice interrupted my thoughts. He breezed past me, and I followed, watching him grab his pack on the way.

"Dmitri, what happened back there? What pulled me backward like that?" I asked, keeping my mouth closed from chattering out loud. He didn't answer. Just kept stomping onward through the snow. *That's it.* I stopped walking, planting my feet in the snow. My hands were curled into fists at my side, and Axel, Rita, and Dax all walked past me, but then slowed when they realized I wasn't moving.

"Dmitri!" I yelled, my voice echoing off the mountains. My breath came out in angry puffs, condensing in the cold air.

Dmitri froze, ceasing his walking. A look of shock was on everyone's face, and they turned their heads to Dmitri to see his reaction. He turned around dramatically slow, narrowing his angry eyes when it reached me. I didn't care how angry he was right now. I was annoyed as well and so tired of him ignoring me unless I needed protection. He stalked my way, angry steps making the snow fly up from under his feet. He stopped directly in front of me, gray eyes hard with anger as he stared into my annoyed ones.

"What happened to me back there?" I repeated through gritted teeth, my breath fogging the air between us before disappearing. I wasn't going to move until he gave me an answer.

"Caspian," he growled.

My heart stopped. "What did you just say?"

"You heard me." He clenched his jaw. Shouts filled the air, and his eyes flitted over my head. Frozen in place, my eyes widened as I watched his face harden.

"Dmitri?" Dax called out, his voice sounding nervous.

Dmitri growled in return, a deep guttural one coming from his chest and throat at the same time. This was a different growl than his usual. It sounded almost animalistic, and I wasn't sure if I found that fascinating or frightening. "Dax, take Meadow, now!" His deep voice carried in the air, making him even more intimidating than he already was. *Take me where?*

Dax was by my side in no time, grabbing my hand. "Come on, Meadow. Let's run." His eyes were wide and cautious as he spoke.

I tightened my hand in his, and we took off, with him leading the way. We ran past Axel and Rita, who both had concerned looks on their faces, staring in the same direction as Dmitri. We continued to run up the mountain, and I tried not to think about what was behind me, why I was being pulled away. Dax was running fast, but still close to my pace. I was actually able to keep up with him, unlike how it was with Dmitri.

"Dax, where are we going?" I asked, my voice coming out a little strained from being out of breath.

"Somewhere, *anywhere* to keep you hidden and safe from what's coming," he answered, looking around quickly before speeding up again.

"He told me it was Caspian," I almost whispered, as if saying his name out loud would actually cause him to manifest.

"I know, I heard. Which is why we need to find a hiding spot as quickly as possible," he said. He stopped when we were far enough away, looking around before speaking again.

"Catch your breath, I don't need you passing out on me." He chuckled, and I relaxed. This part of the mountain seemed safe enough. More snow-covered trees littered the area, bunched together, giving us enough cover.

"Thanks, I definitely need it." I took in a few breaths. I chugged down some water from the canteen, the cold water freezing my insides.

"No problem. Gotta have the energy to fend off Caspian's attempts to kill you." He replied so nonchalantly, I choked on my water. I coughed violently, and Dax pounded my back, trying to help me out.

"Did you have to add that he's trying to kill me?" I wheezed, coughing once more to get the rest of the water out of my windpipe.

"Sorry, I didn't think you would choke on your water. I just need you to keep hearing this, so you realize how serious it is," he responded, rubbing my back as I cleared the remnants of water from my throat.

"I *do* know how serious it is," I grumbled, rubbing my arms to get warm. I really needed to check my pack to see if there was a jacket in there.

"I know you understand a little bit, but not the fullest extent. It is more serious than you think it is."

I sighed and brushed him off, looking at the sky so I wouldn't roll my eyes. "I got it, Dax." I ended that part of the conversation. "So, what's next?" I asked, ignoring his concentrated stare. I understood he wanted to keep me safe, but I didn't want to stress more than I already was.

"We need to find a tunnel to travel in so that Caspian won't find us," he told me, taking the hint.

"All right, let's go find us a tunnel," I said as enthusiastically as I could so that the energy could be cheerful again.

He smiled, and we started walking quickly again. This time, I was more aware of my surroundings. The wind picked up a little making me shiver. My teeth started chattering, and I walked faster, trying to warm up. That didn't really work. Dax picked up the pace and started jogging, so I did as well to keep up, trying not to trip over the lumps of snow. I was panting, and watched as my breath filled the air, Dax's did as well. Random whistles filled the air, and Dax gasped, looking behind us.

"Meadow, run! Go!" He shooed me away, not even looking at me. "I need to create a distraction!" he yelled.

I ran like he told me to, but kept glancing back to make sure that he was okay. When I was a reasonable distance away, I stopped to catch my breath. He was standing in the same spot with his arms spread out. The mountain started shaking, making me crouch slightly for balance.

The snow from the ground rose in the air, creating a thick wall in front of him. I watched in awe as he moved his arms, the middle of the snow wall parting, and I saw movement on the other side. Slapping a hand over my mouth, I held in a gasp that threatened to escape. I ran up the mountain more and hid behind a large tree.

Standing in plain view, between the two walls of snow, was Caspian. He wore his signature purple cloak that rippled behind him as he walked. His blond hair was messed up from the wind, but he actually made it look good, much to my chagrin. His confident strides left no prints in the snow, and there was a huge smile on his face, teeth gleaming even though there was no sun to shine on them.

Seeing him again made my heart hurt. It shouldn't have, but I still couldn't believe that was the same person who knew every little secret of mine. He was there for almost every tear being shed, breakups, undercover jobs, etc. Now he was just...my enemy? That deep connection just severed like it was meaningless. None of it made sense. Blinking the tears away that threatened to spill, I turned my attention to Dax.

"Caspian! Stay where you are!" he commanded, but Caspian kept on walking. Dax lifted his arms, and the snow in the air rose as well, starting to rotate. The snow twisted in the air and started turning into mini snow devils.

Caspian snarled and charged at Dax, making me gasp softly. Dax threw his arms out in front of him, and the snow devils flew Caspian's way, colliding into him. He was thrown backward, but landed on his hands and feet, sliding back as the snow devils continued to attack him. He snarled against the snow, his canines growing, and his eyes suddenly turning a vibrant violet. My mouth dropped, and he threw his arm out to the side, hand curling as he strained against the never-ending snow. There was a loud rumbling sound, and I looked up as snow fell from the higher part of the mountain.

"You want to play games, Dax? Let's play!" Caspian jerked his hand forward, and a boulder rolled down the mountain following his movements. It collided into Dax before he could do anything to protect himself.

"Dax!" I screamed, throwing my pack down and scrambling from my hiding spot. I started running toward him but slowed when I realized what I was doing. But it was too late. Caspian's head lifted, his crystal blue eyes locked on mine, lighting up.

My eyes enlarged, and I reached inside my pocket. I barely took a step before something knocked into my chest, pushing me up into a hard tree. A large, cold hand was wrapped around my throat, and I grabbed at it, trying to yank it off.

"Now, what do we have here?" Caspian spoke, and I finally looked at him, seeing his grin spread on his face. "Hello, darling." His smooth voice lowered, and he used his other hand to tuck a loose hair behind my ear, his eyes caressing my face as if to lock it in his memory.

"Caspian," I greeted in a bored tone, making sure there was a passive expression on my face.

His grip loosened, but he left his hand there, ghosting on my neck.

"What do you want?" I asked, sighing loudly when he didn't speak.

"You know what I want." His eyes darkened, yet the grin stayed on his face.

"Then get on with it," I growled, yanking at his hand, even though it was pointless.

"Ooo, feisty as always, my sweet Meadow. Brings back some rather *delicious* memories." He tsked, moving his hand from my neck.

I rubbed the place where his hand was to relieve the throbbing sensation he caused. I made a face. *Delicious memories?* What was he talking about?

"What made you think I wouldn't be able to find you?" he asked, pursing his lips when I rolled my eyes.

I opened my mouth to answer but paused when I saw movement from the corner of my eye. "I wasn't running away. I came here for my memories. You know I would face you head on if I needed to," I hissed, keeping my eyes trained on Caspian so he wouldn't be aware of Dax sneaking up on him.

He smiled, sans teeth. "How cute." He tilted his head, held up a finger, and adjusted his cloak. "Give me a second." His arm flew back, connecting to Dax's face.

I yelped at the impact and launched off the tree to tackle Caspian. His arm shot out, shoving me back into the tree. Pain shot up my back, and I cried out, arching my back. I thrashed against his hand, trying to get out of his hold. Dax was coughing, and I looked up as he hissed, his head jerking up at Caspian.

His eyes changed to violet, and he quickly lifted up his leg, smashing it to the side of Caspian's face, causing him to loosen his grip on my neck. Taking advantage of this opportunity, I held on to the tree's trunk, lifted both of my legs, and kicked Caspian in the chest.

He stumbled backward from the force, and Dax grabbed his cloak, making Caspian's hands fly up to stop it from choking him. Dax still had Caspian by his cloak, and I ran up at Caspian and hopped up to kick him in the face, but he grabbed my leg, throwing me to the side. All the air in my body left as I was thrown into a boulder, my shoulder taking most of the impact.

The scream that left my mouth was blood curdling, the pain so extreme I had to gasp to breathe properly. It felt dislocated, and I really hoped nothing was broken. I panted heavily as I tried to get up from the frozen ground.

"Meadow!" Dax shouted, and I lifted my head up in time to see Caspian stalking toward Dax, who was focusing on me.

"Dax, look out!" I shouted back, but it was too late. Caspian upper-cutted Dax, sending him flying in the air, and he crashed into a large tree before dropping to the ground. The tree shook from the force, and a loud snapping sound filled the air as it fell to the ground after him.

I couldn't even gasp properly anymore from how much pain I was in, but I staggered up anyway so I could somehow help him. My breaths came out short, the pain igniting in my shoulder from my movements. I grabbed the lighter from my pocket.

"Is this what you wanted? Huh?" Caspian yelled at Dax, who was struggling to get up. He didn't answer as he slowly got to his feet.

"Dax!" I yelled, trying to make it to him in time. His head snapped up, and he bared his teeth at Caspian and charged, bulldozing him. They tumbled to the ground, and Dax was on top, punching Caspian in the face. Something red flew up and landed in the snow.

Blood.

Caspian roared and hooked a leg over Dax and flipped him over, now on top. He delivered punches to Dax, just like what was done to him.

"Get off of him!" I shouted, picking up my pace. I tossed the lighter up in the air, catching the flaming staff as it fell. Caspian glanced up at me mid-punch, and his eyes widened. Dax took advantage and head-butted Caspian, making him yell out and clutch his face. Dax punched him in the chest, the connection creating a loud sound in the air. Caspian flew backward. Dax jumped up and jerked his hands up quickly, sharp, transparent objects raising with his motion. They were icicles.

Caspian got on his feet, and Dax threw his arms forward, the icicles flying at Caspian. He looked up and threw his arm in a circle, the icicles changing direction and flying back at Dax.

"No!" A scream escaped my mouth as Dax flew back, icicles pinning him to the ground. He let out a groan and flexed his arms to escape, making more blood drip down them from where the icicles were lodged. Two were in the middle of both arms, and two more in each thigh.

"Caspian, stop! Leave him alone!" I shouted as he walked toward Dax. He held an arm out, lifting Dax in the air without touching him.

"Meadow, don't worry about me! You have to run now and get to safety!" Dax yelled, breathless.

"I'm not leaving you!" I yelled back, slowing as I got closer. I adjusted the staff in my hand and chucked it at Caspian. He just swiped his hand in the air, making it fly in another direction away from him. I let out a frustrated yell as I continued their way, clutching my arm again. Caspian's arm shot out when I was almost there, and my body completely stopped moving.

I jerked forward, trying to continue, but I couldn't move. "Caspian, let me go now!" I growled as I strained against the force. I felt weightless. I had no control over my body anymore. Caspian ignored me as he dropped his arm, slamming Dax back into the ground.

Dax started coughing, and he spit out blood, groaning when he saw it in the snow.

His lips were busted and swollen, just like his left eye. His breathing was haggard, and he lifted his head weakly, eyes darting around, panicked. When his eyes landed on me, they relaxed, but he winced in pain when he tried to move.

"Poor Dax," Caspian tsked. "You know you did this to yourself, right? All you had to do was hand over Meadow. That's it!" He scoffed, his smile widening and face implying that it was that easy.

"I would n-never betray m-my friends," Dax panted, pausing to take a few breaths.

"Well, look where that got you. And look, I still got Meadow!" He cackled in Dax's face like he just told the funniest joke.

"Caspian, stop it! Let him go!" I pleaded, not wanting Dax to be more hurt than he already was.

Caspian laughed. "Stop? Why would I do that? Not when I have such a lovely audience to witness the magic that's about to happen." His wicked eyes gleamed with mischief.

My panicked gaze flew to Dax, who wasn't healing at all and had a look of defeat in his eyes. Caspian smiled, and I knew something terrible was about to happen. My heart wouldn't stop beating quickly, and my eyes tingled, but I kept blinking rapidly. No tears.

"Meadow—" Dax started coughing before continuing. "Never g-give up. Never s-stop fighting. You are powerful."

Something warm rolled down my cheeks. I was crying.

"I love you, Meadow, my dearest friend." He smiled weakly, his bruised mouth making it hard for it to fully form the words.

"I love you too, Dax," I whispered, my voice cracking. The need to kill overcame me, a sensation I'd never felt before. I wanted to destroy Caspian.

"Hm. That's cute." Those were the last words I heard from Caspian before my shrill screams filled the air. Caspian shoved his hand into Dax's chest. A choking sound left his mouth. Blood bubbled at his lips, and Caspian snarled, yanking his hand upwards. The most sickening sound filled the air.

"No!" I sobbed, clawing at the air with one hand to try to make it to him, but I still couldn't move.

Dax's body went limp, his head rolled to the side as I stood there in shock. My eyes traveled to Caspian, who held something in his hand, blood dripping from it. I choked on a gasp when I realized what it was.

"Dax! Oh my god, Dax, no!" I cried out, and the hold against me was gone. I stumbled over to where he was, my injured arm limp at my side. I couldn't stop the wails coming from my mouth as the image of Caspian holding Dax's spine stained my mind.

I dropped to the ground, mumbling his name over and over as I brushed his hair from his bruised face. His body didn't look out of sorts, but his back was limp, and there was a gaping hole that went down his entire chest, blood dripping from the sides.

22

I couldn't breathe. His blood was on my hands, and I stared at them, breathless. I slowly looked up at Caspian, my mouth slightly agape.

"What did you do?" I whisper-screamed, my eyes murderous, tears rolling down my face. He smirked, and I looked down at my limp arm, the need to kill coming back to me. I breathed out, counted to three, and popped my arm back in place, pain igniting in my shoulder. It traveled to my chest, and I gasped from the pain, biting down hard on my lip, almost drawing blood.

"Come on, Meadow. I know you're not crying over him. He was useless, anyway. It had to be done. Plus, I have some good news, I don't have to kill you anymore!" Caspian spoke, validating my anger.

My head snapped up at his statement, and I narrowed my eyes. He had that annoying, cocky grin on his face and was wiping his bloody hands on his cloak. *That's it.* I let out a yell and jumped up, charging after Caspian when he looked down for a second. I was surprised I was able to tackle him to the ground. I landed a punch to his face, ignoring the pain that sparked in my hand. I raged, drawing back to land another blow, but his hand shot up, stopping my fist.

"You're a fool to think you can fight me." He cackled in my face before throwing me backward.

I slid in the snow, throwing my arms out to stop myself. I jumped back up quickly, breathing heavily. My staff was in the snow next to my foot, flameless.

"Come with me willingly, Meadow. I don't want to hurt you," Caspian lied, holding his arms out.

"I would rather die than go with you," I spit out, curling my hands into fists, wincing at the pain in my shoulder.

He narrowed his eyes. "You're going to regret that." He ran at me in a purple blur. My eyes couldn't keep up, and I was slammed back into the ground with a grunt. My hand wrapped around my staff as his hand wrapped around my throat, constricting my airflow.

"You are weak. I don't care what your story is, your reason for being the way you are. You came out a weak man." I sneered in his face. The heat from the staff traveled through my veins like before, and the pressure built. The pain I was feeling was gone.

His eyes darkened in anger, and then glowed vibrantly violet. He raised his arm, the hand curled into a claw. He bared his teeth, and my breathing quickened. I jerked my arm back and shoved my staff into his side, and flames ignited, engulfing him immediately. He yelled, clawing at his face. The pressure filled my chest and my head as I stood, fear altogether leaving me. My body tingled, and a blue light started glowing from my chest. The blue light grew, and the pressure released, my scream echoing as the light shot out of my necklace, straight into Caspian.

He fell to the ground, unmoving, and the pressure was gone.

I touched my necklace, in awe at the power it wielded. Augustus wasn't lying about protecting me. I walked gingerly toward Caspian and stood next to his body, hesitant to touch him. Taking in a deep breath, I grabbed his shoulder and turned him over, jumping back slightly when his arm swung to the side, landing in the snow. His face was streaked with black lines, his mouth parted a little bit. *I hope he's dead.*

Where was my team? Why didn't they come and help Dax and me?

Dax.

I glanced at his body and forced myself not to break down and cry. I *couldn't*. There was a huge weight on my chest that made me feel like I couldn't breathe. The snow around his body was red, and I had to tear my eyes away from him to focus on what I needed to do. I had to find my team. That was what he would've wanted me to do.

At that moment, I had no idea where they were or even where they were going. I only knew I had to follow the yellow path.

Clearing my mind, I walked over to where my pack was still hiding. Dusting the snow off revealed the rest of my pack, and I slung it onto my back. I needed to get to the top of the mountain and get my memories back. Hopefully, by following the yellow path, I would be able to find the others.

I retraced the steps I took with Dax and trudged through the snow, looking for the path. The wind picked up, and I wrapped my arms around my middle, ducking my head to avoid the snow that kept flying into my face. I peeked up a few times to see if I would be able to spot anyone, but I couldn't. Just piles and piles of white snow, blanketing the entire mountain.

The snow was thickening my lashes, making it harder to see in front of me. As I continued to walk, I passed chunks of ice that had an interesting blue hue to them. More appeared the longer I walked, and my eyebrows scrunched together, trying to figure out where the ice came from. Some of the ice didn't even look normal. The chunks were getting bigger as I continued on, and it started to make me a little cautious.

One big chunk stood directly in my path, and I walked up to it, my curiosity piqued. I slid a finger over the ice and looked at it. There was no water on it. Odd. I slid my hand over it harder and gasped, yanking my hand back, hissing from the sharp pain. My palm had a little burn on it, the red spot throbbing painfully.

"What is this?" I questioned out loud, walking around the chunk. It didn't melt when I touched it, but it burned me. I glanced around again at the chunks, and realization dawned on me. I remembered the fight at the building Caspian owned and how the vampires were stabbed with Jestraetrium and broken into pieces. These were dead vampires.

My heart began racing, and I became more aware of my surroundings so I wouldn't be caught off guard. Dmitri did say something about Caspian bringing a small army with Victor. But that was a maybe. I didn't think it was a high probability.

Now it made sense as to why they couldn't get to Dax and me. They had been preoccupied with fighting a vampire army. It also meant that they couldn't be that far from where I was. I continued walking and kept my head down, making sure to glance around a few times until I saw something blinking a few feet ahead of me. It was the yellow path I needed to take. I ran to it just in time to see it disappear, meaning something else was about to happen.

Did something happen the last time the path disappeared? I was so preoccupied with Caspian, I didn't keep track. The sky was darkening, which meant I had an hour or less before it was completely dark. Finding my team was my number one priority, but finding shelter was a close second. I didn't want to be left alone out here in the dark.

I stepped on the yellow path, a little hopeful about finding my team promptly. As I walked, the wind picked up so much, it pushed me off balance, and I stumbled on the uneven ground. The heavy pack on my back yanked me down, and I coughed from the force, curling in a ball so that the snowstorm didn't pull me away. The storm yanked and pulled at me, but thankfully my pack was so heavy, it held me in place.

Many minutes passed, and I thought I would be curled up in that ball forever. But the storm finally died down, and I peeked up from my arm to see that all of the snow was gone.

Ice replaced the snow. My mouth opened slowly as I got up. Something dark moved under the part of ice I was standing on, and I yelped, hopping out of the way. *What was that?* It looked huge, and I wasn't a fan.

My heart pounded as I took everything in. I hopped again lightly and tried to calm myself. It looked like I was standing on a vast ocean, completely iced over, with a thick yellow streak going down the middle. Gingerly, I followed the path. It wasn't as freezing as it was before, just a little chilly, but it didn't seem cold enough for all of this water to be iced over like this. I kept glancing down to keep a lookout for movement under the ice, but I didn't see anything anymore.

Nothing else was around me except ice. How was I going to find shelter if there was literally no place to hide or even sit? It was almost completely dark, and soon I wouldn't be able to see a thing. Wind started blowing, and it got stronger. White particles, snow, swirled in the air in front of me, making it hard for me to see. I officially hated snow.

I put my arm in front of my face to block the wind and squinted a little over it when I happened to see movement ahead of me. I walked faster to get a clearer view, and when the wind completely stopped, I stopped as well, gasping. Dmitri and the others were a good distance away, but I could still make out that it was them, standing on a snowy bank. They looked like they were arguing about something.

"Dmitri! Axel! Rita!" I yelled, and they all whipped around. It was actually them. I waved my arms in the air and started running their way. Relief spread through me as I ran. Now I wasn't going to have to worry about surviving the night on my own.

I ran, slipping as I went, trying my best not to fall. The closer I got, the more I realized they didn't look happy, and their waves were frantic. It sounded like they were yelling something, but I couldn't hear them because I still wasn't close enough.

"What?" I yelled out, hoping they would hear me with their great hearing and realize that I couldn't hear them. I slowed to a jog when their waves became more frantic and tried to figure out what they were saying.

"Stop!"

I heard a faint shout, and I completely stopped, but it was too late. A loud crack filled the air, and I looked down, panic setting in. A large crack in the ice stretched from where I was standing to their position on the bank.

"Meadow! Don't move!" Dmitri yelled, eyes darting around my feet. "I'm going to try and find a way to get you to safety!"

"Please hurry!" I gasped when something dark swam underneath my feet. "Dmitri! There's something swimming right under me!"

"I know! I see it! Try to stay calm for me, and whatever you do, don't move!"

I nodded, afraid to make any sudden movements. Easier said than done. I was standing in the middle of ice with a possible giant sea creature swimming underneath my feet. This was not a calming setting. Dmitri paced on the edge of the snowy bank, eyes trained on my feet.

He stopped and tilted his head, eyes traveling up to my face. "Toss your pack to the side to lighten the load!" He yelled, pointing at it.

I grabbed the shoulder straps, looking at them. "But what if it doesn't work? Why can't you just come to get me?" I asked with a shrill.

He sighed and scratched his head. "I can't. There's a barrier that won't let me through!" he answered, his voice echoing over the ice.

That made me panic even more, and I was about to take my pack off but stopped when I saw that any movement made it worse. The ice cracked more, fracturing around and under me. I looked at Dmitri with wide eyes. "Dmitri," I whispered, and there was a hushed silence.

Then I dropped.

23

The water was bone-chilling cold. I thrashed around, trying to swim up, but my pack weighed me down. Yanking the straps off, I let go of the dead weight and fought my way to the surface, my lungs burning. My air was almost gone, and I thought I wouldn't make it, but I gave my legs a final thrust, and I broke the surface, immediately inhaling and treading water.

"Dmitri!" I screamed, blinking the water out of my eyes.

"Keep treading, Meadow! Try to swim to me!" he yelled, gesturing at me from the snowy bank.

"I can't! The ice is in my way!" Around the gap where I fell was a large chunk of ice that wouldn't budge and kept me trapped in the small hole.

"You have to try, Meadow!"

I tried to move the ice out of my path. It was denser than I thought, thus making it even harder. I even tried to climb on the ice, but it crumbled under my weight. I had to stop and tread so that I wouldn't sink. As I tried to catch my breath and not think about my tiring muscles, something moved under my feet.

"What was that?" I shouted, kicking my feet. "Dmitri, I think something is in the water with me!" I yelled, breathing heavily.

He looked as if he was trying to stay calm, but his eyes were panicked, and his pacing didn't help. "Get on one of the ice blocks now!" Dmitri shouted, his hands on his knees as his eyes darted around me.

I scrambled to get on one, but I was suddenly yanked down. I had no time to inhale for more air, so my chest burned as I ran out of air and I continued thrashing, trying to get away from whatever was dragging me down. The yanking suddenly ceased, and I hurriedly tried to swim back to the top, eyes trained on the hole in the ice, a little light shining around it.

I was almost there when I was yanked back down even further away from the hole, igniting more panic inside me. I kicked and thrashed, hit something hard, and swam toward the hole again. I stretched my arms to grab the sides of the gaping hole when a dark object swung in my view, and before I could dodge, it smashed into me. Pain spread through my head and face, black spots dancing in my vision. Water went in my nose and mouth, filling up my lungs. My last thought as I lost consciousness was that I had failed.

I WAS DANCING. It was weird because I didn't dance. But there I was, on a ballroom dance floor, twirling around expertly with my chin on a shoulder. I tried to move my head backward to see who was leaning on, but I couldn't.

"You look absolutely stunning," a familiar voice whispered in my ear.

My heart swelled at the compliment. "Thank you," I replied automatically as a blush rushed to my cheeks. But I didn't blush easily, and how did I start speaking without realizing I was opening my mouth? That wasn't even what I wanted to say. I wanted to ask what was going on and where I was because this fancy place didn't look familiar. I also wanted to see the speaker. The voice sounded familiar, but I wasn't able to identify it. We twirled again, and I finally lifted my head off of the shoulder—and came face-to-face with Caspian.

My heart rate sped up, and I opened my mouth to scream. "You look handsome yourself," I complimented him instead, shocking myself. *Why did I just say that?* I tried to yank myself away, but I kept dancing, barely noticing the people around me. To my right, I spotted Dmitri and got excited, trying to call out his name. But all I could do was smile at him, giving him a look, and tilted my head at Rita, who was in his arms dancing with him. There was a large smile on her face and her eyes were closed. She looked happy.

"I am so glad you got them together. They look delighted," Caspian commented.

"They really do," I agreed, my smile growing. *Wait, why was I agreeing?* Dmitri and Rita together? What? Was this real life or a dream? Why could I not get away or yell for Dmitri to help me get away from Caspian? He wrapped his arm around my waist, bringing me closer to his chest, and I wrapped my arms around his shoulders. His smile widened, and I smiled back, getting lost in his beautiful sapphire irises. *Beautiful irises?* What had gotten into me?

"I love you," he whispered, leaning closer to my face.

"I love you, too," I told him breathily and leaned forward as well, glancing at his lips. No, this had to stop. I was trying to yell, trying to stop this.

A loud roar came from behind me, and I turned quickly, finally able to move my body again. Water flooded the ballroom, and I looked around to see if anyone else noticed. Everyone was still dancing, even Caspian, and a gasp left my mouth when I saw another me in his arms, getting closer to his face.

I shuddered in disgust and turned back to find a tsunami in front of me. I didn't run, content with the fact that I couldn't outrun it. Hopefully, this wasn't real, and it wouldn't actually kill me. The water hit me, and I gasped, sitting up quickly, coughing. Water spilled from my mouth, making me choke as it left my lungs. My chest burned, and my throat was drier than a desert. I looked around frantically, trying to figure out where I was.

How in the world did I get in here? The ballroom had been replaced by...a cave, I thought. I didn't remember how I got there. The last thing I remembered was drowning, and that thought made me nauseous. I leaped up and ran to the corner of the cave. Water poured out of my mouth, making me choke like before as I tried to get it all out. The action made me dizzy, and I groaned, holding the side of my head. My mouth tasted like salt, and my lips were extremely dry, on the verge of cracking. The throbbing sensation in my head drowned out every other sense.

I tried to remember what hit me, but all I could make out at the time was a dark shadow. I was so close to reuniting with them, and now I was back to square one. I didn't know how I would be able to make it to them again, but I was going to have to find a way. Holding on to the cave side, I looked out the entrance and saw the moon shining through, the only source of light in the darkness.

I stumbled to the entrance, looking for a way out. It was no longer cold, and the ice and snow were gone. The mountain was back, covered in green moss. No flowers this time. I couldn't see the path from that angle, and a waterfall roared directly beneath me as it crashed into the rocks below. There had to be a way out of this cave.

AFTER WALKING through the cave for what felt like hours, the sight of sunlight on the ground ahead quickened my pace. A way out. The landscape spawned jagged hills and sparse vegetation.

"You got this. Just think," I whispered to myself, pausing to look ahead of me, shielding my eyes from the bright sun. What would Dmitri do in a situation like this? He would be calm and probably look for anything in the surrounding area to get a clue as to where he was. Maybe? I groaned at my idea. That was not a good one, but it was the best I could do while rocking a probable concussion.

I started jogging again and glanced around for anything to help me. I would even accept a strand of hair at this point. My eyes landed on a bush up ahead and paused when something winked at me. It was as if someone was waving a mirror around to catch my attention. I went in the direction of the winking and reached a green bush.

Pushing the leaves and small branches aside, I looked for the source and gasped when I found it.

It was one of the daggers, hidden skillfully in the bush. I checked around for a trap or anyone else. No one was around, so I picked it up carefully, in awe of its beauty. It looked so beautiful up close and not in my abdomen. I chuckled at the thought.

The blue blade winked in the air as I turned it, and I could see the little gold flakes in it. The handle was a beautiful gold color, with blue flakes. I never realized how big it was until I held it in my own two hands, both ends stretching past my palms. This confirmed that they were in the area and that I might be getting close. The sun was shining brightly in the red sky. I walked for about an hour, which meant I had four hours to find my team...*again*.

My pack was nowhere to be found, so I had no supplies. Finding the others was very important. I continued walking along the yellow path.

The entire time, I was really hoping it wouldn't blink because I was worn out from trying to escape and not die. Turned out, not dying was harder than I thought in this world. The air was calming, and the breeze felt great on my skin as I walked. The ground was soft, and little blades of grass littered the path I was walking on. Totally opposite from the freezing snow and ice from the day before. I'd be lucky if I didn't get sick from how much the weather had changed in the last few hours.

As I continued my journey, I couldn't help but think about Dax. Was his death my fault? What was I going to tell my team? Would they blame me? I was so caught up in my thoughts, I didn't hear movement until it was too late.

"Hello." A voice came out of nowhere, causing me to jump and yell, looking around for the culprit. Someone was to the left of me by the cluster of trees, but I couldn't see their face because the shadows hid it.

"Who are you?" I asked, squinting.

The person chuckled, walking out from the shadows. It was a tall woman, and her bronze skin gleamed beautifully in the sun. Her eyes were a total contrast to her skin, sparkling soft baby blue, a color I'd never seen on anyone before. She was in a two-piece blue and purple suit and had on black heels with purple stripes.

"Are you lost, love?" The woman asked, a concerned look on her face, but with a smile at the same time. She had on purple lipstick, and her teeth were pearly white.

I shifted nervously as I shook my head. "No, I'm not lost. Who are you?" I repeated. I felt as though she ignored my first question on purpose.

"Oh, I'm sorry. My name is Impy," she introduced herself, a slight gleam in her eyes. Did I imagine that?

"Okay, thanks. I'm going to go now." I chuckled nervously, pointing over my shoulder. I glanced around, trying to look for a way to dodge this suspicious woman. Where did she come from anyway?

"Where are you going?" Impy continued the conversation as if she didn't hear me dismiss her.

"I'm just traveling for fun," I answered, walking backward slowly. I glanced down, and my body automatically stiffened as I stared at Impy's wrists. Her sleeves were rolled up a little bit, revealing violet streaks in her wrist area. My eyes widened in fear, looking back up at her. Impy smiled, and I noticed her canines were longer than usual. Impy was a vampire. My hand automatically went to the bulge in my pocket, where the dagger was wrapped with a piece of fabric from my pants.

"For fun? No one travels this mountain for fun, sweetie," Impy responded, and her skin began to sag like it was melting off her bones and turned gray, eyes flickering from blue to vibrant violet.

I walked sideways slowly, keeping my eyes on her as I tried not to gag at the grotesque sight. I thought she was a vampire, but I wasn't so sure anymore. She crouched, hissing at me, and I grabbed the dagger from my pocket.

"This is for Maddox!" Impy screeched and lunged at me, igniting a scream from me.

I swung the dagger and smashed the hilt into her face. Another person trying to kill me in the name of Maddox, a mythical being, according to Dmitri.

Impy tumbled to the side and jumped back up, crouching on her hands and toes like an animal. Her jet black hair was wild and her face drooped, jiggling with her every move. Her suit had ripped in the tumble and had large holes in the jacket. Streaks of violet peeked out from the holes. The streaks went up her arms all the way up to her shoulders. She stretched her neck up at the sky and screeched, no longer sounding human, but animalistic.

I watched in horror as the violet streaks crawled up her neck. I could actually hear it moving as it tattooed her graying neck. Tearing my eyes away, I looked around for the dagger that had flown out of my hand. I needed to get to it before she did. "Hey!" I yelled, waving my arms in the air to catch her attention so she could stop making all of that noise.

Her head whipped at me. She growled, walking on her knuckles and toes.

"What are you waiting for? Come and get me!" I yelled, and she screeched as she charged at me. She was slower than any other vampire I'd encountered. I ducked easily when she leaped at me, rolling on the ground away from her and toward the dagger. I swiped at the ground for it and hopped up, waving it in the air.

"I bet you don't even know how to use that weapon, human," Impy hissed, her voice raspy, and her skin flapped as she spoke, tongue flickering out of her mouth like a reptile.

"Try me," I challenged, and she charged at me again. I ran toward her as well, elbowing her in the face when we collided.

Impy howled and lunged at me, clawing my arm. Searing pain shot up my arm, and I screamed. She cackled in my face. Anger coursed through me, and I sliced at her. Her hand blocked the weapon, but my elbow knocked her in the chest, making her fly backward.

I hissed when searing pain shot up my arm again, and my eyes widened as I spotted five long talons sticking out of my arm. Before I could get them out, Impy tackled me and we tussled, fighting to be on top. Impy sat on top of me, snapping her teeth for a bite of my face. I struggled to get my feet up, and when I did, I kicked Impy in the chest. She crashed backward into a shrub.

There was a loud snap when she collided, and she shrugged to get up, clawing at the scrub for help. I took advantage of that and ran at her, dagger raised. Impy had her back to me, and her suit was ripped almost completely, exposing her entire back. I slowed and held in a gasp as I zeroed in on two large, glowing scars on her back. One starting on each shoulder blade, going all the way down her back, glowing the same violet color as her eyes. It looked just like Dmitri's back. Small streaks of violet weaved together on her back as well, connecting into the two patterns.

A growl from Impy snapped me out of my trance, and before she could get up, I shoved the dagger in between her shoulder blades, leaning in to thrust it deeper. The blade cut through bone with a sickening crunch, and I almost lost my hearing as Impy screeched from the pain. She continued to shriek, the sound echoing off the mountains. A crackling sound filled the air, and I watched in slight awe as the ice from the dagger spread over Impy's back until it covered her entire body.

I left the dagger in until I was sure she was completely iced like I had seen Dmitri and the others do. Once I was sure, I yanked it out and used the hilt to hit the ice, shattering it into different pieces. I let out a huge breath and swayed, catching myself on the closest tree. My body was exhausted, and my head throbbed even more than before.

I was starting to regret coming to this mountain. Was it even worth it anymore? Sighing, I decided this time to keep the dagger in my hand in case someone or something else attacked me. I wanted to be prepared. I finally looked at my arm, the five brown talons still there, sticking out. Grabbing one, I eased it out, panting from the searing pain it caused.

I gritted my teeth and closed my eyes, pulling until it was completely out, and let out a short scream as fire shot down my arm to my hand. I dropped the talon and held my chest with my other hand as I got my breath back. I decided to leave the other four there until I was with my team to help. I didn't want to pass out in the middle of nowhere. I rejoined the yellow path, more tense and paranoid than before.

This time, I wasn't going to get lost in my thoughts. The sun sank in the sky, making me nervous. I didn't want to spend another night out here by myself. I wasn't sure if my brain was playing tricks on me, but I swear I could hear creatures rustling in the bushes or someone laughing softly, almost inaudibly.

There was a loud movement, and I held the dagger up, slowing so my feet would make less noise and I could hear my surroundings better. The noise stopped when I slowed, and my heartbeat pounded in my ears. My eyes darted around, looking for the source of the sound, and I turned the corner.

"Meadow?" a voice whispered, and I screamed, swinging the dagger at the source of the sound. A hand shot out and gripped my arm, twisting my wrist almost painfully. The dagger fell out of my hand.

My eyes widened, and I threw myself at him, hugging him tightly. "Dmitri!" Relief spread through me. All the stress and emotions—from Dax dying to almost drowning and nearly being killed by Caspian and Impy—left my mind and body.

24

"What happened to you?" Dmitri asked as he rubbed salve on my bruised arm after taking the talons out himself.

"Where's Dax?" Rita chimed in at the same time, not giving me time to answer Dmitri's question. Dmitri wrapped my arm with a bandage, and tears sprang to my eyes at the thought of what happened to Dax, my chest tightening.

"Caspian. He—" I choked on a sob and paused, taking in a deep breath so the tears and the lump in my throat would go away. I looked at my lap and fiddled with my thumbs, breathing in and out slowly. Dmitri let go of my arm, and I passed a hand over the bandage. He had to cut my sleeve to get the rest of the talons out safely.

"Caspian attacked us, and he—" I stopped again, unable to finish. The tears in my eyes threatened to spill over, and I didn't want to cry in front of them. Lifting my head back up, I saw that they all had long faces, showing me that they probably assumed what happened without me finishing. There was a long, uncomfortable silence, and I kept my eyes on the cave wall in front of me, not wanting to see the emotions I knew would be on their faces. I shouldn't blame myself, but it felt like my fault. It *was* my fault Dax was killed. There was no denying it. I sucked in a breath.

"We can't dwell on it, guys. We need to get ready because Caspian will be coming back with Victor and even more young. We fought some that ambushed us and lost the dagger that you ended up finding. We thought somehow Caspian would end up with it," Dmitri spoke, breaking the uncomfortable silence.

I groaned, putting my head in my hands. "I am so tired of this," I whispered into my hands, frustrated. When would this be over?

"I told you this journey would be a tough one," Dmitri reminded me, making me raise my head.

"I know that," I huffed, leaning back into the cave wall. "I almost died on the way here. There was this woman who said her name was Impy. She attacked me, but luckily, I had the dagger. I had to kill her," I said the end softly.

Axel chuckled, and I turned to him, confused as to what was funny about my story. "I wondered what happened to her. She disappeared a few decades ago, and no one knew where she went."

"At least you survived. We have to make it to the top of the mountain as soon as possible now that Caspian knows where we are." Dmitri gave me a pointed look.

"Actually, I stabbed him with my staff, and my pendant blasted him with light, knocking him out. Would that have killed him?" I asked.

"No. It's not that easy to kill Caspian. We still need to be careful and quick. We have to travel by night as well now." His deep voice bounced off of the cave walls from how quiet it became after his response.

"Dmitri," Axel started, gesturing at him.

"Come on, man." Rita joined in, scoffing.

Dmitri held his hand up. "I know, I know. But we have to. If Caspian captures Meadow now, she will never get her memories back. We have to take the risk," Dmitri explained.

"Actually, before I stabbed him, he did say something about not having to kill me anymore," I added, my words making Dmitri narrow his eyes.

"What is that bastard up to?" He growled, pacing as he clenched his fists. I was confused. Wasn't that better than killing me?

I looked out of the cave, wondering what kind of creatures were out there waiting at this very moment. We'd never traveled at night before because it was dangerous, according to Dmitri.

"Because of the circumstances, we now have to get to the top of the mountain in a shorter amount of time, but we will make it," Dmitri reassured us. It didn't help me, but I stood up anyway, ready for it. Everyone else stood up after me, and we followed Dmitri to the cave entrance. Dmitri put his finger up and we stopped. He tilted his head, listening for anything. "It's all clear," he confirmed, and we walked out of the cave and into the chilly night.

I noticed nothing happened to Axel this time. He caught me staring at him and smiled, touching his necklace. I smiled back. My deductive skills were correct. That necklace helped him somehow.

"What kind of creatures are usually out at night?" I asked Dmitri in a low voice, not wanting to alert anything out there. I looked up at him as he thought about my question. Well, I assumed he was thinking about it.

"Some call them shadow creatures. They are shadows that creep up when you least expect it, and they try to consume you."

Goosebumps spread up my arms. "How can they be destroyed?" My question came out as a whisper.

"The only way that we know how to destroy it so far is with light. The one thing we don't have anymore. We lost it fighting Caspian's followers." He stopped talking, and his jaw ticked. He was pissed. "I really hope we don't encounter them," Dmitri continued, his voice low. His eyes darted around, then relaxed just as quickly. I followed his eyes and didn't see or hear anything. Maybe he was just cautious.

The moon was in the middle of the sky, and the night gave me a chilly, creepy vibe. The only real sound came from the waterfall below us, my loud feet, and my occasional huffing as we climbed. The moon helped give us some light, along with a glowing yellow path, even though I was probably the only one who needed the sources of light. Dmitri suddenly stopped, and a small smile grew on his face. Confused, I looked up to see what he was looking at but saw nothing.

"Do you guys see that?" Dmitri asked in a hushed tone.

I looked again at where his attention was but still saw nothing. "See what?" I squinted at the dark clouds in the sky. That couldn't be what he was talking about, could it? They were just clouds. Rita and Axel gasped, making me even more confused.

"You won't be able to see it quite yet, Meadow, but keep looking at where the dark clouds are gathering."

I kept staring, and after a minute, I gasped as well. Something glowed as the clouds moved, unveiling an obsidian-colored temple. There seemed to be a red color on it as well, but it was so far away, at the top of the mountain, and I had to squint a little to fully see it. It glittered even in the darkness, making it a little easier to see.

"That's our destination right there. We're high enough for a glimpse of it, but still a couple of days away," Dmitri said. I was in awe of the temple's beauty and didn't take my eyes away from it until the dark clouds moved again, concealing the temple. Seeing that made me more excited than I had been for days.

It gave me hope that I could actually make it there. We kept walking through the dark, up the steep mountain. Every now and then, I glanced at Dmitri, and he was always tense. I didn't think he ever relaxed. He was always ready for a fight.

Dmitri's arm shot out, and I ran into it before I could stop myself. The path blinked and then disappeared. There was a waterfall right below us and a vast ravine between us and the mountain's other side. A loud, shrill rasp made me jump and move closer to Dmitri.

"The shadow creature is coming," Dmitri spoke, eyes narrowing as he looked in the direction the sound came from.

"Axel, Rita, one of you guys, take my pack. Meadow needs to get on my back. I also need one of you to jump across to make sure it's clear on that side."

"I'll gladly go first," Rita spoke up, walking past us to the open space. Dmitri and Axel backed up, and I followed. She stepped backward and crouched, putting her head down. Her head popped back up quickly, eyes glowing violet. She started running and yelled as she did, launching herself off the edge. She landed on the other side on both feet, crouching and throwing her arms up like she'd achieved a perfect landing in long jump. "It's clear!" Her voice traveled to our side.

"Now it's our turn." Dmitri reached to grab me, but a small gust of wind blew me back.

Axel launched himself in the air, shouting as he soared. He landed on the other side and rolled as soon as his feet touched the ground.

Dmitri cursed at Axel's unexpected action but didn't dwell on it as he turned to me.

"Ready?"

I shifted my weight on my feet and crossed my arms, looking at where Axel and Rita were, gauging the distance from where I was.

"You'll be fine."

I looked at him when he spoke and then back at the water. The fall had to be at least one hundred feet with pure water at the bottom. I trembled at the thought of drowning again.

Dmitri stepped in front of me, his body heat warming me. "Hey." His voice was low as he slid a finger underneath my chin, guiding my face toward him. "Trust me?"

"I do," I whispered back, afraid my normal voice would crack from all the emotions. His touch sent a shiver down my spine and gave me goosebumps.

"It's here," he whispered.

Next thing I knew, I was on his back, and we were floating in the air.

The dark beauty of the night magnified the mountains and the water. The wind was harsh this high up in the air, striking my face with slaps that stung. I couldn't understand how he was making it to the other side with the momentum he had, but we continued to move in the air.

The other side was getting clearer the closer we got, and we were almost there when suddenly, we lurched downward. The action ripped my breath away, yet my scream escaped, and my heart dropped when we started falling. We were almost one with the water, and my scream grew shrill when something dark wrapped around Dmitri's ankle.

"What is that?" I screamed, almost hyperventilating.

"Hold on!" he shouted, and I locked my legs around his waist as soon as we jerked to the side, slamming into the rocky wall by the waterfall. He let out a groan and clawed at the mountain to get a grip, but he started slipping. He let out a curse as we fell again.

"Dmitri!" I screamed, clinging to him so tightly, I was probably choking him. The fall was long, and some water from the waterfall hit my face on the way down. My scream continued, and I closed my eyes when it was evident that we were going into the water. I prepared myself for the freezing cold. Nothing happened. My body jolted to a stop, and my eyes snapped open. Dmitri hovered, with his arms spread over the rushing water. The torrent crashed against the mountains, spraying mist in my face.

"What is happening?" I whispered breathlessly in Dmitri's ear. I wanted to scream out of fear, out of shock, scream for everything that had happened to me since I started the journey. Scream for Dax, scream for what was to come, scream out of frustration. *Everything.*

"The shadow creature has found us. You might want to hold on even tighter." The words barely left Dmitri's mouth when we were yanked upward.

I held on for dear life, and my eyes almost left their sockets when I saw that we were being held up in the air by a literal shadow. It was pure black, something I could see even in nighttime. It somehow made that raspy, shrill noise with no discernible mouth.

A shadow in the shape of a human body. Dmitri raised his arms slowly, the shadow's hand around his neck not seeming to affect him, and his hand curled. Something dark moved in the corner of my eye, and one of the trees tucked in the mountainside shook loose from the crumbling rock. Dmitri flicked two fingers to the left, and the tree rammed into the shadow. It howled and let go of Dmitri. We fell, and the air around us contorted. Everything disappeared for a second and then came back, the ground underneath us.

We landed so hard, a cloud of dust and grass exploded on impact. I coughed and waved a hand in front of my face. The shrill rasp rang in the air, and I covered my ears, the ringing was almost painful. When I hopped back up, Dmitri was already on his feet, fighting the shadow creature. The creature swiped at him, and Dmitri ducked, punching it in the chest area. It threw its arm out, smacking Dmitri backward through the air. He disappeared—and then reappeared on the shadow's back.

"Meadow!"

My eyes flew up to Dmitri.

"You need to use your pendant!" he yelled, pointing my way.

"What do you mean?" I cautiously glanced at the shadow creature as I backed up to make sure I wasn't in its reach. Dmitri was struggling to keep the shadow creature in his grasp as it thrashed.

"Your pendant is the only source of light we have to use to destroy this creature!" he yelled, and at the same time, was knocked backward off the creature. It screeched and went after him.

I grabbed my pendant, trying to figure out how to use it. The only other time I ever did something was when Caspian tried to attack me and grab it.

"Do it now, Meadow!" Dmitri's muffled voice came from somewhere behind the creature. *How?* I couldn't understand what he wanted me to do with my pendant. The shadow creature tossed him in the air, and I yelled in frustration and fear. I immediately regretted it when the shadow creature turned to me. The obsidian creature became shapeless until arms started reaching for me. I was frozen in place.

The shadow creature grabbed my arm, the contact sending a chill up my spine.

I screamed. The creature stopped growling and slowly brought its faceless head close to me until I could feel the coolness it radiated. I didn't know where Dmitri was, and I couldn't hear anything besides my breathing and the creature's. Seconds passed while I maintained a staring contest with a creature that didn't even have eyes.

My breathing slowed, and I took one slow step backward. The raspy cry hit my ears, almost deafening, and my heart pounded again as the creature grew. My poor heart. It lunged at me. I covered my face and energy left me, a blue light shooting out of the pendant, almost blinding, and hit the shadow creature. It shrieked along with me, so loud my ears started ringing. I couldn't move. So much energy poured out of me and the light grew, spreading until it ripped the creature into pieces. Gone.

The light retreated into my pendant with enough force to knock me backward to the ground. My head was pounding, and it made me lightheaded, my ears ringing so loudly I didn't know Dmitri was yelling until he came into my line of vision. His mouth was moving, eyes frantic, but I couldn't hear what he was saying. I blinked a few times to get the dots out of my vision and rubbed my ears, shaking my head to unclog them. Was he trying to say something?

"What?" I asked, tilting my head to hear what he was trying to say.

"Get up!" The words reached my ears, and he held out a hand for me, and I grabbed it. He yanked me up, and I looked around, trying to understand what had happened, and he snapped his fingers in front of my face.

"Hey, hey, we need to go. Let's go, hop on." He tapped his back, and I jumped on without hesitation, this time tucking my face into his shoulder. I felt him jump and the wind hitting against me, but I didn't lift my head until I felt his body dip from landing. I lifted my head, and Axel and Rita were rushing toward us.

"Are you guys okay?" Axel asked, looking at us and across the mountain, eyes wild.

"I'm okay, I'm okay," I huffed as I hopped off of Dmitri's back.

"I'm good," Dmitri answered him, eyes also cautious and looking around.

"How did you do that?" Rita asked, looking at Dmitri and me.

He looked at me, and I glanced down at my pendant, stroking it slowly. I was still trying to figure out how my pendant gave off the light myself. Augustus' words about putting protection in it came to mind.

"I don't really know," I answered, still stroking it. Axel and Rita looked at me with weird looks on their faces, glancing at my neck where the pendant lay.

"How do you not know? It's *your* necklace," Rita asked, scrunching her dark brows.

"My pendant gave off the light when I screamed, and I don't know how it did that, sorry." I dropped my hand from my pendant so I could stop drawing attention to it.

They both looked at Dmitri, and he shrugged. Strange that Dmitri wouldn't have an answer, since he was the one telling me to use the pendant, so he should've known.

"Did Augustus alter the pendant when you visited him?" Axel asked, eyes glancing between my face and my neck.

"Only gave me a powder to protect me."

Axel nodded, but Rita narrowed her eyes at me, not saying a word.

"We need to leave now," Dmitri spoke.

I took in a deep breath and started walking with the others, looking out for the yellow path. After a few minutes of walking, it appeared. We all walked for a while in silence, and the sun finally started rising, the sky slowly changing from dark blue to a bright red. My body was so tired, I needed to rest for a second.

"Hey, can we stop somewhere so I can rest and eat and drink some water?" I asked, slowing down. They all slowed, and Dmitri glanced back at me. He didn't respond as quickly as I wanted, so I spoke again. "I need to use the bathroom. I know you guys probably don't have to do any of those things, but I'm human at the moment, so…" I finished, dragging my feet obnoxiously to catch their attention.

Dmitri sighed and glanced at Axel and Rita. "We're so close to making it up to the top of the mountain, and it's only going to be one more day. Can all of those things not wait?" He asked, not looking at me anymore as he continued to walk.

I gawked at his back. Did he not understand how the human body worked? It wouldn't slow us down that much. "No, this can't wait. I need to do this now." I rolled my eyes and stopped walking altogether. The others stopped as well.

"Fine." Dmitri made his way back to where I was standing. We looked for some type of shelter and found a cave.

"Let's rest here." Dmitri dropped his pack, and Axel and Rita followed suit. Dmitri walked over to where I was sitting and dropped a sleeping bag in my lap while they got comfortable. I thanked him, and he nodded, walking back to his spot. We ate whatever was edible in their packs, and I chugged water until I was satisfied. I took care of my personal necessities and got comfortable in my sleeping bag but couldn't sleep.

I didn't know what it was, but I had a feeling. Every time I closed my eyes, a sliver of chill went up my chest and forced my eyes open.

"The cave, come to ussss, the cave."

I shot up. Who…? I looked around, but everyone else was sleeping.

"Come to ussss."

I quietly slipped out of my sleeping bag and stood, making sure they were still sleeping. I needed to explore the cave. They were calling out to me. I crept to the back of the cave to explore.

25

I should've trusted my gut. Though the cave was calling to me, I had a gut feeling that I shouldn't follow it. I didn't listen. If I had, I wouldn't be stuck in this position.

"Don't say a word," he hissed in my ear, a hand clamped over my mouth. How on earth could I say a word when his hand was preventing me from saying anything? How did he even find me? I thrashed and tried to elbow him in the chest, but he had a steel grip on me.

"Are you going to scream if I let you go?" he asked, and I shook my head. He slowly let go of my face, and I passed an arm over my mouth to wipe off his scent. I turned and faced him, fists curled at my sides. He had the most arrogant smirk on his face and winked at me, his blue eyes sparkling with mischief.

"Caspian, let me leave," I said through gritted teeth. I was disappointed that the stabbing and the blast from my pendant did nothing to him. He looked as if he came straight off a runway.

"Or what? You'll blast me with your little necklace?" He chuckled to himself as if he'd told the best joke ever.

"The blast that knocked you out cold?" I retorted, tilting my head to the side and crossing my arms.

His lips pressed together, and his brows dipped for a second before a grin spread on his face. "That's the only time it will ever happen, so don't push your luck."

I rolled my eyes. "Okay, but can I leave?" I asked, taking a cautious step back, hoping he wouldn't notice.

His eyes narrowed and he grabbed my arm, yanking me to his side. "Absolutely not. You're not getting your memories back. Plus, you're great bait so I can get to Dmitri and kill him instead of you," he said nonchalantly.

"Why do you want to kill Dmitri?" I wondered as he tugged me along through the dim cave.

"Because we have a long history. He ruined my life."

I scoffed. "Okay, so what are you going to do with me then?" I asked. We obviously had some kind of history that made him feel this much hatred for me, but I couldn't think of what it could possibly be.

He stopped walking and faced me, his goofy face changing to a serious one. "My boss wants you," he answered simply. I waited for more, but that was it. He said nothing else and continued walking, a hand secured around my wrist.

"That doesn't really answer my question, Caspian."

"You talk too much. Don't be annoying, Meadow." He flashed me a confusing grin; I couldn't keep up with his mood swings. "Ah, here we are." Caspian halted, letting go of my wrist.

"Where are we?" I asked, trying to look over his shoulder. He was blocking the entrance, so I couldn't see anything.

"Are you sure you really want to see?" He glanced over his shoulder at me with a sly smirk.

I raised my arms at his question, giving him a dirty look. "Yes, I do." I pushed him out of the way. Why was he still wearing that dumb cloak? I shook my head and walked through the entrance. "Oh my god!" I stumbled backward, hitting my back on Caspian's hard chest. My hand flew to cover my pounding heart. Fear coursed through my body, breaking my tough act.

"See, this is why I asked if you really wanted to see. I knew you weren't prepared." Caspian's words caressed my ear in a whisper and he gripped my arm. He was right. I wasn't prepared at all for it.

"So, this is where you're hiding your army?" I breathed, eyes flitting around the large space. There were at least a hundred men and women combined, down below on the ground. Some were shivering and tucked into corners, the others roamed around aimlessly. All of them were wearing black suits.

"Yes. They are my creations. I brought them here myself."

I looked at him in horror as he grinned and rubbed his hands together.

"I know you're not about to take all the credit for my work now, are you?" A new voice came out of nowhere to my left, and my jaw dropped when Donatella walked down the rocky steps that I just noticed. She wore an all-yellow tracksuit and long green nails. Her hair was no longer blonde. It was highlighter-blue, bone straight into a shoulder-length bob. The black booted heels she wore made her tower over me.

"Nice to see you again, Meadow," she greeted, her teeth pearly white against her purple stained lips.

"Wow, so Caspian was the boss you were talking about?" I ignored her greeting.

She pursed her lips, tapping a manicured nail against her cheek. "I mean, I wouldn't call him my boss per se. I was exaggerating only slightly." She chuckled as she walked up to Caspian. He let go of my arm and I moved out of her way, rubbing my throbbing arm where Caspian had gripped it.

"Sorry for taking all the credit. How could I forget about your excellent hunting skills that delivered them all to me?" Caspian hummed and grabbed Donatella by the waist, pulling her closer to him.

She giggled and wrapped her arms around his neck. One hand slid down his shoulder, and the other cupped his jaw, a finger tapping against his cheek. "It's okay, my love. You can make it up to me later." Her sentence trailed off at the end as their lips touched, and I automatically whipped my head away from the scene in front of me. Donatella and Caspian?

I glanced back quickly, and they were still locked on each other's faces. Perfect. I slowly walked forward into the cave and continued to the stairs that Donatella had descended earlier. I had to watch my step as I climbed so I wouldn't fall over the edge and onto the ground below with the rest of the young. I reached the top of the steps, and there was a large platform with a brown stone seat in the middle of it.

Past that stone seat, there was an exit. I didn't know where it led to, but as long as it got me away from this area, that was all I cared about. Without hesitation, I ran up the platform, kicking rocks as I went. A force hit my chest, and I stumbled backward, hitting the ground hard. Pain shot up my elbow, and I grunted from the force. In front of me, Caspian and Donatella blocked my way to the exit.

"Now, where do you think you're going?" Caspian asked, chuckling at my attempt to escape. He held his hand out for me to grab, and I ignored it, getting up on my own.

"Nowhere now." I groaned, rolling my eyes as I dusted off my clothes. I mean, I didn't *really* expect to make it to the exit, but I was trying to be optimistic about it.

Donatella laughed, tilting her head to the side in pity. "I wouldn't suggest trying that again. You might slip up, and you never know who's hungry over here." Her eyes flashed violet and flickered to the ground below us. I followed her eyes.

"Look a little closer at them," Caspian said, a slow grin forming on his face. They all looked normal to me until the small details jumped out at me. The men and women tucked in a corner all had violet streaks tattooing their faces. The ones walking around didn't have streaks on their faces, just on their hands.

"So, you see, I would be careful if I were you because one of them might be hungry enough to take a bite out of you at my command," Caspian warned, clapping his hands together.

An actual shiver of fear went down my spine as I imagined teeth sinking into my skin.

"Now that we've cleared that up, time for my meeting." Caspian turned to Donatella. "Make sure everything is in place for later."

She nodded and walked away through the exit I was trying to escape through.

"What are you planning?" I asked, watching him closely as he made his way over to the stone chair, sinking into it. He flicked his wrist, and I was yanked backward and pinned to the wall, with no control over my body.

"Hush, Meadow." Caspian rolled his eyes but grinned at me from his spot in the chair.

"No. Let me go." I tried to yank myself from the wall but failed.

"I won't let you go, but you can sit down." He flicked his wrist again, and my body fell to the ground. I slumped down, my arms snapped behind my back, and I felt something wrap around my wrists, locking my arms in place.

"Is this really necessary?" I complained, trying to snap the thin rope. No success.

"Of course, it is. You remember what you just did, right? I can't have you trying that again while I'm distracted." He paused and situated himself on the uncomfortable-looking chair. "Now, sit still and stay quiet while I conduct my meeting." His humorous demeanor disappeared, replaced with a serious one, and his eyes flashed from his brilliant blue to violet, then back to blue.

If he was trying to intimidate me, it wasn't working. Well, *almost* not working. A little part of me was worried about his reckless side. He could decide that he didn't actually need me and throw me to the hungry vampires below.

I huffed in annoyance and sank against the hard, cold wall. There was no point in fighting it. I couldn't escape. I could only hope that my team would come for me, though they didn't even know where I was. As I tried to figure out a way to leave the cave successfully, there was movement in my peripheral.

Victor, the man I had been investigating, walked through the exit in the same black suit as the vampires below. I hadn't seen him since the boat incident, and now that I was actually getting a clearer look at him, he didn't look as old as I thought, despite his salt-and-pepper hair. He looked way younger than he'd looked on the ship. He had a troubled look on his face as he slowly walked to Caspian. He was so focused on him, he didn't even steal a glance my way.

"Update me, Victor," Caspian spoke before he even made it to his side.

Victor fiddled with his fingers, an obvious nervous tick. He must've messed up on something and was afraid to let Caspian know. I chuckled to myself.

"Um, sir. You know the plan we had for the cruise ship?" Victor stuttered, clearing his throat a few times.

"Obviously. It was my idea." Caspian had a bored look on his face and waved his hand to hurry him along.

"Well, it doesn't look like we will be able to execute the plan on schedule," Victor whispered the end, taking a small step back as Caspian sat straighter in his chair.

"What happened?" Caspian raised his voice, his jaw ticking in annoyance.

Victor shifted like he had to use the bathroom, and I wanted to tell him to hurry up because I really wanted to know what was going on as well.

"Someone destroyed the yacht."

I barely heard what he said because he spoke so low, but by the look on Caspian's face, he heard him clearly.

He stood slowly, his cloak flowing behind him. "Excuse me? I just want to make sure I heard you correctly." Caspian chuckled humorlessly, clasping his hands together. He walked up to Victor and towered over him, tilting his head to the side, waiting.

A little laugh slipped from my mouth, and Victor's eyes flew my way for the first time since he entered the room. I couldn't wave, so I gave him a smile.

His brows dipped, and mouth opened, staying agape. "What is she doing here? I thought you didn't want to include her in the plans any—"

Caspian snapped his fingers and pressed his index finger and thumb together, cutting Victor off. His lips were pressed together tightly, and his eyes were wild as Caspian slowly walked around him. "Why must you talk so much? You know plans change all the time. Now, back to the original topic." He did a couple of circles around Victor and stopped when he had circled back in front of him. He spread his fingers apart, and Victor opened his mouth, moving his jaw around when he had control again.

"The yacht that we planned to use for the shipment was destroyed," Victor repeated with more confidence this time. Shipment? What were they trying to ship, and where?

Caspian had a shocked look on his face, but it seemed fake. He blinked a bunch and put a hand over his chest, scoffing. "Someone dared to touch what belongs to me and got away with it?" Caspian asked, sinking back into his chair.

"About that. It seems, based on the extent of the damage, it was done days before we found it," Victor answered, his voice wavering from nervousness.

Caspian didn't say anything, but his face was cupped in his hand, a finger tapping quickly against his tensed jaw.

"Would you like to know the rest of the information I found out about the yacht, sir?" Victor broke the silence, earning a dirty look from Caspian.

"Why wouldn't you tell me everything at one time? Of *course*, I want to know. I want to know everything!" Caspian shouted, throwing an arm in the air. Rocks from the ground flew up with his arm, and Victor flinched, his arms flying up to protect his face. I even tried to scoot back a little bit from reflex, even though the rocks weren't even close to me.

Caspian didn't seem to notice what happened, or maybe he just didn't care. It was probably the latter. Victor didn't say anything and dropped his arms, pulling at the sleeve of his black suit jacket. Caspian looked at him and raised his brows, indicating that he was waiting for Victor to speak.

Victor cleared his throat. "There was a cross left on the side of the yacht," Victor whispered and bowed his head immediately.

Caspian jumped up out of his chair, hissing. His eyes quickly turned violet, and he stretched out his arm. Victor flew forward into his hand, throat first. "A cross was left on the side of *my* boat?" Caspian growled, his mouth so close to Victor's ear, it looked as if he was biting it.

Victor didn't respond, but nodded rapidly, not daring to open his mouth. A small wheeze started coming from him from how tightly Caspian was gripping his throat.

He growled and pushed Victor away. Victor wheezed again, a few deep coughs following.

"That damn Dmitri. I knew he was coming for me. I just didn't think he would actually attack the boat," Caspian muttered to himself, pacing angrily in front of his chair.

I perked up at the mention of Dmitri and smiled at how upset it made Caspian.

"It's a yacht, not a boat," mumbled Victor, and Caspian whipped around, glaring at him with blazing violet eyes.

"What did you say?" Caspian raised his hand.

"Nothing, nothing," Victor quickly responded.

"Forget about the boat for now. That plan can be fixed. Right now, instead of waiting for Dmitri to come to me, I'll go to him." He cackled and rubbed his hands together, eyes sparkling. "Victor, watch the girl. Make sure she doesn't get away. Here, have my seat." Caspian gestured to the chair behind him, and Victor hesitantly walked to it.

Once Victor was seated, Caspian clapped his hands twice and faced the vampires below. They were all standing and staring up at Caspian. The ones who were in the corner were no longer there, and the ones who were pacing were now still. Their undivided attention was on Caspian.

"My children!" Caspian raised his arms. "I promised you a fight, a way for you to prove that you are indeed worthy of being a part of my family."

The vampires collectively shouted 'yes', making the cave walls vibrate. "I now offer you the promised fight! We will go now, and you will prove to me that you are worthy enough to serve me! Are you ready?" Caspian shouted, his arms raised high in the air.

What kind of narcissistic speech was that? They *had* to be brainwashed. They all had empty looks in their eyes when I checked them out earlier, but I figured that was because they were hungry.

The group shouted again and started chanting Caspian's name. He was pumping his arm in the air and looked back at me, his mouth open with a huge smile. He nodded along with the chanting and held his hand out, moving it like an invitation for me to join in.

I made a face and shook my head, not wanting to join in on that foolery. He frowned and flicked his wrist. My body scooted back into the wall, and my arms raised uncomfortably above my head. I gritted my teeth and mouthed a curse at him, and he smiled, shrugging his shoulders. Victor didn't react at all to anything and kept staring straight ahead, probably not wanting to be a target again.

"My children, we go now!" Caspian shouted, his arms raised as they cheered, pumping his fists. Caspian looked over his shoulder again and winked at me before running out the entrance we came through, and my arms dropped. The rest of the vampires ran with him, fading into a large blur. In one blink, they were all gone.

It was quiet. The only prominent sound was my breathing. Victor still stared straight ahead, his back straighter than a pole, and just as tense. I was finally alone in the same room as him, and it didn't even matter anymore. My case no longer mattered.

I shook my head. "You know Caspian is gone, right?" I asked, wincing at the rope biting into my wrists.

"What's your point?" he responded a few seconds later, surprising me. I thought he was going to ignore me.

I scooted, elated that I was able to move now, and tried to move into his line of vision. His eyes flitted my way without moving his head and just as quickly looked back in front of him.

"My point is, you don't have to be so tense. I'm not going to hit you or anything." I shrugged when he glared at my words. We stared at each other until I blinked, losing the staring contest. The corners of his mouth raised a bit.

"Look now, that wasn't fair. I'm human. Well, in a human form and you're...not?" I guessed, not really sure what he was.

He raised a brow at me and sighed, scooting back into Caspian's chair. "I'm human," he answered, and I made a face.

"You're lying."

He chuckled at my response and shook his head. "What makes you say that?" He finally looked at me fully, eyes large and curious.

"For one, you look nothing like the picture I found of you on the internet or how you looked on the boat."

That earned a hard chuckle from Victor. "I forgot about that picture. Maybe they just got an unflattering angle of me. Maybe it was too dark for you to see clearly." He smiled, throwing me off. He looked even younger when he smiled with teeth.

"Nope, it's not that." I shook my head, not accepting his answer. "Even on the boat, you looked like an actual old man. Now you look like a man in his early thirties who just started graying early."

He laughed. "Thank you for the compliment. Any other reasons you doubt me?" he asked, leaning on the arm of the chair, chin in hand.

I pursed my lips, tilting my head to the side a bit. "Caspian doesn't seem to value humans. To have one work for him wouldn't really seem ideal. I feel like he would accidentally kill a human if one worked for him. Maybe even on purpose."

He nodded, seeming like he was thinking hard about a response. "I understand. I can see why you think the way you do, but sorry to disappoint. I really am human." When I opened my mouth to explain more, he held a hand up. "I am human, but I'm not like normal humans. I'm a priest."

I waited for him to elaborate, but he didn't say anything more. "Is that supposed to mean something?" My head jutted out for him to explain more.

"I forgot that doesn't mean anything to you in your current state." He chuckled lightly, brushing a graying lock of hair from his eyes. "In this world, there are very few priests. Priests in this world are basically immortal," he explained.

Immortal priests? Now that was a new one.

"Why are priests' immortal?" I questioned.

He opened his mouth to respond but quickly shut it when a sound came from the entrance I came through earlier. My eyes widened when he got up from the chair, glancing back at me with narrowed eyes. I shrugged, just as confused as he was about the sound. I didn't have anything to do with it, but it was a great distraction. That was my chance to escape. Victor walked gingerly toward the entrance, glancing back at me one more time before disappearing through the opening. I yanked my arms apart, trying to get the thin rope off. It felt looser, but it still wouldn't come off.

"Come on, come on," I grunted and leaned back a little, rubbing the rope on the hard ground. My wrists were twisted in an uncomfortable angle, slight pain igniting in them, but I had to continue. I kept my eyes on the opening, hoping Victor stayed there for a little longer. I stopped rushing and yanked my arms apart again, this time, hearing a little snap. I could actually wiggle my wrists comfortably now.

New confidence started building inside me, and I leaned forward and hopped up, stumbling to catch my balance. Once I could stand still properly, I turned to the exit I was originally running toward, adrenaline coursing through my body. I barely took a step forward when hands grabbed my bound wrists.

"Where do you think you're going?" Victor growled in my ear, yanking me down.

"Escaping!" I yelled back as he pushed me forward.

He made me keep walking, past the chair and toward the steps by the cave entrance. Panic set in.

"Where are we going?" I asked, struggling against his hold. He didn't answer me, which I took as a bad sign. I had to act quickly, or I would probably never see the light of day again. Near a wall by the entrance, an idea popped in my head. When I was close enough, I yelled out and jerked backward, raising my feet to the wall. My feet connected, and I pushed back with all my might, catching Victor off guard. He growled, arms wrapping around my waist, and we fell backward off the steps, Victor on the bottom.

He was my cushion, yet I still hit the ground hard, making my back arch as pain shot up my spine. Victor's arms went limp, and I let out a pained breath before jumping up, eyeing him on the ground. He was knocked out, his mouth slightly agape, and a red trail of blood trickled from his mouth and down his cheek. A small bout of guilt crept inside me.

"Sorry," I whispered, and he groaned, eyes still closed. Struggling against the rope, I didn't stop yanking until I heard a pop from the restraints snapping off my wrists. "Yes!" I cheered and ran at the same time, rubbing my sore wrists. I ran with my eyes trained on the exit, determined to finally make it there. And I did. I paused to catch my breath and took in my surroundings, trying to find a way out. The space was narrow, and I crept through it, wary of the bugs that might fall on me in the tight space. It was dim in this part of the cave, with many twists and turns. I had no idea where I was going, taking left turns at times, and right turns other times, hoping to find some type of exit. I couldn't let Victor catch up to me.

After a few minutes of weaving through the confusing cave and swatting at random bugs, I saw light from my right side. I followed the light and pumped my fist in the air when it led me straight outside.

The sky was darker than it was when I first came in here. The air was chilly and felt nice against my hot skin. I ran, looking for any sign of Dmitri and the others. I was really hoping to make it to him before Caspian, even though that was probably unlikely. Caspian had a head start and his ability to run fast. As I ran, a cackle filled the air, halting my steps. I listened, and the cackle came again, this time even louder. It sounded like Caspian.

Fear slithered up my spine, and I ran up the incline and saw the backs of Dmitri, Axel, and Rita standing in the clearing. Caspian stood in front of them with his possessed army.

They were all standing in the middle of the yellow path, and it started blinking, though I thought I imagined it because none of them were reacting to it. I glanced at the ground for a second, and black boots appeared in front of me.

I was yanked up, and a face came close to mine, piercing silver eyes narrowed with a hard look in them. I breathed out a sigh of relief.

Dmitri didn't say a word. He just shook his head and pulled me along with him. I knew he was furious with me for leaving the group. He would get over it though, hopefully. We made it to the clearing, and I looked up to see Caspian staring hard at me, his eyes narrowed when we locked eyes.

"Ah, Victor, what a useless man," Caspian hissed, crossing his arms over his chest.

I smiled at my accomplishment, while Dmitri, Axel, and Rita had their full attention on Caspian.

"Like I was saying, you know I can't let you all make it up the mountain. *At all.*" Caspian smirked, eyes trailing over the four of us, lingering on me the longest. He kept his eyes on me, his intense stare making me a little squeamish.

It was as if he had a secret plan already and was silently taunting me. I sighed inwardly, wishing I had just stuck with the plan.

26

―――――――――

"What do you want, Caspian?" Dmitri asked darkly.

Caspian chuckled menacingly at Dmitri's question, his funny demeanor disappearing.

"Dmitri, you out of all people know what I want," he answered, starting to pace back and forth. His hands curled into fists, his jaw ticking.

"You can't have her," Dmitri growled. The passion in his voice startled me.

"Then you will die!" Captain snarled, his chest was heaving and his fists were curled and pressed into his side. I heard a low hiss and looked at Dmitri to see he leaned forward, teeth bared at Caspian.

"If only you would just see it from our side and actually listen, you would understand why it's so important for her to get her memories." Dmitri threw his hands in the air, exasperated.

"Dmitri, I *know* why it's so important, which is why I have to stop you," Caspian responded, a slow grin forming on his face.

Gasps filled the air, and I saw shocked looks on Dmitri, Axel, and Rita's faces. I didn't understand what made them react that way.

"You didn't!"

"How could you?"

"Caspian, you better be lying." They all growled at the same time, making Caspian guffaw loudly, clutching his belly.

He wiped a tear from his eyes, a huge smile on his face. "Did you guys really expect anything less? I needed help, and they were the only ones willing to provide the services I needed." Caspian waved his hand in the air nonchalantly.

"Killing innocents is never the answer! Nothing should be so serious that you'd go back to The Comitye!" Dmitri shouted at him, breathing heavily.

My mouth dropped at Dmitri's statement. He'd told me about The Comitye and how it was an organization that he thought was for good, but they wanted him and the others to kill. But he didn't want to kill innocents. It clicked. The pale males had to be the ones who failed to transition.

There was no way I would've been able to solve this case. That was why there were so many cold cases. I didn't know Caspian was a part of The Comitye as well. Their history went deeper than I thought.

"The Comitye is the only answer! I can't believe I let you brainwash me to leave!" Caspian yelled, shaking his head.

"Our lives were going to change for the worse if we stayed! There was nothing good associated with The Comitye!" Dmitri threw his words back at him.

Caspian cackled humorlessly and punched the side of a tree, causing it to vibrate. "Leaving The Comitye changed my life for the worse! We were a brotherhood, a family! And you tore us apart!" Caspian spat, his voice cracking from emotion. His eyes were blazing in anger, his chest heaving from his outburst. All the emotion in his voice almost made me feel sorry for him. *Almost.* He was still panting heavily and hissed, his eyes turning violet. "I'm going to make sure you pay for ruining my life. Starting with her!"

I took a step back when he pointed at me, glowing eyes trained on me. Genuine fear engulfed me. I had never seen him so angry and emotional. He almost looked animalistic.

Dmitri took a step in front of me, partially blocking my view. "You're going to have to go through me first," Dmitri hissed, crouching.

Caspian crouched himself. "With pleasure." He glanced back at his army that hadn't moved a muscle the entire time they'd been there and whistled. All of them crouched like Caspian, hisses filling the air.

Axel and Rita crouched, their hisses just as loud as they prepared themselves.

"I hope you didn't lose your staff," Dmitri said in a low voice, glancing at me.

I shook my head. It was still safe in my pocket. My heart started racing when I realized every single one of them were looking my way. The look in their eyes was pure hunger. How were we going to defeat them?

Caspian lifted his head, snapped his fingers, and pointed our way. His mouth moved, and lips curled over his teeth as the vampires started racing our way.

"Let's go!" Dmitri yelled, reaching to the pack on his back and grabbed a machete. I took out my lighter, tossing it in the air. Catching my fiery staff, I slashed the air, ready for them to come my way.

"Take this too." He lifted his hand, and in it sat one of the daggers. I grabbed it out of his hand. "I kill, you ice." He grabbed my hand and started running, easily catching up to the other vampires. A female jumped in the air at him, and he shoved the machete into the air, the female landing right on it. There was a nasty crunch that made me cringe, and blood trailed down his hand and arm.

He held her up by the machete. "Slice her arm."

I gripped the dagger and sliced her arm, opening a wound that gushed blood. It changed immediately, and the blood froze, turning the wound an icy blue.

Dmitri tossed the body to the side, and we ran through the army, stabbing and slicing anyone that got in our way. My energy was never-ending. I wanted more. I was in my element.

"Rita, phase!" Dmitri yelled, and she turned to us, eyes glowing violet. Dmitri chucked his machete at her, and I gasped when it reached her face and went right through her. An earsplitting shriek filled the air as the machete hit a vampire in the head, lodging itself right in the middle of his forehead. The air around us contorted, and it was completely black for a second before we appeared in front of the male vampire.

Dmitri yanked out his machete, and a spray of blood flew up.

I sliced his arm. The process was the same, and we moved on to the next. Dmitri joined Axel as he shot two vampires who tried to jump him and sliced one more that was sneaking up on Axel from behind.

I did my job of making sure I sliced each one and defended myself at the same time. Multiple vampires jumped in front of me, and with no hesitation, I sliced them all in half cleanly with my staff. The sky was getting darker, the once red color now battling between orange and purple.

"Dmitri!"

He whipped around quickly at Caspian's call, and I turned as well, to see Caspian holding Axel by the throat, his feet dangling off the ground.

"Axel!" Rita shouted, a gasp leaving her mouth. She threw her arm back with her double-bladed sword in it, prepared to chuck it at Caspian.

"Rita, wait! Don't do anything." Dmitri threw his arm out to block her.

She looked up at him with a confused and hurt expression on her face.

"Look at his hand." He continued, gesturing Caspian's way. I gasped along with her when I saw what was in his hand. He was holding the other dagger.

"How did he get that?" I whispered.

"Axel had the other one and was going to finish what you couldn't," Dmitri whispered back, pulling me closer to him as he eyed the other vampires who stopped fighting. Seeing Axel fight and thrash to get out of Caspian's grip was too much for me after what happened to Dax. I shook my head get the images out.

"Caspian, please. Don't do this, not to Axel. He's my best friend. I can't lose him," Rita pleaded with Caspian, shrinking her weapon and pocketing it.

My heart tugged at her voice full of emotion, and I hoped Caspian would find a grain of tenderness in his heart to let Axel go. We weren't as close as I had been with Dax, but he was still a part of the team.

Caspian chuckled, holding the dagger close to Axel's throat, who was still swinging his legs in the air from the tight grip around his throat. "Give me Meadow, and you can have your precious Axel back." A large smile grew on his face after his proposition.

Rita's eyes swung to me quickly and then settled on Dmitri. I chuckled humorlessly and silently at the look on her face. She had no problem trading my life for Axel's. I mean, why would she? I was literally nothing to her, and Axel was her life.

"Absolutely not, Rita! Don't even start to think about that," Dmitri growled, and I felt the anger radiating off of him.

Rita scoffed, crossing her arms and relaxing them just as quickly. "That's not fair! Just give her to him. Her life isn't worth Axel's death! Look at what she already did to Dax!" she yelled, not even looking at me.

I flinched at her words. That one actually hurt deeper than I thought it would. But deep down, I kind of agreed with her. Who was I to them, and why should my life be more valuable than his? "She has a point, Dmitri," I spoke up, earning a shocked, furious look from him.

"No! You have no idea what you're talking about, so you definitely have no say in this." He dismissed me, turning his attention back to Rita. "We will find another way," he said, making her hiss.

"There is no other way," Caspian interjected, lowering Axel to his feet. He let go of Axel, who coughed and wheezed as he tried to get air back in his lungs. He straightened after his coughing fit and took a step forward.

"Uh, uh, take one more step, and I'll rip out your spine," Caspian hissed at Axel, who froze in place. When Rita tried to step forward, Caspian held a hand up, and she flinched backward. "If you want your friend to live, I suggest you stay right where you are." He let his hand fall when she didn't move again. Her fists were shoved into her sides, eyes filled with fear for Axel, and it looked as if she was about to cry.

Dmitri glared at Caspian, his eyes darting back and forth. My heart clenched at the situation, and it hurt. I couldn't let Axel die. If surrendering myself to Caspian was going to save his life, I had to do it.

"Everyone, stop! I'll go to Caspian." The words had barely left my mouth when Dmitri started yelling.

"Absolutely not! You aren't going anywhere!" He reached for me, but I moved away from his grasp.

"I have to do this. I can't let Axel die because of me." I mouthed *I'm sorry* before I started in Caspian's direction, and Dmitri hissed harshly, his eyes flickering from silver to violet with conflicting emotions. I faced Caspian and walked slowly, my heart pounding. Whispering to my weapon, I turned it back into a lighter and pocketed it.

I couldn't believe I was willingly doing this. Dax's death scarred me deeper than I realized if being a martyr didn't seem so bad.

Caspian grinned, and I didn't realize what was happening until it was too late. While I walked toward Caspian, he grabbed Axel by the throat again, lifting him high in the air.

"No!" Dmitri shouted, and I turned back to see why he was shouting, but he disappeared. I whipped back around in time to see Dmitri appear next to Caspian, but Caspian threw his arm out, sending Dmitri flying back.

Caspian laughed and shoved his hand into Axel's abdomen, and I almost stopped breathing.

"Caspian, no!" I screamed, running his way. I tripped and fell hard, my arms catching my fall. Tears welled up in my eyes when I looked up to see Axel's spine in Caspian's hand, blood dripping to the ground.

Rita's shrill scream filled the air, and wind from her speed rushed over me as she tried to attack Caspian. He simply swiped his hand in the air, tossing her into Dmitri, who was trying to get up.

I couldn't move from my spot on the ground out of shock and could only watch as Caspian dragged the dagger across Axel's throat, a blue line following his movements. Rita cried out, and my vision got blurry as tears spilled down my cheeks. The pendant sizzled against my chest, and I swallowed a gasp. I didn't need any explaining as to what was happening. This was it. This was the price I had to pay. I offered myself to Caspian in exchange for Axel's life, yet he still killed him. The price was bloodshed.

I choked on a sob and scrambled to my feet when Caspian locked eyes with me. His attention turned to Dmitri when he was punched from behind, and I took this opportunity to run to Dmitri's side. His eyes were glowing vibrantly, his teeth bared in anger. Rita joined him, weapon out and ready to do some damage.

"I told you to give me the girl or your friend would die," Caspian said, shrugging.

"She was on her way to you! How could you?" Rita cried out, angry tears streaming down her face.

Caspian glanced at me before turning his attention back to Rita. "She was taking too long." he replied nonchalantly.

A gasp left my lips at the same time as Rita's, and her eyes swung to me, pure fire in them. I couldn't look her in the eye and instead looked at what was left of Caspian's army. They gathered behind him, only about forty of them left, yet Caspian still seemed pretty confident.

There was a long silence filled with hard staring, Rita's heavy breathing louder than my own. The tears stopped running down my face, but my heart still felt the pain. Axel's body was no longer there, only an ice sculpture in its place.

I didn't dare move a muscle, not wanting to be the one to break the tense silence.

Caspian's eyes slowly went over each of us, starting with me and ending with Rita. He locked eyes with her, and I watched as he raised his leg over what was once Axel and dropped his boot on the ice sculpture's head.

"No!" Rita roared and charged after Caspian. Dmitri didn't even stop her. Before she could reach him, everything started shaking. The entire mountain rumbled. Rita lost her balance, falling to the side a few feet away from Caspian. He had a look on his face that resembled fear, but it was quickly replaced by shock.

"Crap," Dmitri muttered under his breath, his eyes trained on the ground.

I crouched, trying to keep my balance, but it was hard. "What's happening?" I shouted over the rumbling, looking around for the source. I had to squint to see anything clearly since the sun had fully set. The only light source were the stars casting a bright twinkle to the ground, giving me barely enough light to see the others and the area.

"It's an earthquake!" he shouted, eyes now darting around the area.

I groaned and walked closer to him the best I could. Even Caspian and his followers were having a hard time keeping their balance.

"What are we going to do now? Are we going to take this time to try and evade Caspian?" I whispered to Dmitri. I didn't want to waste time when we could take advantage of this opportunity.

He squinted a little bit, looking like he was thinking about the question. "Give me a second." He disappeared, appearing next to Rita. He quickly grabbed her and appeared by my side in a second. "We're going to run before the mountain starts shifting." He patted his back, and I sighed, reluctantly getting on the best I could without falling.

They started running, and like before, I clutched my arms around his neck, terrified of falling off. I didn't tuck my face in his shoulder and spotted Caspian getting up from his fallen position, trying to run after us.

The mountain shook harder than before, making Dmitri and Rita almost lose their balance. My pulse rushed in my ears, and I hoped Dmitri wouldn't fall and crush me. I heard a snarl and saw the followers running after us.

"They're coming!" I yelled over the rumbling, and Dmitri grunted in acknowledgment, picking up the pace. He took another step and was suddenly in the air. My scream was lost from the force, but I couldn't stop it as I looked down, seeing a wide pillar carry us in the air.

"Hold on!" Dmitri shouted and leaped into the air, my arms locking around his neck. I shoved my face into his shoulder, trying to control my breathing. The wind rushed against my skin, and Dmitri grunted hard when he landed. My mouth dropped open when the mountain started shifting, massive pillars shooting up in the air around us. Several narrowly missed us. My eyes darted back and forth as I tried to take in what was happening. The mountain didn't even look like one anymore. It was chaos, the surface cracking, making way for the pillars to come through.

"Rita, look out!" I shouted when I saw one of the vampires running after her.

She jumped up from her fall and turned around in time to dodge her attacker. Before he could grab at her, a pillar shot up, carrying him into the air.

My eyes followed as he jumped off the pillar, falling from the scary height, but then started flailing. I squinted to see what was happening, but he was too high up for me to see properly.

"What's happening to him?" I asked when Dmitri started moving as more pillars shot up closer to us.

"He's dying," Dmitri answered simply, glancing up.

Dying? "How?" I asked as I started seeing what was happening clearer. Dmitri didn't answer me, but he didn't really have to at the moment because I saw it for myself. The vampire's skin bubbled like it was boiling, but the bubbles never popped.

He finally landed, and I had to turn my head away after his impact. There was a hiss, and Caspian looked in the direction of his fallen follower. He stared at the sky and growled. The moon had finally showed up, shining brightly in the sky.

"Let's move," Dmitri said in a hushed tone when Rita made her way over to us. She glanced at me with hard eyes and looked back at Dmitri, nodding. I knew she hated me. But that was the least of my worries.

They took off, and the scenery around me blurred. Dmitri kept jerking to keep himself from falling, which rattled me. I looked up to see where we were headed. At the top of the mountain, part of the temple still stood unaffected by the earthquake.

"I see it!" Dmitri yelled before I could say anything.

The temple was closer than before, and I felt like we could actually make it tonight.

Dmitri growled and turned around, punching one of the vampires that leaped in the air. I ducked when her arm swiped at me. Dmitri ran backward while fighting the vampire, whose eyes glowed violet along with the streaks going down her face. Her snarls filled the air, and he hopped up and kicked her in the face, causing her to fly back into the male vampire behind her. He whipped around and continued running, grabbing one of my arms that lost its grip and locked it back around his neck.

"Thank you," I breathed, too short of breath to yell.

He nodded and continued to run up the mountain. The rumbling faded, but the pillars wouldn't stop coming.

"They're not going to stop unless we stop them. I'll take care of it," Rita yelled, glancing behind her.

"Be careful. Meet us at the top when you're done before Caspian can catch you," Dmitri responded, and she gave a curt nod, jumping backward and twirling her weapon in the air. I heard her battle cry loud in the air but didn't look back. Dmitri dodged and weaved between the pillars, all of them coming close to knocking him off the path again. The yellow path was up ahead, the only spot on the mountain that wasn't moving. We were so close.

Dmitri jumped up and started running on the pillars that shot up in front of him, leaping off each one as they got higher. He landed on both feet on one that was a few feet away from the yellow path. He grabbed my arm and flung me into the air.

"Dmitri!" Half of my scream was stuck in my throat from the sudden action, and I clawed at the air for a second before landing in Dmitri's arms. He rolled on the ground, protectively curling me to his chest. The rumbling was over, and no more pillars were shooting up in the air on this side.

"Why would you do that? You almost gave me a heart attack!" I yelled, jumping up out of his embrace. My heart was pounding loudly in my ears.

A small smirk formed on his face as he rose from his sitting position. He shrugged.

"I just wanted to see your face when you thought you were about to die." His teeth made a rare appearance, eyes sparkling with humor, and I crossed my arms, glaring. "Come on. We only have a little way to go before finally making it to Aloysius." Dmitri glanced around the area before walking straight down the path.

"What about Rita?" I asked. I couldn't see where she was from my spot on the mountain. I hoped she was okay.

"Rita will be fine. She'll find her way back to us. What you need to worry about is meeting Aloysius."

I was confused. "Why do I need to worry?" I questioned as I caught up to him. He paused his walking, making me stop as well. I followed his eyes but didn't see anything.

"Wait for it," he whispered, eyes facing straight ahead.

I looked as well, tapping my foot impatiently, wondering what he was seeing. After a long, agonizing minute, the dark clouds parted, and I saw exactly what he saw. "Are those stairs?" I squinted, hoping it would help me see better. Yep, those were definitely actual stairs floating above the mountain, only a short walk away from where we stood. They were gold and wide, casting a light glow onto the mountains. The clouds moved, and I saw clearly that the stairs were connected to the temple.

"Yes. Aloysius is an extravagant man. He loves for everything to be over the top and for everyone to see his wealth," Dmitri explained, rolling his eyes.

I pursed my lips and nodded. Augustus seemed to be about the same, so I expected his brother to be similar. "Is that why I need to prepare myself?" I threw that question out again when we started walking.

"Part of it." He paused to lift himself onto the stairs, and then steadied himself and reached down, waving his hands for me to reach up. I put my hands up to grip his, and he lifted me effortlessly. "Another part is that only you will be able to enter the temple. Aloysius loves to pull tricks. I won't be there to help you, so you have to prepare yourself to not get sucked into his act."

2 7

On the way to the temple, Rita joined us, not a hair out of place. Everyone from Caspian's army was dead, and Caspian was nowhere to be found. She didn't know where he went, and I hoped he'd given up trying to capture me.

"These stairs weren't this long last time I was here. He must've expanded it," Dmitri commented, eyes narrowing a bit in suspicion.

"Is that a bad thing?" I asked.

"I'm not sure. I hope not," he answered, looking around warily. The stairs glittered and shined, their beautiful golden color mixed with the blue accents, made me feel slightly euphoric.

I actually made it. I mean, I wasn't completely there yet, but I was closer than before. I made it through drowning and creatures attacking me and being captured by Caspian. I considered this a win. My eyes traveled up the beautiful stairs and stopped when I saw the large temple. It shone brightly against the dark sky. It didn't look like there was a door, but then again, I was still far away, so I couldn't see every detail.

This is it. There's no turning back.

A blue color appeared whenever we took a step and disappeared when our feet lifted. I bounced and hopped up the stairs, laughing at myself as I tried to create my own rhythm with the blue color every time it appeared.

Dmitri was shaking his head at me, but there was a soft smile on his face. That gave me the hope I'd been missing the entire trip. The confidence I needed to get me through this challenging journey was now here, and I welcomed it with open arms.

Rita wasn't smiling at all as we traveled, but I didn't really expect her to. She may not be showing that she was grieving, but I knew she was. Her best friend was just killed by Caspian. There was no way to bounce back from that after only an hour.

"How much longer do we have? What would be your guess?" I asked Dmitri as we continued to make our way up the stairs.

"Probably another thirty minutes at the rate we're going," he answered, giving me a side glance.

I scoffed and laughed at the deeper meaning behind his answer. "Hey, now, I can't help that I can't just speed my way up the stairs like you guys." I waved my hands in the air for emphasis.

His smirk grew, and he nodded to himself. "I mean, I could help you, but I'm assuming you would rather take your time."

I smiled at him. I guess he did know me well, huh.

As we climbed, I took the time to get lost in my thoughts and gaze at the sky. I stopped keeping track of time, but I figured a good bit passed by from the sky's color. It was getting a little brighter, the dark sky being replaced with red streaks.

For some reason, I didn't really want the day to come just yet. I kind of enjoyed the night, despite the destruction that came with it. It was calming. The dark clouds hovering above the temple also started changing colors, from almost black, to a muted yellow. As we continued, the temple got closer, and I could see more detail than before. It turned out I was right about the temple not having a door, at least not one that I could see.

The front was smooth, with no lines or cracks that would indicate an opening. The entire temple was pure black with red streaks gracing the pillars. The shine from it was almost blinding. The clouds above it seemed to absorb a lot of the shine so that it wouldn't blind us.

It looked like lightning shooting through the pillars. The colors were constantly moving. I tried to see the shapes on the front of the temple, but I wasn't close enough. I did notice that the top of the temple was dome shaped, the same red streaks going through it like the pillars. Seeing the beauty on the outside made me excited to see the inside.

"Only a few minutes left until we are at the very top. Are you ready?" Dmitri asked, staring at the temple like I was.

Am I really ready? My lack of mental preparation mixed with Dmitri's doubts made me believe I wasn't prepared, but thinking about everything I went through to get to this spot, I knew I was ready. "I was born ready," I answered proudly, my steps becoming more confident with each one I took. Nothing was ruining my great mood, not even Rita. Caspian was nowhere to be found, and at this point, I was confident that he wasn't going to show up again. At least not anytime soon.

"Do you know why Aloysius will only let me in the temple?"

"He likes to have a one-on-one interaction with whoever needs his services, so he says. I never really asked why to figure out the true reason," Dmitri answered.

I nodded, thinking about his response. "I guess that makes sense. I might ask hi—" My sentence was cut off from a force that slammed into my back, causing me to stumble forward. I lost my breath and caught myself on my hands, the pressure jarring my wrists.

"Meadow, run!" Dmitri yelled as I got up, trying to regain my balance. I whipped around quickly and almost tripped over my feet. Dmitri was growling and wrapped his hand around Caspian's throat, stopping him from attacking.

I ran. I didn't look back to see if I was being followed. I could barely make out what was in front of me. The steps seemed to go on forever, and I paid more attention to the way I was breathing. The temple was completely clear now. The shape that I couldn't see before on the front of the building was now visible. It was a cross. The same intricate cross I'd seen everywhere, except on the temple, it was upside down. My brain wanted to analyze and comprehend everything it was taking in, but I couldn't. All I could focus on was getting to the top.

"Meadow, duck!" Rita shouted, but it was too late because I was hit from behind. This time I tumbled and rolled down a step with another body. I tried to get up on my own, but I had no control. I was yanked up and an arm wrapped around my throat, cutting off my airway. My hands automatically grabbed onto the arm, clawing at it.

"Let her go now!" Dmitri shouted, eyes blazing in anger.

Caspian's laugh filled my ears, and I continued to claw at his arm, trying to get air back in my lungs. My chest tightened, and it felt like his hands were squeezing my lungs slowly.

"Now!" Dmitri's eyes glowed violet, and Caspian loosened his grip on my neck just enough for me to be able to breathe again. My cough was obnoxious, but I needed to get air back into my lungs.

"Caspian, please let me go," I rasped, pleading with him.

Rita looked at us with cautious eyes, and Dmitri's were hard and narrowed, trained on Caspian.

"Now, why would I do that? I finally have you exactly where I want you. All the other times were just cat and mouse games. But this, *this* is the real deal." He cackled in my ear.

"Don't do this, Caspian." Dmitri walked our way slowly, a hand stretched out.

Caspian walked backward, pulling me with him. I stumbled over my feet to find the next step so I wouldn't fall. Caspian kept an arm around my neck, and his other hand lying flat over my pendant. I tried to glance down to see what he was doing, but I couldn't move my head.

"What are you doing?" I asked breathlessly. I tried to speak with confidence, but some fear seeped through. My eyes widened when I looked at Dmitri and Rita. "Why are you guys staring at me like that?" I questioned them, trying to understand their faces. Neither of them answered me or even paid attention to me. All of their attention was on Caspian. "Caspian, answer me!" I growled, trying to use some bass in my voice.

"Oh, sweetheart. What I'm about to do to you is a gift that, in due time, you'll come to appreciate," he whispered in my ear. A shiver went down my spine. He gripped my pendant tighter and yanked, detaching it from my neck. The gasp that escaped me was loud and hoarse. My hands flew to my empty chest, and I looked up at Dmitri in shock. He looked as if he was shouting, but I couldn't hear anything.

An explosion rocked my vision, and pain ignited in my head immediately. My vision was so blurry. Flashes of images hit me at full force, each one more painful than the other. None of them were clear enough for me to see. More images slammed into my head after the other set was over, drawing the biggest scream out of me.

I couldn't figure out if I was standing or sitting. I didn't know what was happening around me. I thought I heard Dmitri yelling my name, but music blocked a lot of it. Where was that music coming from? Something else slammed into my mind and it had me gasping for air. I couldn't breathe.

"What's happening to her?" I heard Rita shout, and I didn't hear a response. Something ran into me, and I felt like I was floating and drowning at the same time.

Drowning.

Drowning.

Drowning.

The word was repeating in my mind, and I started choking. I wanted to claw at the air, but I couldn't move. What was happening? *Let me breathe!* I wanted to scream, but my mouth wouldn't open.

"Don't worry, I've got you. We're almost there." Dmitri's voice reached me. His voice echoed in my head, another image following behind it. The image started moving. It slammed into me, and I was no longer floating. I was on a dance floor. It seemed familiar, and I looked around until my eyes landed on Dmitri. He was staring at me. I smiled at him over Caspian's shoulder, and he smiled back, eyes soft. Rita was in his arms, but he paid no attention to her.

Static replaced the dance floor, and now I was looking at Dmitri's back. I looked around, and I was in my apartment sitting on the couch. *How did I get here?* I glanced up and gasped as I saw myself standing in front of Dmitri, a surprised and frightened look on my face. Before I could decipher it, another image slammed into my head, white lights spotting my vision.

I wasn't on the couch anymore, but looking at someone in the air, from behind a boulder. The area was dark, and I heard shouting. Dmitri and everyone in my team, plus Caspian, were running on the beach, arms raised and waving. Another woman I didn't recognize was running with them. The angle changed, and I was face-to-face with the person in the air. I couldn't make out who it was because her face was down, and everything started getting blurry.

No, no, no. I wanted to see who it was. I was starting to be pulled back away from the woman, and I waved my arms around, trying to get everything clear again. I was about to be too far to see when she raised her head, and I choked on a gasp when her golden eyes locked on mine, auburn hair turning black right in front of me. Before I could see anything else, the scene disappeared, and I was drowning in darkness.

Many images raced toward me and began slamming into my mind like before, not slowing down for me to see anything clearly. It felt like someone was smashing a hammer over and over again on my head in the same spot.

"Hold on, *please*. We're here, just hold on a little longer." Dmitri's voice penetrated the force, and it sounded like his voice was filled with...pain? But why?

"Let me in! Drop the barrier, *please*, Aloysius!" Dmitri was shouting, but it sounded muffled. I was being rocked forcefully from whatever he was doing, and another scream left me when it felt like my head was about to explode.

"What is happening to me?" I screamed, clawing at my head when I realized I was able to move again. My screaming wouldn't stop. I couldn't stop the pain. It spread through my body and seeped into my bones. It was everywhere.

"Your memories are coming back, but in a deadly way. Your pendant was holding them back. It wasn't supposed to be taken off yet," Dmitri whispered, jerking when I screamed louder.

My eyes snapped open, but I couldn't see him. I saw a moving image of the beach, but it quickly disappeared, and it was dark. But then many moving images came back, surrounding me, then forcefully moving all at once. It was so overwhelming. I didn't know how much longer I could hold on and take this.

"Come on, man! She's dying!" I heard Dmitri shout, and tears started rolling down my face.

Dying.

Dying.

Dying.

I was dying.

The pain wasn't letting up. I could barely breathe, and it was getting harder to stay conscious.

"You know I can't let you through." A new voice that sounded familiar filled the air. It must be Aloysius.

My scream joined in when the memories all started slamming into my mind all at once. I couldn't do anything but lie there. So, this was what it felt like to die a painful death.

"Then take her! She can't die like this!" Dmitri pleaded.

I was numb to the pain by that point, so I could hear the silence between the two. Red spots dotted my vision and my eyes closed again as the memories became fuzzy. I was losing consciousness, and that was okay with me. It meant the pain would be over soon.

"Fine. Hand over the witch."

ACKNOWLEDGMENTS

This feels weird. I've read many acknowledgement pages from many books and now I have my own. I will keep this short and sweet.
The first person I'd like to thank is my twin sister. Thank you Kalilah for sharing your stories with me and encouraging me to write my own. You pushed me to find my own voice and made sure I knew that I was a talented writer and reminded me that everyone tells their story differently.
Thank you to my other sister, Malika, for letting me bounce ideas off of you and our late-night crocheting and talking each other's ears off about characters, tropes, and plots.
Thank you to my brother, Josiah, and his amazingly creative mind. Thank you for listening to me go on and on about my world building and my characters and for helping me shape them into who they are now.
Thank you to my parents for listening to all my ramblings about this book and encouraging me to forge my own path and to pursue my passions.
And lastly, thank YOU, reader, for picking up this book, taking the time to read this story, and showing love to my book baby. I really

appreciate it and hope you continue to join me on my writing journey.

ABOUT THE AUTHOR

Kahilah Harry is a full-time writer and avid reader. She spends her time creating worlds with words and playing with her cats. In her spare time, you can find her using a crochet hook to bring yarn creations to life. You can also find her documenting her writing and author journey on her self-titled YouTube channel. Visit her online at www.kahilahharry.com and on Instagram @kahilahhh.

CPSIA information can be obtained
at www.ICGtesting.com
Printed in the USA
BVHW071344090921
616446BV00013B/876/J